ROSE'S EVER AFTER

CHRISSIE BRADSHAW

VALLUM PUBLISHING

DEDICATION

For my daughter, Rhona

CHAPTER 1

DECEMBER 28TH 1955

*R*ose wheeled Lily's pram along the bumpy path leading to her mother's grave, her head filled with the changes there had been in the family since her last visit a few months ago. The tall wych elm had been shedding yellow leaves the last time she saw it, and now its bare branches stood out starkly against the grey winter sky.

She put the brake on the pram, carefully lifted the sleeping baby out of her cocoon of blankets and took a deep breath. Even after six years, it was hard to see her mother's name on her headstone.

Virginia Kelly
Beloved wife of John Kelly
Mother of Rose Virginia, Stanley, David and Terence
10th June 1909 – 28th Dec 1949
Laid to rest beside David Kelly
26th Oct 1936 – 23rd Jan 1945
RIP

1

She crunched over the frosty grass, crouched level with the inscription and traced over the writing with her free hand.

'I've brought Lily along, Mam. Your granddaughter has come to say hello.'

Rose took a handkerchief from her pocket and wiped her eyes. They were streaming with the icy chill of the air as well as sorrow. 'It's been a busy three months since this little one was born, that's why I haven't been for a while. I think about you a lot though, and I wish you could have held her. I hope you know that.'

The grave looked well tended, with a fresh holly wreath by the headstone. Dad must have been before Christmas to lay the wreath for David but had he spoken to his wife, told her of his plans? She was glad her mother had been laid to rest beside her little brother. It meant Dad couldn't ignore her altogether because he paid regular visits to David.

The air was still, but the freezing temperature and the heavy grey sky warned of snow, so Rose carried Lily back to the pram and tucked the blankets snugly around her, before returning to the graveside with an armful of Christmas roses and a few sprigs of holly.

'I brought these from Dad's allotment for you and David. You always loved to see the Christmas roses appear.' Her hands trembled as she arranged her offering and words tumbled from her. 'So much has happened, Mam. So much! I wonder if you know? I wonder if you understand how I feel?'

Rose knelt on the frost-tipped grass by the grave and clasped her numb hands together. She would love to hear a message or see a sign to show her that her mother was listening, but in her heart, she knew Ginnie Kelly was far beyond this world's worries and any upset within the family made little difference to her now. Knowing that still didn't take away her need to spill the whole tale out to her mother.

'I'm stunned by the bombshell Dad dropped on Christmas Day. I just wasn't expecting it.'

Dad's announcement still hadn't sunk in and maybe, if she told her mother, she could make more sense of it herself.

On Christmas day they had a wonderful lunch with Dad, her youngest brother Terry, and Danny's sister, Grace, who looked after Terry and the house for Dad. Grace, who was about forty, had never married, and for the past year she had kept house at number one. She stayed over when Dad was on night shift, so Terry wasn't alone and Rose didn't have to worry about either of them. Grace did most of the cooking but Rose helped, and afterwards Dad offered to help Grace clear up. 'You and Danny go for a bit of air while Lily is asleep. I'll help Grace with the dishes before all of the others arrive and then we can settle down and listen to the Queen's speech.'

Rose had been happy to leave them to it and take a walk with Danny. She was glad to have his heart, and now they had a beautiful daughter, she felt blessed. When flakes of snow started to fall, they ran back to First Row, hand in hand, to be in time for the Christmas message which was due to be broadcast to the nation at three o'clock.

They opened the door to laughter and a full house. For the first time, Rose's family, the Kellys, and Danny's family, the Dodds, were all gathering together for Christmas afternoon. Rose squashed herself on the sofa in between her husband and Grace; Rose's dad and Mr Dodd sat at the kitchen table on dining chairs. Mrs Dodd, stouter every year that passed, took the comfy chair beside the range, and that left Stanley, Rose's elder brother, sitting beside his girlfriend, Brenda, and Terry, her younger brother, cross-legged on the rug in front of the sofa.

The family connections were complicated and it was a bit of a squeeze, but they all wanted to be together, and they didn't need a good view of the screen because the Queen was to be broadcast in sound only. Queen Elizabeth ended the speech by asking her listeners to resolve to keep the spirit of Christmas with them as they journeyed into the unknown year that lay ahead.

Grace broke the silence after Queen Elizabeth finished by saying what Rose had been thinking. 'What a lovely message. Though it would've been nice to see the Queen at Sandringham and see what she was wearing for Christmas Day.'

'She couldn't have looked any nicer than you or Rose,' Danny answered, giving Grace a hug, and Rose's heart melted at Grace's beam. She did look especially nice today in a new dress.

'You're right there, Danny. The ladies did us proud with their cooking too.' Dad stood up, looking flushed and animated. 'I have something to say to you all in a moment when Grace has handed you a drink.'

Grace, stuck on the low sofa, was pulled to her feet by Danny. 'Thanks, pet. I've got the glasses all ready.' A moment later she appeared from the scullery with a tray filled with glasses of sherry. She handed one to Dad and two to her own mam and dad before bringing the tray over to Rose and the rest of them.

What was going on? Mr and Mrs Dodd seemed as puzzled as Rose felt. Her heart thudded with apprehension. Sherry? A speech from Dad? Grace standing by him looking rosy cheeked and... and in love. No, surely not? Yes, it looked that way. Was Dad going to announce an engagement? No!

'I'd like to take this opportunity to tell all of those closest to us that Grace and I...' Dad clasped Grace's hand and smiled at her. 'Grace and I, we got married last week. We wanted it to be quiet and to keep the news for today when we're all together. So now I would like you all to raise your glasses to toast my wife, Grace Kelly.'

Rose tried to paste on a smile. She mustn't make a show of herself. The room was going out of focus as though she might pass out. Lily, asleep upstairs, let out a cry, and to Rose's relief the room stopped turning and she had an excuse to leave. She dashed upstairs into the cool bedroom, held Lily to her and took in gulps of air to stop herself from crying.

How could her dad have sprung such news on her like this?

'What's wrong? You rushed up here without even saying congratulations.' Danny stood in the doorway.

'Lily was crying and… and anyway, I'm not sure I want to be congratulating the new Mrs Kelly.'

Danny strode across and hugged her. 'Rose, come on. Your dad has been on his own for years, and they seem so happy together.'

Rose shrugged him off. 'I know *you'll* be pleased for them, but don't expect me to be.'

Danny held her away from him and a puzzled frown darkened the blue of his eyes. 'What's got into you? How can you begrudge a bit of happiness to a woman who has never been married and had a family of her own, who has looked after your dad very well for the past year, and loves your brother Terry as if he was her own little lad?'

Rose's cheeks burned. All he said was true, but she didn't want her dad to replace her mother. 'They were fine as they were. They didn't need to marry.'

'If they discovered they loved one another, they did. They needed to marry for Grace's sake, and don't you forget who she is to me – that's my flesh and blood you're slighting. I'm surprised at you, Rose. I'll tell them you're feeding the bairn, but you'll have to come down and face them soon.' Danny strode out of the room.

Rose sank onto the bed to feed Lily. Why had she been so mean and hurt Danny? Although the Dodd family kept up the story that he had been a late baby for Mrs Dodd, it had been whispered along the rows for years that Grace had given birth to him at seventeen. Rose and Danny had discovered the whispers were true, but none of them openly admitted it. Danny adored

Grace, and for his sake she'd have to compose herself and wish them well when she went downstairs, but she didn't feel it in her heart.

Danny was right about Grace being good for both her dad and her little brother. She just hadn't imagined that Grace would supplant her own mother.

As Lily suckled at her breast she calmed down. What had their Queen said about this year's journey ahead? Something about keeping the spirit of Christmas going. It would be hard, but she'd have to try her best.

When she'd finished feeding Lily she lay her on the bed before checking her face in the dressing table mirror for evidence of crying. She wiped her eyes, powdered her nose and rubbed a dab of lipstick into her cheeks to give them some colour. Picking up Lily, she nuzzled into her neck and kissed her cheek. 'Come on, little one. Let's face the music. This is one way you'll get to call Grace her rightful name of Grandma.'

Remembering her mother's advice, she told herself, 'What's done is done, and I'll just have to make the best of it.'

And for the past three days, making the best of it was what she had been trying to do. 'I congratulated them both, Mam, but my heart felt as frozen as my fingers are now.' Rose felt better at getting the story off her chest.

'At first I was vexed, but I've thought it over and I'm sure if it hadn't been for your secret, for what you did to the family, Dad would never have looked at another woman, no matter how long he was on his own. Dad has good reason to feel let down by you. You can't argue with that, so please don't think badly of him.'

Rose shivered. She'd broken the news and made her mother take her share of the blame. 'It was six years ago today that you left us, and I still miss you. I wish you were here to be a grandma too.' Her face felt tight with salty tears that had dried in the chill air, but she still did not move until she heard Lily stirring. 'I'm going now. Lily will be wanting to be fed soon. Bye Mam, Bye David.'

Pushing the pram towards the cemetery gates, Rose's heart felt heavy with loss. She could accept that death had taken her mother and brother, but it was hard to accept that her sister, Terry's twin, was lost to the family because her mother thought it was for the best. That was something she could never accept.

Danny, who was working between Christmas and New Year, was picking her up from First Row to take her home when he finished, so she had to return to the newlyweds for a while and make an effort to look happy. As she wheeled the pram though the back gate of number one, her friend Lottie, who lived next door, was hanging nappies out on the line.

'Do you think they'll dry in this weather?' Rose asked.

Lottie came over to the adjoining wall. 'I don't care. They'll probably freeze on the line, but I want them out of the house. You'll soon get tired of nappies steaming in front of the fire on a winter's day. Paul uses his potty and he's dry during the day now, thank goodness, but he needs two around his chubby little bum at night.'

'Pop in for a cuppa when you're done.' Rose hadn't seen Lottie for a while.

'I will. What about your dad and Grace? Isn't it lovely news?' Lottie called over her shoulder as she finished pegging out nappies.

'A real surprise.' Rose forced a smile as she opened the back door and manoeuvred the pram inside.

CHAPTER 2

*R*ose left Lily sleeping in her pram in the narrow hallway leading upstairs; she would wake for a feed soon. The hallway was just off from the scullery which was a small room with a larder, a bench and a sink. The open range in the large kitchen was where food was cooked, and the coal fire burned brightly to keep them warm.

As she entered the kitchen to join her dad and Grace, Lottie from next door knocked and walked in, bringing her little boy, Paul. It was easy for Rose to blend into their conversation as Paul proudly showed off his pull-along Donald Duck toy, and Lucky, turning from old fireside dog to playful puppy, tried to pounce on it.

Lottie was eager to hear about Grace and John's wedding. 'Fancy living next door to Grace Kelly! I loved *To Catch a Thief*. What film are you making next?'

Grace's cheeks flushed and John grasped her hand. 'My Grace is just as lovely as yon film star, and even better, she's a dab hand at the pastry. Aren't you, Mrs Kelly?'

Grace nodded. 'Talking of pastry, I'd better take that apple tart out of the oven.'

'Did I hear apple tart was on the menu?' Danny said as he arrived at First Row after finishing work. He was picking Rose and Lily up to take them home to Alnwick. He hugged Grace.

'Yes, you heard correctly, and I hope you're staying to have some.'

'Is that okay with you, Rose?' he asked as he shuffled beside Rose on the sofa.

She nodded and he kissed her cheek. 'If we're staying a while, I'll just check on Lily and help Grace with that sink full of dishes.'

Lottie said, 'Grace, now you're an official grandma, maybe you'll babysit Lily on New Year's Eve and these two can go to the dance at Burnside with us?'

'I've offered to babysit for that little poppet at any time. If you want to take Rose to the dance, we'll have the bairn here, you know that, Danny. We've still got the cot from when Terry was a little'un.'

'We'd be celebrating our first wedding anniversary too. What do you think, Rose?' he called through to her from the kitchen.

Rose took a deep breath and dried her hands. If she played happy families for long enough, she might grow to accept Grace as her dad's new wife. She walked to the kitchen doorway and Grace's anxious look made her feel ashamed of her earlier behaviour. 'If you're offering, I'd be delighted to have a night of dancing and to see the new year in with Lottie and Dennis.'

Lottie hugged her. 'Like old times! We'll Lindy hop and bop, and you can stay next door at number two with us because Paul's sleeping over at Dennis's mam's.' Lottie and Rose talked about their plans for the evening and what they would wear, before Lottie took Paul home.

As Lottie left, Grace's dad called to bring her a bunch of beetroot from his allotment. Rose returned to the dishes but listened in to the chatter coming from the kitchen; they were discussing Clement Attlee's recent retirement earlier in the month.

'We could have won this year's election, but there was too

much in-fighting between old labour and Gaitskill's fans. Clement put up a good fight.' Rose had heard Dad's opinion on the election many times.

'Aye, he did fight well. But that Tory, that Eden fella has a way of talkin' – like Churchill. He can get folks on his side,' Mr Dodd said.

'Clement Attlee might be mild-mannered, but he got things done.' Dad was a staunch Attlee supporter.

'I do think twenty years of leadership is enough though. Labour needed a new man,' Danny ventured his view.

Rose heard sounds of Lily stirring in the hallway, so she picked her up from her pram and took her into the warmth of the kitchen.

'Maybe you're right, Danny,' John nodded. 'I hope Clement Attlee is enjoying his Christmas break with his feet up and a glass of good cheer, but I don't think that Gaitskill will unite the party.' He raised his mug of tea to his lips.

'Who could unite or even control both the Bevanites and Gaitskillites? You're not suggesting Morrison?' Mr Dodd asked.

'I'm blowed if I know.' Danny shook his head.

'I'd rather have given Nye Bevan a go,' Dad said.

'They're not in power anyway. We'll have to give Sir Anthony his chance and see how things pan out.' Danny looked over and gave Rose a wink. She could read him like a book; he was enjoying egging the two older men on.

Mr Dodd stood up to go. 'Aye, we will see how he handles things, and Bevan will be a thorn in his side as the shadow colonies minister.'

As they were leaving for home, Grace took Rose to one side and hugged her. 'I'll never be your mam, pet, but I'll do my best for your dad and Terry, and I'll love being a grandma to that lassie of yours,' she whispered.

'I know you will, Grace. It's just a shock.'

'Aye, we were shocked when you and Danny tied the knot on the quiet, like you did, but we got over it. In fact, it was thinking of how easy it could be done that got your dad thinking of doing the same.'

What could she say to that? When Dad wasn't speaking to her, furious with her after discovering she had known Mam's secret and not told him, she'd turned to Danny for support and they had married, on the quiet, last New Year's Eve. She didn't regret it, but she knew not walking his daughter down the aisle would have hurt her dad.

Danny was in high spirits as they drove home. 'Grace looks radiant. She'll bring Terry up more strictly than she could with me, you know. She had no say in what I did because Mam and Dad spoilt me.'

Danny had been a live wire and ran a bit wild, but he'd turned out to be a hard worker and the best husband. 'I shouldn't have reacted like I did to their news, but it was a shock. I'll try my best with Grace, promise.'

She was glad she was going to the dance at Burnside for New Year. It would be fun sleeping over with Lottie and Dennis, and they'd only be next door if Lily needed them in the night. They'd welcome 1956 in, celebrate their first anniversary, and as their young Queen said on Christmas Day, they'd journey into it with good spirit and give Sir Anthony Eden a chance.

CHAPTER 3

1956

*O*n a blustery March day, Rose decided to take Lily on the bus to see the family at Linwood. She set off early so she would have the chance of a cuppa with Grace before Terry and her dad came home. They'd had a rocky time at Christmas, but it was hard not to like Grace; she was kind-hearted and one of those women who loved to cook and look after her family. Terry was thriving and her dad was back to his old self, painting brighter pictures and ready to chat and put the world of politics to rights.

After leaving her own mother's hearth Grace had blossomed, and her once dumpy figure looked trim now she was running her own household and eating fewer of Mrs Dodd's cakes and puddings. Folk in the rows said she'd been a bonnie lass in her youth, and you could see that now, even though she must be over forty.

Rose opened the back gate of number one to find Grace leaning against the wall and looking grey. 'What's wrong? You don't look well.' She balanced Lily over one shoulder and took the pail of coal out of Grace's hands. 'Let me carry this. You look like you'll keel over.'

Grace didn't object but followed her and sank down on the chair by the fire. Rose saw some colour returning to her cheeks and said, 'I'll make us a cup of tea. You just sit there.'

She was used to the way Grace had rearranged all of the scullery shelves now, and the changes didn't annoy her anymore. She was glad the house was running smoothly, and Terry was doing so well at school; he'd just had his tenth birthday and would be sitting his eleven-plus later in the year.

Rose placed a cup of tea beside Grace but she shuddered. 'I'm right off tea at the moment, hinny. I'll just have a cup of hot water if you don't mind.'

Rose went back into the scullery. She'd felt like that for a while when... Crikey! Grace, she couldn't be... could she?

She carried the cup of water over. 'Grace, is there something you want to tell me?'

'About what, pet?' Grace's wan smile showed she had no idea about Rose's fears.

'About feeling poorly and being off your tea?'

Grace wrung her hands together and twisted her new wedding ring. 'I think I'm starting with women's problems. It's a bit early, I'm only forty-one but... I've missed, you know, and I'm that tired. It'll be the change, I'm thinking. Mam suffered for years.'

Rose swallowed hard. It *could* be early menopause, but it could be a baby. Grace seemed unaware; she'd had Danny in her teens but that was well over twenty years ago, so maybe she couldn't remember the symptoms. 'Grace, have you considered... have you thought you might be expecting?'

Grace's face revealed she hadn't even dreamed of such a thing. 'Expecting? I don't think so. I'd die of shame if I was at my age. What would your dad say?'

'For goodness' sake, Grace. You can have babies in your forties, and Dad knows how it happens. He'd probably be delighted, but you'll have to go to the doctor's for a check-up first. When was your last monthly?'

'Do you know, I've been that busy I can't recall. I think it must have been in the new year.'

'Two or three months, then? Oh Grace, get to the doctors with a sample as fast as you can. I won't say a word until you tell me the result.'

A week later, Rose got a phone call .

'You were right, pet. I'm expecting. I've got used to the idea and your dad, well, he's over the moon, but Terry isn't impressed.

Rose gulped and managed, 'Congratulations.'

'Now I know your dad's happy about it, I don't mind shouting it from the rooftops. I never thought I could have a bairn... I mean, one I could call my own. I'm the luckiest lass alive.'

Grace talked for a while about travelling to the antenatal clinic in Ashington and how she'd be booked into Princess Mary's maternity hospital for the birth before Rose put the phone down. Her head was spinning with this turn of events for the family. Fancy her dad becoming a father again. He was a fit fifty-two-year-old, and he'd need to be because babies were hard work. Terry was ten and would come around, eventually. Hadn't she got used to the idea when her mam fell pregnant at that age? Crikey, her dad was too bleedin' fertile. Luckily having twins had been all on her mam's side.

This news would certainly have the colliery rows buzzing.

Next day, Rose caught the bus to visit Grace and took her a bag of lemons, some root ginger and some honey to have with her hot water until the nausea went away. 'That's kind of you, pet. I still can't look at the tea caddy.'

'It's awful while it lasts, but I bet a cup of tea is the first thing you ask for once the baby is here.'

'My date is the end of October so I've a long wait. I bet folk are counting the months since I married John, so I hope it doesn't come early.'

Rose nodded. She understood how Grace must feel; because of the whispers about her and Danny over the years, she wanted this pregnancy to be gossip-free.

'I think it'll be a boy, and we're calling him John – after his dad.' Grace beamed.

'We'll have to wait and see,' Rose said.

Grace took a long envelope from behind the clock. 'A letter came this morning and it is addressed to you. I propped it here so I wouldn't forget. My brain is cotton wool at the moment.'

'For me?' Rose took it and puzzled over the neat handwriting and the Southampton post mark. 'Grace, watch Lily for me. I'm just going to take this upstairs to read.'

Rose had a strange feeling about the letter. Her fingers trembled as she sat on the bed in her old room and ripped the envelope open.

A photo fell out, a school photo of a ten-year-old girl with curly blonde hair tied to the side with a ribbon and a mischievous grin on her face: Terry's twin, her secret sister; she had the green Kelly eyes and Terry's dimple. Rose unfolded the letter.

March 10th 1956

Dear Rose,

I'm writing to let you know that Joy is a happy child and she is doing well at school. She is creative and loves music and art. This birthday she started riding lessons, and no doubt she'll soon want a pony as well as the dog she loves.

We moved to Yorkshire because I realised the chance of bumping into a member of her birth family was too great, and your mother and I never considered how much like her twin brother she would look. Mr Fletcher must never know the facts of her birth and it is a burden I have to live with. I see how happy they both are and know it is worth it.

Lately, I have considered that Joy will have no close family after her father and I die; I expect my own parents will be laid to rest by then. That is why I am writing, to keep in touch. I have made up my mind to reveal the truth to Joy in my will, or after Mr Fletcher's death, which-ever comes first. I hope it is not for many years yet, and if she ever needs to find you I hope you will make room for her in your warm-hearted family.

You may show your father this letter if you think it right to do so. I only feel safe revealing this to your family because, by the time this reaches you, we will have set off for Australia. Mr Fletcher has a manager's position with a coal mine in New South Wales and we are starting a new life.

When we reach Australia I think I shall finally relax and stop looking over my shoulder. Mr Fletcher will be involved in the mine, but we will have land and raise animals and Joy will love this.

If your family moves from First Row please leave a forwarding address with the next tenants. I am forever grateful to your mother for her gift to me of a daughter, and she is always in my prayers.

Kind regards

Mrs Fletcher

What was she to make of this? She was glad Joy might, one day, know the truth, yet sad she was going so far away; and relieved, yes relieved, that there would be nobody else bumping into her and putting two and two together. If Joy found this secret out when she was Rose's age, would she be furious? Rose knew, if it was her, she would be devastated to have been denied the truth for so long.

Then came the niggle of when Dad should tell Terry about his twin. The ripples of her mam's deception spread in ever wider circles to involve the whole family.

Danny would tell her she was overthinking things, and now

Dad knew the truth she would leave the whole quandary of who should know in his hands.

She took another look at the photo and replaced it in the envelope. Taking the letter downstairs, she handed it to Grace. 'It's from Mrs Fletcher, and Dad needs to read it and keep the photo somewhere safe. Give it to him when the house is quiet, Grace.'

'There'll be no end to this carry-on, will there?' Grace stuffed the envelope into the large front pocket of her apron.

'No Grace, I don't think there ever will.'

CHAPTER 4

The sun shone through freshly cleaned windows into a spotless kitchen as Rose admired her newly mopped floor in the flat above Alnwick bakery. That was it, thank goodness; her jobs done for the day and Lily was still taking a nap. Between them they'd got into a routine of sorts, and Rose had the rest of the day free before preparing the evening meal.

She *could* bake a cake, but her efforts with the gas oven were still hit and miss, and wouldn't it mess up all her hard work? Besides, she lived above a bakery, and she couldn't compete with their fresh Border tarts. Rose shrugged off her apron. She'd check on Lily and maybe read a book.

Lily was sleeping so Rose riffled through the pile of books she'd borrowed from Alnwick library. She picked out a new romance by Jennifer Kent and walked to the front room window. Looking out onto Bondgate Within, the bustling street below, she saw day visitors to the market town, mothers out with their bairns, and one of her neighbours cleaning their step. She felt restless; she'd take Lily out for the afternoon as soon as she woke up. They both needed fresh air and a change of scene.

Until Lily woke up, Rose would grab an hour's reading. She was soon transported to Africa by the Mills and Boon romance.

The church bells chimed two as she wheeled Lily towards their favourite spot by the river Aln and Rose's head was still in Africa. She'd love to travel to exotic places like that, but she wouldn't be looking for romance, oh no. She'd be looking for the wildlife – the zebras and hippos – and just imagine the thrill of seeing an African elephant in the wild...

The only elephant she had been near was Wilhelmina, the mechanical elephant that lumbered up and down Whitley Bay promenade giving rides to adults and children on its colourful howdah. When it arrived to compete with the donkeys one summer it had thrilled and terrified Terry in equal measure, and she had been given the big sister's duty of riding Wilhelmina with him on every summer day trip for years. In a year or so it would be Lily's turn to take a ride and sway along the lower promenade.

It was warm for July, but Rose was confident her spot by the river would be quiet because the schools hadn't broken up for summer yet. Today, for a treat, she'd spend as long as she could down by the river and then call in to buy a fish and chip supper on the way home. Danny didn't mind if his meal wasn't home-made, as long as it was hot and filling.

She wheeled over the grass, found an even spot beneath the tall sycamore she loved and spread a large blanket in its shade. Watching Lily kicking, her little hands trying to catch the shadows the leaves made, was relaxing. Lily giggled as she rolled over onto her tummy. Soon she would be crawling and into everything.

Such a perfect, peaceful day! The running water of the Aln was soothing. Rose decided to go to the water's edge and dabble her feet in there before getting stuck into her book.

'Hi, do you mind if we join you? Rose tented her eyes to see a little girl of three running towards the river and a smiling blonde-haired woman following her with an empty pushchair.

'No, no, not at all.' Rose stood up and walked back to the sycamore to check on Lily.

'This is our favourite part of the river. It's shallow enough for Jennifer to paddle in and it's off the main track so it doesn't get many visitors,' the woman explained.

'Yes, that's why I like it too. Not that I mind you being here.' Rose felt a blush rise to her cheeks.

The woman laughed. 'Don't worry. We won't stay long if you're after peace and quiet, because you won't get that with my chatterbox about.' She held out her hand saying, 'I'm Helen.'

Rose shook her hand. 'I'm Rose, and this is Lily.' She looked towards the gurgling baby.

'She's so happy and contented. Jennifer screamed for most of her first year.' They both watched Jennifer as she leant forward to drag her hands through the running water. 'Jennifer, stay away from the river until I'm with you. Come over here to see the baby.'

The little girl laughed and dabbled her hands even harder as she turned to see her mother's reaction.

Then she toppled in.

Both Rose and Helen darted to the riverbank, and when Helen pulled her out Jennifer screamed at the top of her voice.

'Now look at you!' Helen removed the sopping dress from her sobbing daughter. 'You're soaking wet, and we have no dry clothes. That was very disobedient of you, Jennifer.'

Rose bit her lip trying not to laugh at the puce-faced child who had learned a chilly lesson, because even on a warm July day the river Aln remained cold.

'She can dry off on one of Lily's spare nappies, and I'm sure her clothes will dry quickly in this heat,' Rose offered.

'That's so kind of you. Say thank you, Jennifer.'

Order was restored, and Jennifer seemed happy to run

around naked as her clothes dried. She didn't go near the river again until her mother took her for a paddle.

When they came back, Jennifer sat chatting to her own baby doll and to Lily on the blanket in the shade of the tree.

'You look like you're in need of a cuppa.' Rose pulled a flask out of her bag. 'I've brought tea and a packet of ginger nuts. Would you like a cup? I packed a tin mug and there's the flask lid.'

'Thank you.' Helen beamed and settled next to Rose on the blanket. 'I have until four then I have to head back home to Seabottle. My mother picks up my eldest two on Thursday and makes dinner for us all, so it's lovely to get away with Jennifer. She loves the bus ride into Alnwick.'

'I just have Lily and she keeps me busy most of the time. I can't imagine having three.'

'The other two are at school – five and seven – and I can't wait for them to break up so we can have days out together. To tell you the truth, just having one around my feet is harder work. When there are a few, they entertain each other. I love kids anyway. I was a bit lonely after having Susan, my first. Once I had Mattie and Susan started school, I got to know the other mothers and it all got a bit easier I'd say.' Helen dunked a ginger nut into her mug.

'I know what you mean. I've moved away from my home village because Danny, my husband, works in Alnwick, so the days when he is at work can be long. I love looking after Lily, but when she's napping it would be nice to have adult company or something different to do.'

'You're welcome to visit me. There's plenty to be tackling on a farm, but I always have time for a chat.'

'A farm? You live on a farm? I'd love that. My brother does and I envy his life at times.' Rose plucked at the daisies and started making a chain for Jennifer who watched with interest.

'You'd like all the muck and hard work? My husband Matt is a farmer, and I spend most of my time cleaning after him and cooking to fill him up.'

'I'm a pitman's daughter, and well used to muck and hard work. From my teens I was looking after my dad and brothers. Before I had Lily I was lucky enough to work for a brilliant vet, and we were always up to our necks in clarts and worse. I loved working with animals.'

'That makes sense. I miss my job even now. I was a nurse – a children's' nurse – and I had to leave when I married Matt. Married nurses weren't a thing in the forties. Leaving was a hard decision.'

'Work or marriage, it's a difficult choice and we shouldn't have to make it. Mr Campbell was happy for me to carry on being a vet's assistant until I was pregnant, but that didn't take long.' What Rose really missed now that she was married, with Lily to look after, was the pleasure of working with animals and nurturing them back to good health. She wouldn't ever swap her life, she loved Danny and she was enjoying seeing the changes in Lily every day; but she did miss working at the vet's and being out and about at the local farms. 'Lots of careers are forsaken because of the idea that work and marriage don't mix.'

'There must be a way we can change that one day. When you think about what women did during the war, we all stepped up to the plate and kept the country going, so of course it's hard to slip back into domestic routine. I loved nursing!'

Helen's face flushed with indignation and Rose recognised that pleasure of finding someone who understood, who could be a real friend. She had Lottie in the rows when she was growing up and Brenda from her first days at Morpeth Grammar School; and now she'd met Helen who wanted work *and* marriage, just like her.

'I love having a husband and baby, but the rest of it – the polishing and cooking – leaves me cold.' Helen laughed when she added, 'I'd rather make a poultice for a horse than a cake.'

Jennifer wore her daisy crown and they took her and Lily down to the river's edge, where all four dabbled their feet in the chilly current.

Just before four, when the sun was lower in the sky, Helen began packing up. 'Blackthorn Farm is just a short walk from Seabottle bus stop on the Alnwick to Morpeth route. I live at Corner Cottage, just inside the farm gates. Why not call around next Tuesday? It's a baking day so we can have a pot of tea and you can take a walk around the farmyard. Jennifer will introduce you to our geese and hens, won't you Jennifer?' Helen struggled to get Jennifer's wriggling feet into her shoes.

Jennifer nodded and escaped her mother's grip to give Rose a hug. 'You'll bring baby Lily too?' she asked.

'Thanks, I will.' Rose waved Helen and Jennifer off then picked up Lily to feed her. 'We've made new friends today, Lily. Hasn't the afternoon flown by?'

CHAPTER 5

The following Tuesday, Rose took Lily on the bus to visit Helen and Jennifer. Blackthorn Farm had not been on Campbell's Veterinary Practice's list, but Rose passed its fields every time she travelled to Linwood. It was a small farm on the outskirts of the coastal village of Seabottle, with a mixture of crops and dairy cattle.

They got off at the nearest stop and Rose wheeled Lily towards a display of produce just outside the gate. A large basin of eggs, a few fresh cabbages and a basket of tomatoes from the farmhouse garden were arranged on a bench. The prices were marked in chalk on a piece of slate, and a tin money box sat beside it for payment. Rose decided she'd buy eggs and tomatoes on her way home.

Corner Cottage was to the right once she went through the farm gates. She spotted its front door wide open and a tabby cat sunning itself on the step. 'Hello?' Rose knocked on the door and Jennifer came running down the hallway.

'We're making a tart to have with our tea!' Jennifer announced.

'That sounds lovely.' Rose parked Lily by the door, covered

her pram with a cat net to protect her from insects as well as the sleepy tabby, and took the little girl's hand. 'You show me the way to the kitchen.'

Helen, her hair tied up in a scarf, was just putting a tray into the oven. 'I've made a Border tart and a couple of rhubarb pies, and now I'm just putting in a corned beef and potato pie.' She rubbed a stray strand of hair from her brow with the back of her hand. 'It's thirsty work, so I'd say it's time to stop for a cup of tea.'

'I came just at the right time then.' Rose smiled and took off her cardigan because the kitchen itself was like a giant oven.

'We'll have it in the garden where there's some shade. While I'm setting a tray, why don't you wheel Lily through the side gate and into the back so we can keep an eye on her.'

Jennifer helped Rose to wheel Lily through to the back garden and bumped the pram about so much that Lily woke up. 'Hoorah, baby Lily is awake! Now we can play tea parties with my dollies.'

Jennifer set up her tea set on a shady piece of lawn and carefully spread out a blanket for Lily. 'You can be my biggest baby today,' she informed Lily as Rose placed her beside a row of dollies. Rose took a seat on a bench nearby and admired the fruit bushes and neat rows of vegetables as Jennifer chattered away to Lily.

'Matt does all this,' Helen explained as she placed the tray on a wooden cracket and sat beside Rose. 'He loves the outdoors and growing things. When we met he'd been drafted as a Bevin boy and worked underground. He hated leaving his family's farm and would have rather been in the forces, but they had no choice. Then he met me and had to stick to mining for a year or so after the war.

'We got engaged and I thought we might have to move south to his parents' farm once we were wed, but as luck would have it, my dad – he's a blacksmith – introduced Matt to Ted Fairbairn at the county fair. Ted was getting older and looking for experienced help with his crops, and Matt seemed like just the man. He's really fallen on his feet here, and we both love it.'

'The Bevin boys had a hard time being accepted during the war, didn't they? My dad is a miner, but like many of them he's happy to be outdoors and digging above ground. His special talent is sketching and painting, but he had an accident last year so his hand is stiff nowadays.'

'Is he one of the Ashington Group? I've seen the work of the pitman painters on display.'

'Yes, he is. He does most of his painting down on his allotment. Your vegetable plot reminds me of the allotment when I was younger. He grew most of the fruit and vegetables we ate during the war years. It was never so neat though!'

'It's just Matt's way, to keep things organised – but he doesn't mind Jennifer running amok through his rows, and he's happy for me to sell any surplus produce at the gate beside Mrs Fairbairn's eggs and veg or to give it away. Saying that, you must take some rhubarb home. We have loads.'

'Oh no!' Rose said. At Helen's startled look, she went on to explain, 'I don't mean to sound ungrateful, but that would mean me having to bake and I'm not keen. I can do it if I have to, but I'd rather not.'

Helen laughed. 'At least you're honest.' She handed Rose a mug of tea and lifted a cloth from the tray. 'Rhubarb pie or Border tart?'

'I'll have a slice of the Border please, it looks like it would melt in your mouth.' She took a bite and the pastry, filled with a moist mixed fruit filling and topped with a thin coating of icing, was even more delicious than it looked.

'I talked to Daphne Fairbairn – she's Ted's wife – and she knows Jennifer is taking you to the farmyard this afternoon. Just be careful with gates and you'll be fine.'

. . .

Jennifer, who turned out to be a great guide, took Rose into both of the barns and explained who did what job. Matt and a farm-hand called Uncle Harry looked after the crops it seemed, while Mrs Fairbairn looked after the poultry and Farmer Fairbairn and his son saw to the cattle and other animals.

Jennifer led Rose along a track to a field where four sturdy ponies grazed. 'These are the pets of the farm. Farmer Fairbairn says they're old men like him so I can't sit on their backs, but I can bring them an apple or carrot.'

Rose recognised them at once. Pitmen called them gallowas or ponies regardless of their breed or size. These pit ponies were retired from pulling coal tubs, bless them. 'It's kind of Farmer Fairbairn to give them a home,' she said.

'They're from the local mines. Farmer Fairbairn thinks they shouldn't have to travel far away to find a retirement home. This way their workmates see them.'

'Their workmates? The other ponies from the pit?'

'No, silly!' The four-year-old laughed and shook her head. 'The *men* who worked with them and looked after them down the pit. Their marras, that's what Farmer Fairbairn calls them.'

'Oh, I see.' Rose had to smile. The little girl had an old-fash-ioned turn of phrase and was forward, but she wasn't trying to be cheeky. A bit like herself when she was younger.

'See Spike, the grey over there?' Jennifer stood on the gate and pointed to a pony standing at the far edge of the field with his back to them. 'He can be mean, and he's so grumpy to everybody but his marra, Bob Bradley. Bob comes twice a week, and Spike knows the times and days because he always comes right here to wait.'

Rose sighed. 'I wish we had brought some slices of apple now.'

'You can come again. I'll bring you.' Jennifer smiled and hopped off the fence. 'Let's go back to see baby Lily, shall we?'

With Jennifer in charge they returned to the yard by a different track and passed a small herd of Ayrshires. The other fields held the black and white Holstein dairy cattle that had become popular since the end of the war. Their numbers were growing because of the generous amount of milk they produced, but Rose, like many others, thought their milk wasn't as creamy as that from an Ayrshire.

There were a dozen of the Ayrshire red and white beauties of various ages and Rose suspected they might be show stock, with one or two kept for the farm's own milk. A young heifer stood up and walked towards the fence. Rose could see she was slightly lame in a hind leg. Preventing cattle from becoming lame was a major job for a dairy man because it affected milk production and fertility, as well as being painful for the animal. Had it been noticed?

Mrs Fairbairn waved as they passed the main farmhouse and Rose walked over to say hello and mention the lame Ayrshire.

'A lame Ayrshire, you say? They're my husband's pride and joy. We did so well at the county show this May. I'll let Jim, my son, know right away. He never mentioned it at lunchtime. We just had the hoof trimmer in to them last week too.'

An hour later Helen was about to start peeling potatoes for dinner and was serving Susan and Mattie bread and jam, so Rose said her goodbyes with promises of coming back another day. As she wheeled Lily around to the front of Corner Cottage, a young lad strode towards the path. He stopped and gave her a hard stare.

'Are you the woman who spoke to my mother about the lame Ayrshire?' he asked.

'Yes, I noticed she was lame on her left hind leg when she first got up but seemed better after walking for a while. I thought it would make sense to check her out,' Rose explained

'Did you now?' The lad, she assumed he was Jim but he hadn't introduced himself, was frowning and didn't look too pleased.

'That herd's hooves were fully checked last week, and I go over the herd every day. *I* haven't seen any lameness.'

Rose knew when she was about to lose an argument. She'd visited farmers in this neck of the woods for years, and lots of farm folk didn't like being wrong and didn't like unsolicited advice. 'I hope I'm wrong. Sorry if I've upset you, but it won't harm to check her. It's the nicely marked heifer, show standard I'd say.'

'I'm not upset, just annoyed at uncalled for interference by a... by a visitor! I'm on my way out and I get a message to put a stop to my plans. Our trimmer came last week and he's the best around here. He'd have noticed any signs.'

'Is he John Gill?'

Jim's head jerked back. 'Aye, do ye know him?'

'Just tell him Rose Kelly who worked at Campbell's thinks the heifer is lame and ask him to check for the beginning of bruising. It could easily have started since he's been. Act quickly and you won't need the expense of a vet.'

Rose released the brake on Lily's pram and walked off, leaving an open-mouthed Jim. It was up to him to investigate further, but at least she'd set him straight.

*a*s Rose lifted two perfectly poached eggs out of the pan, she smelt burning. The toast! She rushed to retrieve the bread from the toaster. It had just caught at the edge, so she scraped the burnt bits into the sink.

'Something smells good,' Danny called from the bedroom.

Rose smiled. He wasn't being sarcastic; Danny never criticised any of her offerings and often said he always felt lucky to be fed and loved by her. 'Hurry up then or it will get cold,' she warned.

Her husband, smart in a shirt and tie with his dark curly hair almost tamed, took two strides from the kitchen doorway and wrapped her in his arms. 'A bowl of cereal would have done, but thanks.' He sat down at the table and rubbed his hands together. 'Lovely. Is there tea to go with it?'

'Of course. I'll just pour you a cup.'

'Aren't you having any?' Danny sliced into his eggs on toast.

'No, I munched on a slice of toast while I was cooking, and I don't want much because I'm meeting Helen and we're taking the girls to Esme's tea rooms for an early lunch.'

'That's nice. Make sure you fasten Lily carefully into the high chair. She's as lively as a lop.'

'Don't I know it. Jennifer will keep her occupied. Lily could watch her all day long.'

Danny piled egg and toast onto his fork, saying, 'You seem happier to have a friend round these parts. What about meeting up in couples like we do with Lottie and Dennis?'

'You're forgetting we have grandparents when we go out near Linwood. We don't have a sitter to go out here.' Rose took his empty plate to the sink.

'What about inviting your friend and her husband around for something to eat one night? No sitter needed.'

Rose turned from the sink, her eyes wide. 'Danny! I'd never relax or enjoy that. Helen is a great cook.'

'Get her to invite us around then.' Danny's eyes were glinting with mischief.

One look at her face stopped the mirth. 'Sorry, only joking. What about a picnic one Sunday? Do they have a car?'

'They use the farm's Land Rover – I'll ask. A picnic is a better idea.'

Danny stood up and planted a kiss on Rose's brow. 'I'm off. I've got deliveries to make up, stock to order, then phone calls to make – all before lunchtime. I'll grab a sandwich downstairs because I'm off to see Mr Williams this afternoon. See you later.' He grabbed his jacket and was off.

Rose sank back and sipped her tea. She just had a few minutes, then Lily would wake up.

Before she met Helen, a long day ahead of her like today would have her feeling restless, but now she had the morning to look forward to, and she could tidy up and make dinner once they got home.

They had just settled into Esme's tea room when Helen opened with, 'You caused quite a stir last week with the Fairbairns.'

Rose groaned. She knew she'd upset Jim, the son. Why

couldn't she ever just keep shtum? 'Sorry Helen, but I saw the heifer was lame and it looked to be prize stock.'

'Nothing to be sorry about. John Gill came the next morning and you were proved right. There was the beginning of bruising in the hoof, and it was early enough for him and Ted to treat it without a hefty vet's fee.'

Rose breathed a sigh of relief. 'I was sure, but then I doubted myself because Jim was so adamant I was mistaken.'

'He was very sullen the next day. It was nobody's fault, but Jim's often too eager to get away from the farm to meet up with his friends and his dad can be hard on him. Ted told him he had to thank you next time you visit.'

'There's no need for that.' Rose didn't want a fuss.

'There is if Ted says there is.'

Rose drank her tea and fed Lily a buttery crust from her sandwich. Lily had a few teeth now and was showing a lot of interest in the food Rose and Danny ate. 'I've got an idea, Helen,' she said.

'Come on then, out with it. I can see you're planning something.' Helen tucked a napkin into Jennifer's pinafore because she was about to tackle a chocolate éclair. Rose couldn't help smiling at the little girl's delight. Wasn't it so nice that rationing was finally over?

'I would like to come each week and help with the pit ponies – tidy them up a bit, check them over and lead them around the fields to give them some attention. Do you think Mr Fairbairn will agree?'

'I think he'd be delighted – I'll ask to make sure. I hope you'll still call and see me. I'm getting the impression you prefer animals to people, Rose.'

Rose laughed. 'I love being with animals, and I haven't had much chance since I left work at the vet. An upstairs flat above a baker's on a high street that doesn't allow pets is the exact opposite of where I'd choose to live,' she explained.

'Is there any chance of moving?' Helen asked.

'Yes, we will. One day. Danny and I hope to save enough to put a deposit on a house, a new one with a garden and room for pets. We would be the first in our families to buy our own property, but lots are managing to do it nowadays.'

'I don't think we'll ever be able to buy with three hungry mouths to feed. But we do have plenty of room, and I love Seabottle,' Helen said.

Jennifer had finished the chocolate éclair and given Lily a tiny piece of the end. Both were covered in chocolate, so Rose and Helen headed for the ladies' room to wipe them down before taking a stroll down by the river.

They walked to the bus stop before three because Helen had to be back home in time for Mattie and Susan finishing school, and Rose suggested a weekend picnic at the beach near Seabottle.

'What a great idea,' Helen agreed. 'If you prepare lots of sandwiches, I'll bring pies and a cake because I know you're not keen on baking.'

'It's a deal. All we need is sunshine on Saturday.'

Danny and Matt hit it off and a pattern was set where the two families had a day out together every two or three weeks. Between times Rose called regularly to Blackthorn Farm. Lily was about to have her first birthday and wanted to be on her feet but couldn't balance yet. She didn't like to be in her pram for too long, so some afternoons Helen offered to have Lily for the couple of hours that Rose was with the pit ponies, and Jennifer loved to entertain her.

On a mild September afternoon, as Rose returned from the ponies' field, she was surprised to see Danny's car parked at Corner Cottage. Her heart missed a beat and she started to run. Lily! Was she okay? Why was he here instead of at work? She burst into the cottage to find Danny having a cup of tea.

'Danny! You gave me a fright. Why aren't you at work?' The colour flooded back into her cheeks and she felt hot.

'I called here on my way back from Linwood with some news for you and Lily.' He looked pleased with himself.

'What is it? What's happened?'

'Grace went to Princess Mary's maternity hospital during the night. She has given birth to a ten-pound boy, John Junior. They are both grand.'

With the heat from the kitchen and the news, Rose felt her legs give way from under her. Quick as a flash, Danny caught her and sat her on his chair. 'Here, take a drink of this.' He handed her his cup, and after a sip or two of sweetened tea Rose felt better.

'Thank goodness it's good news. When can we visit?' she asked.

'She's in for a few days and it's just John who can visit the ward, so we'll have to wait to meet our... our newborn addition, our little Johnnie.'

'I think we should all have a sherry to wet the baby's head...' Helen reached into the cupboard for the sherry bottle and three glasses. 'He's your half-brother isn't he, Rose? And Grace is Danny's sister, so what relation does that make him to Lily?'

Danny caught Rose's eye and winked. The relationship between Danny, Lily, herself and this little lad would take some working out, but he would be a welcome addition and be loved.

The autumn afternoons were becoming more chilly, and nowadays Rose went to Blackthorn Farm straight after lunch to spend an hour or so tending to the ponies because the nights had started to draw in early. When she called back at Helen's to collect Lily, she was persuaded by Jennifer to stay for a cup of tea. 'I hardly see you and Lily now I've started school. I've just got home. Please let me play with Lily a teeny bit longer because I'm teaching her a new rhyme.'

Helen was by the range knitting a cardigan for Susan; her fingers never seemed to stop. 'Matt told me something interesting last weekend after we'd been out to Plessey Woods with you and Danny.'

'Oh, what was that?' The men had walked off looking for conkers with Mattie and Susan because there was a conker craze at school.

'They started talking about how they met their wives. Danny mentioned he'd known you from being five and gave you your first conkers.'

'Yes, that's true,' Rose smiled at the memory.

'So Matt explained how he was sent north to be a Bevin boy and met me through the woman he was lodging with at Burnside colliery.'

'Burnside? That's next to our village.' Rose remembered the Bevin boys arriving when she was a little girl.

'Well, it gets even more interesting. It turned out Danny knew the woman who Matt lodged with – Mrs Simpson from Burnthouse – and said you're friendly with her granddaughter.'

'That's right, I am.' Rose had been friends with Lottie since forever. Where was this going? she wondered.

'A further coincidence is that I nursed Sid Simpson, Mrs Simpson's grandson, in the isolation hospital in 1944 during that dreadful epidemic.'

'*I* was there! I was there at the same time.'

'Exactly!' Helen exclaimed. 'Danny explained you were in there over Christmas.'

'I didn't think you were that old?' Rose clamped her hand over her mouth. Trust her to be blunt.

Helen laughed. 'I was twenty-two that year. How old were you?'

'I was ten.'

'I would have remembered you, I'm sure, but I nursed the boys' wards.'

'Can you remember Douglas Fletcher or David Kelly?' Rose's heart ached at the mention of their names; two boys lost too young.

'Remember? Of course I do. I never forgot any little lad that diphtheria took. I was at both their funerals. Saying goodbye, it helped me to get back to my duties.'

Rose sat quietly for a moment. 'It's a bigger coincidence than you think then, Helen. I was in the same class as Douglas. And David... David Kelly was my little brother.' A tear escaped from her eye and she brushed it away.

Helen's eyes filled as it dawned on her. 'You're David Kelly's sister? You got home but he was rushed in later during the epidemic and didn't make it. It's a really small world, isn't it?'

After that Helen and Rose became even closer, and Rose confided in her, like a sister almost. Though she didn't confide that she had a sister who was being raised in Australia, and how that had happened. That secret wasn't one she shared with anyone.

CHAPTER 7

1959

*L*ily grew into an inquisitive little girl, and Rose's days were always full. She now spent a couple of afternoons at Blackthorn Farm with the pit ponies. Some of them were hitting thirty yet they still had their health. They'd lost one old chap and gained two new retirees since she'd started helping out.

As well as the time they spent with Helen and Matt's family, there were weekly visits to see family and friends in Linwood. Lily and little Johnnie were great friends, and it wouldn't be long before they started playing down by the burn or beside the allotments for hours, just as Rose and Danny had in their childhood.

She saw her brother and Brenda, his wife, regularly too. It was through her friendship with Brenda and the family that Stanley had gone to work on their farm near Rothbury. From her brother having a young lad's crush on her best friend, their love had grown. Rose was delighted they had married in spring, with Lily as a flower girl and Johnnie as a page boy.

Ever since leaving school, Brenda and Rose had kept to an arrangement of meeting up in Morpeth by the clock tower every other Saturday. They'd take a walk around the shops to look at what was new and then go for tea at the Clock Tower tea room where they'd chat and put the world to rights. It wasn't set in stone, but if one of them didn't turn up it was for a very good reason.

They'd encourage each other to try the latest fashions in Rutherford's. Brenda worked in a solicitor's so wore smart clothes for work and loved reading up about fashion. Rose always enjoyed dressing in her best when she met Brenda, and sought out her opinion when she bought something new.

'Shall we try on those new extra high stiletto heels they're displaying in the window? They're not a look for a solicitor's office, but I'd love to try to walk in them,' Brenda confessed.

'I'll try a pair too, but they would be wasted on the Blackthorn ponies. They might cause a stir at the Burnside dance, but I think I'd fall off them!'

After a relaxing weekend that took in an afternoon of shopping with Brenda, an overnight stay at Linwood to go to the Burnside dance with Lottie and Dennis, and then a family Sunday including a roast lunch, Rose and Danny returned home to Alnwick laden with pies and cake from Grace.

Danny turned on the TV because it was Rose's turn to settle Lily for the night with a story then her prayers. While she undressed, Lily chatted to Rose about when she could go to 'big school' with Jennifer. Lily loved going to the Methodist Sunday school at Linwood colliery with Johnnie before Sunday dinner, the same one that Rose and her brothers had attended. She enjoyed the stories and songs, and was eager to start 'big school' and learn to read.

After saying goodnight, Rose curled up on the sofa beside Danny. 'We need to talk about Lily starting school.'

Danny put his arm around her. 'Is there anything to talk about? Don't we just put her name down for the local school?'

'That's what we need to decide. She can attend Alnwick

primary because it's nearest, or we could send her to Seabottle village school where Helen's children go.' Rose loved the little village school and had a feeling Lily would be happy there.

'Is there much difference? All schools teach the same, don't they?' The deep line between Danny's brows told her he was puzzled. 'I hadn't thought about choosing a school for a four-year-old.'

'I hadn't either, but then Lily started chatting about going to school with Jennifer, and the more I've thought about it the better it seems.'

'Why's that?'

'She knows a few of the Seabottle children because we're over there a lot – plus it's a smaller school that does well.'

'Okay, I can see you might have a point, but it would mean a bus or a two mile walk to get there. I can't drop her off every day in the car.'

Rose had thought about that, of course she had. 'At first, it would mean we had to travel, and I wouldn't mind taking her and picking her up. What else have I got to do? But weren't we thinking of buying one of the new post-war houses in a year or so? There's a small development earmarked just behind Seabottle school, and if we moved there eventually she would already be settled.'

Danny scratched the stubble on his chin. 'I'd been thinking of us looking at the new housing that's going to be built around Alnmouth way, but when I think of it, Seabottle isn't a bad spot – it's still near work, and if you'd be happier—'

'I would! I really would. I'd love to be near the beach, I love the village and I'd be near to Blackthorn Farm to see to the pit ponies. Then there's that lovely village school of course.'

'Let's get your priorities right.' Danny smiled and studied her closely. What was he thinking? Was he convinced? 'How long have you and Helen been planning this move?' he asked.

'Danny Dodd! I haven't planned anything with Helen. I just

got to thinking about our future, and you know I'd talk it over with you first before anybody else.'

Danny drew her close to him, his lips kissing her lightly on the brow. 'It seems to me that we have ourselves a plan. Get Lily enrolled into Seabottle, keep saving and get our deposit down for a brand new semi when the Seabottle plots are released. We will have to save like mad to have a decent deposit.'

'I've heard you only need fifty pounds deposit, and the council are giving mortgages on the rest. We can easily do that.'

'It still needs to be paid back. I want to put more down so we don't have a hefty mortgage and big monthly payments. Don't forget, we're rent free because we live above the shop. Still, it's good to know we can move somewhere with a garden before...' Danny stopped mid-sentence.

'Before what? What were you going to say?' Rose looked at him closely. He seemed to be going pink. 'Danny, what were you going to say?'

Danny took her face in his hands and his dark blue eyes sparkled with mischief. 'I was going to say before we have another – a brother or sister for Lily.'

'Oh.' Rose pulled away. Not this again. 'I've told you before. I had Lily really young. I love her and wouldn't change a thing, but I feel I haven't really done a lot with my life. I think, once she's at school, I'd like to work again for a while. I'm only twenty-five and I don't want a semi full of babies before I'm thirty, Danny.'

'It would just be one. Think about it. I don't want Lily to be an only child. I love you Rose, and I'd like us to have more children.'

'Yes, you can go to work and enjoy the house and children and the weekends but I'll be the one stuck in doing things I don't like much – cooking and cleaning and washing. I did all that from the age of fourteen for Dad and Stanley and Terry because I had no mother, but I really thought when I was a bit older I'd have time to follow my own choices, and it wouldn't be house-work ever after.'

Danny took her in his arms and hugged her. 'Don't be upset. Don't you already have time for you? Don't you have free time to go to Blackthorn Farm and mess about with the ponies? You could still do that. You did it when Lily was tiny.'

Rose blinked back tears of frustration. She loved Danny, but it was such a man's world and he honestly didn't see what she had to complain about. She wanted a proper job working with animals. Did he think she was being selfish?

One thing was for sure, she just didn't want another baby right now, and she wouldn't fall so easily as she had with Lily. 'I'll think about it Danny, but let's get Lily settled into school and move into a proper house before we make a decision. There's no room for a baby in this flat.'

'Rose Dodd, your mother and mine made room for how many kids in two bedrooms in the rows? Remember where we come from.'

'I'm not that generation, Danny. Babies weren't planned.' She just stopped herself from pointing out that he hadn't been planned but she still wanted to make her point. 'If you remember, my mother wasn't exactly happy about her last pregnancy. Look what happened there.' Rose was about to stand up, but Danny pulled her back down and onto his knee.

'Let's not argue.' He kissed her and she couldn't be angry anymore. Marriage was a compromise, and wasn't she fortunate to have a man she loved?

CHAPTER 8

1960

A new decade had begun. To Rose, the sixties seemed full of promise and their plans for the future were working out. Northumbrian schools took infants into reception in the term after they were four, so Lily, who'd turned four in September, started at Seabottle school in January. Seven-year-old Jennifer kept a look out for Lily in the yard, and on most school days Rose spent a couple of hours with the ponies and the prize Ayrshires either straight after taking Lily to school or just before she picked her up.

Rose, an early riser, found she could just manage to fit her daily shopping, her housework and her washing into the hours she had spare. She had learned from her teen years to work quickly and efficiently, and although she was no great cook, she had a menu of a dozen meals and puddings she used from her mother; Ginnie's recipe book was her kitchen bible. Fancy stuff came from the shop below, so Danny's sweet tooth was catered for.

It was the second month of this new regime when Ted approached her as she was mixing a feed for the ponies. 'You love this work, don't you lass?'

'I do, Ted. I love the outdoors and being with the animals. It makes me feel useful and... and fulfilled, if you know what I mean.'

'I do lass, I do. It's a love of the job. I'm never happier than when I'm with the beasts, especially my Ayrshires, but our Jim he doesn't have that feel for it. He can do it all and he's good with the books so we make a profit, but he hasn't got the feel you and I have. I've watched you – fulfilled you said, that's a good description of it. Anyway, I'm not getting any younger, and Jim isn't getting any better at the things you and I are both good at.'

'What do you mean, Mr Fairbairn?'

'When it comes to looking over the herd, that second sense that an animal isn't right and then acting on it. You have that skill by the shovelful, and it's a worry that Jim doesn't, I'll tell you.'

Rose wasn't sure how to respond. Ted was usually a man of few words. 'Can I help at all?'

'Aye, that's what I'm coming to. You can help. I've talked it over with our lass and with Matt Wilson, and they think I should put it to you.'

'Put what to me?' Rose was intrigued. She'd never heard the man talk for so long.

'I'd like to offer you six hours on weekdays, nine until three, for a proper wage. You'd still have your ponies to tend, but you'd oversee the cattle too. Jim would be the dairy man, but you'd be caring for the young heifers and the like and helping me with the calving, I hear you're good at that from John Gill. So, what do you say?'

'What do I say? I say it would be a dream job for me, Mr Fairbairn. I say yes!'

'Aye, well talk it over with your man first, hinny. He mightn't be keen to have you out of the house for so long, but if we need to talk again about shorter hours, we can.'

With that, Ted strode off and left Rose with her head in a

whirl. Danny? Talk it over with Danny? He couldn't deny her this, could he?

As she peeled potatoes and placed their pork chops under the grill, Rose went over the discussion she would have with Danny once they had eaten their meal that night. Would he be cross and not want to hear her out? His brothers' wives didn't work; the only women from Linwood who worked were widows, or those who had men who didn't cough up their wages. Danny, a good provider and a saver, might not agree to a working wife, and then what would she do? Would she go ahead anyway?

Should she stress the extra wage she could bring in? They'd save more quickly for their own home. Or should she be direct? She should tell him the big draw wasn't the money but the pleasure she would get from being with the animals.

She cut her finger opening a tin of peas and it throbbed with a dull ache as she held it under the icy tap water. Crikey! She'd better concentrate on the task ahead and speak from the heart after they'd settled Lily for the night.

'You're very quiet, is something on your mind?' Danny asked. He picked up a tea towel to dry the dishes as she washed.

Rose took a deep breath and swallowed the lump that had formed in her dry throat. 'I had an offer today from Ted. It took me by surprise.'

Danny took her hands and dried them with the towel then led her to the sofa. 'I knew something was eating away at you. You'd better sit down and tell me all about it.'

The words came out in a rush as Rose relayed the whole encounter to Danny and ended with, 'I'd love to work there, I really would, but I said I'd talk it over with you.'

Danny slumped back on a cushion and closed his eyes. Rose

could usually read him like a favourite book, but not tonight. 'Danny, it would mean more money to save for a house.'

Danny's eyes opened. 'Be honest, that's not why you want to work there.'

Rose blushed. *He* could read *her* like a book too. 'You're right. I'd just love seeing to the ponies and the herd every day.'

He closed his eyes again. 'Rose, you've had time to think this through. It's a lot to consider, so give me a day or so.'

'Of course! I'm just glad you're not dismissing it out of hand.'

He pulled her to him and kissed the top of her head. 'If I disagree, will you reject the offer?'

Rose had thought hard about this question all day. She couldn't go ahead without Danny's backing, no matter how much she'd like to. 'We're a team, Danny. I'm hoping you'll agree, but I wouldn't go ahead if you were unhappy about it.'

He lifted her chin and his lips found hers. 'I love you, Rose. Let me think it over.'

CHAPTER 9

To Rose's indignation, opposition to her work plans came in full force from her dad and Grace when they visited Linwood. As they sat down to Sunday lunch, Danny brought up the topic. 'Rose has had a job offer we are thinking about. Tell them about it, Rose.'

Why had he done that? She wasn't ready to face their arguments against her working until she had Danny's backing. As she outlined the offer, she could see Grace's jaw dropping and Dad's frown deepening, but they heard her out.

'I would've thought you had enough on your plate looking after your man and that little lassie.' Dad stopped carving the rolled brisket into neat slices and pointed to Lily with the meat fork.

'I can work and still keep house, Dad. I had to do it for long enough after we lost Mam.' Her heart was pounding, and if Dad was ready for a debate so was she.'

'That wasn't through choice. You did a grand job, lass, but you have a good provider in Danny, so you don't need to be skivvying after farmers.'

'I'm not skivvying after anybody, Dad! I'm tending to the

46

animals, a job I was trained for and had to give up when I was expecting Lily.'

Grace joined in. 'But Rose, if you work all week, how are you going to manage washing and shopping and the like? You can't be doing that when Danny comes in from work. A man expects his dinner on the table and his house in order.'

Rose glared at Danny. Why hadn't he just said it wasn't happening? Why bring Grace and Dad into it? 'I'm still waiting for Danny's opinion – he wanted to think it over,' she said, side-stepping Grace's question about housework.

Danny took the plate Grace handed to him and winked at Rose. 'I thought you two might think it strange that Rose would want to work when I give her good housekeeping, but I know how much enjoyment Rose gets from working with animals. Thar's why I've taken time to think it over and I think we might have a solution.'

Rose caught Danny's eye. 'You have?'

'I have! I know how the light shines in your eyes when you come home smelling of the stables, and I know that faraway look you get when you've been washing and ironing all day, and I know which Rose I want to come home to. So I've had to work out what's best for us as a family, and I think that's you working at what you love and us employing help for the house.'

'Help for the house? Grace's eyes grew round. 'Help? We've never needed that before, not in Linwood.'

'Come on, Grace. You were help for John when he needed it. You helped him look after young Terry, and you did his washing and cooking when he fell out with Rose. You have a short memory!' Danny was sitting next to Grace and squeezed her arm. He meant no animosity.

'All right, all right, but that was neighbourly help. No need to bring those times up, Danny,' Grace's eyes flicked to Rose.

Rose understood that Grace didn't want to resurrect old wounds.

Grace added, 'You're right. Maybe Rose *should* have a chance to do what she likes, but finding good help isn't easy and it will cost a lot.'

'That's what I've spent a day or two working through. Meg Mason, the bakery cleaner, does two hours in the evening when we shut shop, but she wants morning work too. She'll be willing to do four mornings and will clean, shop, do the laundry and a bit of cooking. She's as neat and clean as your donkey stone doorstep, Grace. What's more she's honest, and she's a dab hand at baking when we're short-staffed in the bakery, so I reckon she'll fit the bill.'

'What's that going to set you back? You're saving hard for a house,' Dad asked.

'I've worked it out. Meg's wage will come out of Rose's own wages and will leave Rose with only a third of her earnings – but if it's what Rose wants...' He turned towards Rose. 'Do you want to pay for help in the house so you can muck out at the farm?'

'Danny, you know I do. That's a brilliant idea.' She got up, leaned over his chair and hugged him. No more washing and ironing, and tending to the farm animals every day was her idea of heaven.

'Mud and cold and back ache, I say,' Grace muttered to John.

John shrugged. 'It sounds like you two have a plan, so can we get on and eat our dinner? Grace's blackberry pie that's standing on the hearth will be there until tea time if we don't make a start.'

I love you, Danny Dodd, Rose thought as she cut into Grace's delicious Yorkshire pudding. Many a man would put up obstacles, but Danny looked for ways to set them aside and make her happy. She knew how lucky she was to have him.

Mrs Mason was a godsend and Danny's plan worked well. Rose arrived home to an empty laundry basket on Mondays, ironing done on Tuesdays, and a clean house with meals prepared on

Wednesdays and Thursdays. The animals at Blackthorn thrived under her care and she finished in time to collect Lily from school.

She popped along to Helen's for lunch a couple of times a week and, though Mr Fairbairn didn't say anything to her, she found out from Helen and Matt that he was pleased with how she was working.

'Ted says you've freed up his hours so he can spend time training Jim and still have a bit of time to himself at last,' Matt told her.

Jim, *he* was the only murky cloud on the horizon. Rose had never hit it off with him. He'd been surly towards her ever since he'd been made to apologise to her after the lame cow incident.

CHAPTER 10

One summer's day, Jim walked straight past Rose yet again with a grunt in reply to her greeting. It happened when she was on her way to Helen's to eat her lunch in the garden, and as she scrubbed her hands at the kitchen sink she brooded over his surly behaviour.

She raised the problem with Helen. 'I've been working here for months and you'd think Jim would be pleased I'm helping out, doing the parts of the job he doesn't like. I'm delighted to have Mrs Mason doing my laundry, so why can't Jim Fairbairn be happy I'm cleaning cow's hooves?'

Helen handed her a clean towel 'I think that's because you're happy with your lot, but Jim isn't. He doesn't want to be on the farm at all, but he's the only son now. Edward, his older brother, went missing in action during the war, his two sisters have married and moved on, and that means Jim is under pressure to take over the farm one day.'

'I didn't realise he was so unhappy. He's worked for his dad since leaving school, hasn't he? Does he want to do something else?' They walked out into the garden.

'Oh yes, but his dad won't hear of it. He wants to study music.

He plays guitar and saves all his money to buy music stuff. He would have loved to go to a music college, but Ted said it was agricultural college or learn on the job.'

'Oh. I didn't know that.' Rose felt ashamed for judging the lad so harshly. She of all people knew what it was like to love something and be thwarted. Hadn't she yearned to be a vet? Hadn't she wanted to keep working at Campbell's as a vet's assistant after she married? And wasn't this job on the farm perfect for her because it was the next best thing? If Jim loved his music, it must be hard to contemplate a future in farming. 'From now on, I'm going to try harder to get on with him, Helen.'

The next week Rose and Jim were mucking out the barn together, and instead of disappearing over to Helen's at lunchtime Rose walked over to the farmhouse with Jim. She'd try to chat as they had their sandwiches.

They both sat in an uncomfortable silence at the farmhouse table. Mrs Fairbairn was pegging out washing, and Jim was eating the bread and cheese she had left out for him.

Rose bit into her apple. Jim was staring out of the window and didn't look like he would break the silence, so Rose opened the conversation. 'I hear you're a musician, Jim.'

He turned his head from the window. 'Who told you that?' His tone was guarded, almost suspicious.

'It was Helen. She mentioned you're good on the guitar and would have liked to go to music college.'

'Did she now?'

Conversation wasn't exactly flowing, but Rose pressed on. 'She did. I was wondering, how did you get to be interested in guitars?'

He cut another wedge of cheese and seemed to be weighing her up. 'The music teacher at school brought his guitar into our lesson one day. I'd always liked listening to music, but to see him playing along to a record with this guitar, it was something else. I wanted to try, and I asked if I could have a go at break time.'

'Did he say you could?' Rose asked.

'Yes, he let me stay behind, and the minute I felt that guitar in my hand I knew I had to have one of my own. I wanted to make music.'

Rose sipped the tea from her flask, marvelling at the change in Jim. All the surliness left his face and he sat up straighter. 'How did you get your first guitar?'

'Christmas 1953, I asked for one. I was thirteen and my dad was happy for me to play then. I got the guitar and a term's lessons for Christmas, so I quickly learned to play the simpler stuff. I was taught classical guitar through the school and I taught myself the popular stuff we all listened to at night. I like all music and I can spend hours practising.'

'I'm surprised I haven't heard you.'

'I'm not! Dad complains if I play in the house now. He didn't mind until I left school, but he wants me to concentrate on the farm. Most of my gear is kept at the back of the church hall and at a friend's garage.'

'Is that why you're always keen to rush off?'

'I do a fair day's work.' He sounded defensive again.

She hadn't meant to sound critical. 'I'm sure you put in more hours than you need. I've just seen you looking in a hurry to get away.'

'I'm part of a band so I need to get to rehearsals, but Dad always seems to waylay me on practice nights. I'm sure he does it to make me late. I meet the lads to practice in Eric's garage or the church hall. We play at the teen dances on a Saturday night.'

'I never knew that.'

'Well, we've never talked.'

'I'm sorry about that. We got off to a bad start, didn't we?'

Jim's cheeks flushed. 'We did. I was that vexed you were right about Dad's bleeding prize Ayrshire.' He laughed and looked like a handsome young lad instead of the scowling workmate she had come to know.

'I'd like to hear you play one day, if I may,' she said.

'Don't dob me in it anymore with Dad and I might let you.' He smiled at her.

'I won't, Jim. I didn't mean to land you in trouble, but I suppose my passion for animals is a bit like your passion for music and guitars, and I can't help sharing what I know.'

A light dawned in his eyes. 'That makes sense,' he admitted.

After this exchange of views, they greeted each other and sometimes stopped to chat about the animals, and work was even more pleasant for Rose.

It was later in September when Jim sought her out on the top field. She was with the Ayrshires when he called from the gate. 'Rose! Do you want to eat your lunch in the chicken barn later?'

Rose looked up, surprised. 'I could do.'

She walked up to the gate and he explained. 'I've just taken my guitar there. Dad's gone into Berwick for a few hours, so I'll play you a few tunes. That is if you have time?'

With his head down and his hands thrust in his pockets, Rose realised the lad was braced for rejection. 'Of course, I'd like that,' she answered. She had intended popping along to Helen's, but she could do that after she picked Lily up from school.

'Great! I'll be there about twelve.'

At twelve, they washed up at the trough, and Rose settled with her flask and sandwiches not knowing what to expect. Jim tinkered with the tuning and then played something melodious. She wasn't an expert, but he seemed to play well. The sound reminded her of Romanies and foreign lands. 'You're really good, Jim,' she said.

'I can *play* classical guitar, but I'm not *that* good. I can't grow my nails to pluck properly, not when I'm farming.'

He started playing another piece with more confidence and Rose was enthralled.

'It must be wonderful to play like that,' she said when it ended.

He picked up a small object and held it up. 'I'm better playing modern songs with this plectrum,' he explained and started strumming a steady rhythm. Rose recognised it immediately. 'Oh, it's "All Shook Up". Can you sing and dance like Elvis too?' she joked.

He gave her a serious look. 'I try. This is the kind of music we play on Saturday nights at the church hall. We write our own too.' He sang as he played a lively tune about work and Saturdays, and his whole demeanour changed into that of a confident performer. 'That's called "The Best Day of the Week", Mick and I wrote it for the band.'

'It's really good.' Rose meant it. The song was catchy and celebrated looking forward to Saturdays as many young people did; teenagers, they were being called these days.

'When we play it on Saturday nights, everybody is up dancing and singing along. It's a funny feeling knowing the crowd love something we've made up. It's the best feeling.'

'I can imagine.'

'I'm working on playing like Vic Flick who plays with the John Barry Seven. Do you recognise this riff?'

Rose listened to a strong repetitive tune that seemed to need a lot of concentration. 'I've never heard that. It's like film music, isn't it.'

'You're right, you've got a good ear.' He grinned and played a little longer before saying, 'It's the theme from "Beat Girl" – and I'd better put this away before my dad gets back, or he'll be in here and threatening to smash it over my head.'

Rose laughed 'You're joking. He has got to be proud of you being able to play like that.'

'I wish he was. He can't stand the sound anymore. He used to be okay about it, but now… I think he's scared I'll put the music first and leave his precious farm.'

Rose thought about Jim's revelations all afternoon. It must be hard to have a love of something and not have support from your parents. She had made sacrifices for her family after her mother died, but Dad and the boys knew what she'd given up and Dad had persuaded her to go back to school as soon as they could manage.

She was lucky she had always had a supportive family, and now Danny supported her in doing this job. It was wrong, she thought; it was wrong that Jim should have to put his ambitions aside to please his father. Ted shouldn't expect it.

Danny wasn't so sure when they talked it over that night. 'Rose, don't go interfering between a father and his son. Ted has a farm to leave and only the one heir, so that's a big responsibility. Maybe his young'un needs to step up to the plate and learn.'

'He's talented at music though, Danny.'

'Your dad is a talented painter – a pitman painter. He's a pitman first and a painter second. Ordinary folk can't make a living off paintings or music.'

'Some people do just that,' Rose argued.

'As far as I've seen most of those creative folk do well when they're dead. A farm is a far better bet than a music career.'

'Unless you're a working-class Cliff Richard or Adam Faith?'

'Are you saying Jim's group could be the new Shadows one day?

'Anything is possible, Danny.'

Sometimes Danny couldn't see things her way, but at least he listened.

CHAPTER 11

After the harvest, Rose and Jim met up for lunch in the barn. They'd fallen into a pattern of getting together once a week when he'd play his newest songs, but lately he'd been working long hours with Matt and his dad getting the crops in.

For October, it was a bitterly cold day. Rose brought a flask of soup for lunch and cupped her frozen hands around the mug. Jim's singing could be heard through clouds of steamy air, and Rose tapped her feet to the catchy tunes as she tried to keep warm.

After playing for a while he said, 'I've been thinking about what you were saying, Rose. All the time we were working the fields, I thought about how I should follow my own dreams and not let Dad's views stand in the way of what I want to do.'

'Did I actually say that?' Rose certainly believed that, but after her conversation with Danny she had been careful not to put ideas into the lad's head.

'Well, not in so many words, but that's what you think, isn't it? You've said I shouldn't waste my talent and people shouldn't spend their lives doing something that doesn't sit right with them.'

Rose knew she could let her opinions run away with her, but she didn't want to encourage Jim to lock horns with his dad, did she? She backtracked. 'I meant you should work hard for your dad as well as showing him how you love music.'

Jim paced to the barn door and banged it with his fist. 'I've tried that approach since I was thirteen. I've always helped round the farm, but he's never changed in seven years so I doubt if he will now. If I decide to go away with the band it'll be a huge falling out.'

'Go away? Where to?' Alarm bells rang. Was he serious?

'The rest of The Jems are all geared up to go over to Germany. There's a really good music scene over there with live clubs, and Eric's brother – the one who married a German after the war – lives near Hamburg, so we could go there and try to play some clubs. Eric's brother has a few leads for us.

'The other lads are handing their notices in, and if I don't go with them I'm out of the band, and I won't even be playing here on a Saturday unless I form a new one. I know what I want to do, but it'll upset the milkcart in a big way.'

'Oh Jim, it's difficult for you, I know, and you shouldn't have regrets. Can't you ask your dad for a leave of absence? Tell him you'll either get this out of your system or you'll be a success, but at least you'll know.'

'I could put it that way, give it one last try to go with his blessing. I'd rather just slip away quietly in the night if I'm honest, but I suppose you're right. I can always rely on you for good advice.'

Rose smiled. She was still in her twenties too, but she must seem so old to a twenty-year-old with no ties and an adventure in front of him. 'I like the band's name, does it mean you're all gems?'

He shook his head. 'Nothing so fancy. We're Jim, Eric, Mick and Stuart, so if I don't go they'll have to find another J – or another name.'

. . .

The next day, the ponies were flighty under dark fast-moving clouds and the sky was growling with faraway thunder. 'It's just The Old Man Up Above rolling a few potatoes down the stairs,' Rose whispered to Spike. That's what her mam would tell her about the thunder when she was a bairn. She was hurriedly adjusting Spike's coat before the rain set in when Ted stormed along the track looking furious.

She paused. 'What's up, Ted?'

'What's up? What's up?! And it's Mr Fairbairn to you.'

Rose walked away from Spike, whose ears were going back with either the atmosphere of the weather or the tension between her and Ted.

'Don't you walk away from me.' Ted was red in the face.

'I'm not walking away from you, I'm leading you away from the ponies. You're unsettling them and there's a storm heading here.'

'There's a bleeding storm alright! There's a storm at the farm-house, let me tell you – and it's all down to you.'

'What's happened? Try to calm down Te— Mr Fairbairn.' From his high colour, Rose was worried he'd have a stroke or collapse.

'Don't bleedin' talk to me about calming down. You've planted daft ideas in my lad's head! "Rose thinks this, Rose says that," is what I get, and now you think he should go to Germany and try to be successful or get the idea of playing music for a living out of his system. What are you trying to do to this family?'

Rose's heart sank; so this was it. 'I've just been talking through the options with Jim, Mr Fairbairn. He needed a listening ear.'

'Options? He has no options! This is his farm one day and his place is here. You have given credence to his madcap notions and now he's going off.' Mr Fairbairn slumped over the gate to catch his breath.

'He loves music. Don't you see he deserves a chance to do what he wants?'

Mr Fairbairn raised his head and the usual ruddy colour faded from his cheeks, leaving him grey. He didn't look well at all. 'His place is here! He's my heir, my only son. You've encouraged him and filled his head with his runaway dreams, and now he's all for letting me and his mother down.'

'Don't you see you've made him walk in your boots that don't fit him, and you're denying him a choice in life? A choice that makes him happy.'

'You're fired, Rose Dodd. I don't want to hear another word. Finish what you're doing, then go and don't come back.' Jim turned on his heel and headed back to the farmhouse.

A sheet of lightning flashed overhead, and the ponies clustered together. Spike whinnied and Rose went to him to stroke his neck. His eyes showed fear and she murmured soft words into his ear. Her own eyes filled with tears. Who would look after the ponies, now that she was fired and Jim was leaving the farm? Had this been all her doing?

Heavy drops of rain fell onto the back of her neck, but she stayed with the ponies for a while. She was wet to the skin before she headed for Helen's house. She wasn't going near the farmhouse kitchen today.

Helen gave her a change of clothes and a cup of tea. She sympathised with Rose. 'I know you were only hearing Jim out, but his dad won't see it that way. Ted is stubborn, so if he says you're fired then he won't change his mind.'

'I'll just sort my stuff out and go. I'll hand you my notebook on the cattle and the ponies and my charts for their feed. Matt can pass them to whoever takes over.'

'I think they'll all just have to muck in and do more. Farmhands with experience aren't easy to come by around here, and Ted won't be in any fettle to train somebody up to take your position as well as Jim's.'

A knock on the door stopped the conversation. Helen opened it to find Jim on the doorstep. 'Come in, we're talking about you.' She stepped aside so he could walk through to the kitchen.

'Rose! I thought I might find you here. I'm sorry about Dad. I didn't mention you at all today, but he seemed sure you'd been the one to listen to my daft ideas and he needed somebody to blame, I suppose. I'm so sorry you've lost your job because of me.'

Rose's heart softened at his distraught face. The lad needed somebody in his corner. 'Don't blame yourself. You had to make a decision, and we couldn't know how your dad would react.'

'I did know! I knew he'd go mad.' He blinked back tears saying, 'I've packed up, and I'm staying with Mick's family for a few days before we head off for London, then Germany.'

Rose nodded and patted his shoulder. 'Good luck, Jim.'

Helen pulled him into a hug, 'You'd better do well, lad, and show us all you did the right thing.'

'I'll try.' He turned to leave but paused to look at Rose. 'I just want to say I won't ever forget how you've encouraged me and listened, and shown me I'm just as important as the farm. I'll make it up to you for losing your job one day, I promise.'

'When you're famous.' Rose smiled.

'I could be, you know!' The light in Jim's eyes showed he had found self-belief. 'One day you'll see The Jems at the top of the bill at Newcastle City Hall.'

Rose stepped forward to give him a final hug.

Helen followed suit. 'You try your best. Show your dad he was wrong,' she whispered.

He was off, striding back to the farm with head held high and a burden off his shoulders. Helen turned to Rose. 'You did the right thing, Rose. He's a different lad. He'd have been unhappy here and he was never a great farmer in the making, so don't punish yourself.'

CHAPTER 12

*R*ose couldn't help but punish herself. Her talks with Jim tormented her; she may have done the right thing, but she had upset Mr Fairbairn, lost a job she loved, and she was going to put poor Meg Mason out of work too. She wouldn't find another job that suited Lily's school hours and they couldn't afford Meg's help if she wasn't working.

She dreaded telling Danny, even though she knew he'd be understanding and might even be glad to see his wife ironing his shirts again. She chided herself for thinking that. It was unfair; Danny wanted her to be happy, and was more than happy to tuck into Mrs Mason's cooking.

When he came home from work, Danny listened to the whole sorry tale, then said, 'I think he's spoken to you in the heat of the moment. He won't find a worker like you, Rose. Let's not worry Mrs Mason just yet. He might change his mind.'

'He's as stubborn as an Ayrshire bull and just as scary when he's vexed. I doubt he'll back-track, Danny.'

'There's no rush to change our arrangements here. I'll ask Meg to help us downstairs in the bakery tomorrow and then there's the whole weekend. Let's give him a chance to cool down.'

. . .

It seemed that someone else was in the same mind as Danny. Next morning, Rose was surprised to find Mrs Fairbairn waiting for her when she returned from dropping Lily off at school. She had to look twice at the woman standing in the bakery doorway because Mrs Fairbairn was dressed in a good burgundy tweed coat instead of her khaki mac with a black felt hat covering her curls in place of a scarf, and she stood tall in heeled court shoes.

'Hello Rose. I've come into town to talk to you in private. I didn't want other ears wagging to hear our conversation as they would if I met you at the school gates.'

'Come upstairs and I'll make us both a cup of tea.' Rose led the way upstairs to their flat, wondering what had brought this visit on. At least Mrs Fairbairn didn't seem to be annoyed with her.

Mrs Fairbairn removed her coat but not her hat and sat on the edge of the sofa. It seemed strange to Rose that she was making tea and piling some of Meg Mason's fruit loaf onto a plate. She felt all fingers and thumbs as she went about it because it was usually Mrs Fairbairn bustling about the kitchen.

'It's a lovely place you have here, Rose. It's right in the centre of town too,' Mrs Fairbairn called into the kitchen, but she didn't come in and see all the breakfast dishes soaking in the sink, thank goodness.

Rose popped into the living room with her tea tray of best china. 'It's handy to live above the shop, but you know I like a bit of space for animals. We can't even have a dog here because we're above a food premises.'

Rose went back for the plate of fruit loaf then sat opposite. As she handed Mrs Fairbairn her tea she said, 'I'm sure you haven't come all the way here to chat about this and that. What is it you want to say to me?'

Mrs Fairbairn took a sip of tea and put her cup on the table. 'I want you to be patient with Ted. I can imagine he was awful to you yesterday, because he was upset with everybody he looked at. You and I know he had no right to blame you for Jim's decision. Ted was just lashing out and looking for someone to blame – that's Ted's nature. He's slow to calm down, but he will eventually. I just don't want it to be too late, because I don't want you to go, Rose. We need you at Blackthorn.'

'Oh Mrs Fairbairn, I don't want to go either. I love my job.'

'Good. I'm going to do my level best to talk Ted around over the weekend, so unless you get a call at the bakery on Monday morning, just come in as normal on Monday.'

'Can you do that? Persuade Ted to change his mind?' Rose wasn't so sure. She still had visions of that puce face firing her.

'I certainly can. I don't often put my foot down, and I won't do it in public, but when I do make a stand I get my way. I should have made a stand about Jim and the music instead of allowing a young lass like yourself to do it. My father always warned me if you don't make a stand then you're likely to fall into anything, and I've fallen into placating my husband instead of sticking up for my lad.'

Mrs Fairbairn looked determined, but Rose could only say, 'If you're sure.'

The older lady leaned forward as if the walls might hear. 'Rose, I'm telling you this in confidence. Ted is not a well man. He has a lot on his plate and his family have dicky hearts. His father dropped stone dead over by the big barn, in harness so to speak. That's why Matt Wilson and I have tried to lighten Ted's workload over the past year or so. I think the stress of knowing Jim wasn't right for farming has been gnawing away at him. Now he'll have to accept it. My goodness, if he was ever near to having a heart attack, it was when Jim said he was going to Germany!'

'He can't see it as an opportunity for his son?'

'Maybe in time, but it's not just losing his son from farming – it's going *there*. Our eldest, Edward, named after Ted, did have the farming instinct. We lost him fighting the Germans, you know.

Edward would be in his thirties now, probably settled and married like Matt, and ready to take over and let Ted have a well-earned rest.' Mrs Fairbairn took a handkerchief from her bag and dabbed at her eyes.

'I suppose that explains Ted's determination to keep Jim on the farm.'

'Jim has been brought up in Edward's shadow and I'm sure it made him turn to something different to excel at. *I* hope he does well at his music. Farming is a hard life for anyone, so you have to love it. The farm will have to be sold when we're too old to run it, but that's the way of things. Ted will come to accept it and I'll make him see he can't get rid of good help willy-nilly.'

'Thanks for explaining things. I'm happy to return on Monday if Ted will have me.'

'I'll suggest you work under Matt's direction and we'll look for a new worker to replace Jim for you all to train up.'

'I'll train someone to tend to the ponies and the herd willingly. I've been making a booklet for anyone who wants to rescue a pit pony – it deals with their care, the costs and the best way to keep them healthy. I'll be happy to bring somebody on board.'

'Good! After Matt trains them in agriculture they'll be a real asset, and Ted can slow down a bit, semi-retire.' Mrs Fairbairn stood to go. 'I'm so glad you didn't take offence and you're coming back, Rose. You're a good-hearted woman, thank you.'

'I understand about men when they're hurt and angry. I once didn't speak to my own dad for months... but that's another story. I'm glad we've got you as a peacemaker at the farm.'

'While I'm here, I'm going down to that bakery and I'm buying a few things for the weekend. After all the fuss of the last two days I'm having a break from baking, Rose, and the Border tarts in the window look grand.'

'They are, but they're not a patch on yours.' Rose smiled as she saw Mrs Fairbairn out. She closed the door and rested her back against it. A huge sigh of relief escaped her, and a bubbling feeling of happiness arose in its place. Danny had been right! She was going to get her job back. Sharing her opinions and giving advice had almost lost her the job she loved, but when she thought of Jim following his dream, she was glad to have helped him.

CHAPTER 13

On Monday, Rose waved Lily off at the school gates and hovered to watch her playing a skipping game with a group of friends. Jennifer, who was skipping in the middle of the rope being swung by two other girls, called out, *'Somebody's under the bed, Whoever can it be? They make me jolly nervous, So Lily jump in with me'.*

Lily's face lit up as Jennifer pointed towards her and she was chosen to skip into the middle of the ropes. Jennifer chanted, *'Lily lights the candle, and Lily looks under the bed',* as Lily mimed the actions before answering, *'You'd better jump out, you'd better jump out, there's a ghostie by your head!'*

Jennifer jumped out of the rope, leaving Lily to repeat the chant and choose another girl to join her. It was a skipping game Rose had played at that age; childhood games didn't change.

Rose was in no hurry and stayed until the bell rang for the children to form orderly lines by the entrance. She was hesitant about walking up to the farmhouse and decided to head straight up to the Ayrshire herd in the far field. There was less chance of bumping into Ted up there at that time of day, but she still felt nervous.

As she rounded the corner, she saw him standing by the gate observing his show herd. Her heart pounded as she darted into the shrubbery and sent up a cloud of starlings. She tried to catch her breath. Crikey, what should she do? Head back to the farmhouse to check with Mrs Fairbairn that all was well, or brave it out?

She couldn't turn tail, she just couldn't. Hadn't she faced her dad in a rage? Hadn't she learned to stick up for herself from being a young girl in the colliery rows? It wasn't in her nature to tiptoe around somebody, and she wasn't going to start today, even if she did get fired again.

When she stepped out he was watching her. Those screeching birds, they had alerted him to her hiding.

'Don't let me slow you down, hinny. I guessed you'd come here first so I've been waiting for you.' His tone was calm so that was a relief.

'Good morning, Mr Fairbairn.'

'Less of the mister – I'm Ted to you, and I'm not too high and mighty to say I'm sorry you got the hind end of my temper last week.'

Blimey, if that was the 'hind end' then Jim must've had a doodlebug of a row with his dad before he packed up and left. 'Do you want me to carry on working here?' She'd better make sure.

'I do. Daphne and I chatted over the weekend, and she's shown me I've been blind as far as Jim is concerned. Wanting something to happen doesn't make it so. It's not just the music, Rose. It's the fact he's gone to live over *there*. I'm that disappointed in him and I canna change how I feel, but there was no excuse for looking for someone else to blame and I did that to you, a young slip of a lassie.' He held out his hand. 'You're not fired and I'd be glad if you'd stay on.'

Rose shook his calloused hand. It was shaking as she took it, but he had a firm grip and looked her in the eye and she could tell this apology and the realisation his son had left the farm had cost him dear. Now wasn't the time to talk about being at peace with Germany and moving on from the war.

'Consider it forgotten, Ted. Now can we chat about that youngest heifer, the one in the left corner...'

Two weeks later, a thin blue envelope with a red, white and blue border landed on her doormat. A foreign stamp – she knew it must be from Jim.

November 1960

Dear Rose,

We made it! We've settled in Hamburg and live together in such a dump, but it's cheap and near to lots of action. The city is exciting so we are not in the apartment much. We're meeting up with other musicians in cafés and clubs. There is a group from London and one from Liverpool who we are friendly with and, through them, we have been given our own spot.

We've started playing at the Star Club a couple of nights a week. It's well known for bringing on new bands, and we may get a few more gigs if we're popular. The young people really love their music and dancing here.

I do miss home cooking, a warm bed and Mam and Dad but I'm not too homesick because we are having the best of times and doing what we dreamed of.

I'm writing to Mam but putting more of a gloss on the living conditions.

I've worried about you having to deal with Dad's bad mood after I left. I wish I hadn't mentioned talking things over with you. It did help to have a listening ear these past few weeks and I hope that one day I can repay you for giving me confidence in myself.

Has Dad cooled down? Is it safe for you to visit Blackthorn Farm?

The Germans are lovely people, but after losing Edward in the war, Dad isn't going to believe that. Is Mam okay?

I'd love some home news when you have time to write.

Auf Wiedersehen für jetzt (Goodbye for now)

Jim

CHAPTER 14

On the third Saturday of December, Danny lugged a huge Christmas tree up the stairs and Rose's eyes widened at the height of it. 'Lily chose it so don't blame me.'

He grinned as Lily protested, 'Dad! You told me to choose the tallest we could find.'

'We'll need to buy more tinsel and baubles,' Rose warned, as the tree stood at ceiling height in the corner of the living room.

'I'll buy some tomorrow,' Danny promised. 'I need to get rid of all of those farthings in the change jar. They aren't legal tender after the thirty-first, so it'll save me taking them to the bank.'

He lifted Lily up onto his shoulders as they all stood back and admired their grand tree. 'If you sit on my shoulders, you'll easily be able to reach up and put the star on the top. Get the star and we'll do that now.'

'The star is supposed to go on last, Danny.'

'Who says that?' he asked.

'I say that.' Rose tried to look stern but broke into a smile. It was like having two children at times, but Rose loved the enthusiasm her man brought to everything he did.

'Well, *I* say that from now, the Dodd tradition is to put the star on *first*. Those in favour say "Aye!"'

'Aye!' Lily giggled as Danny slid her from his shoulders.

'Come on Lily, let's find the box of decorations and make a start.'

Rose smiled. Christmas had started, and who was she to stand in the way of a new tradition?

On Christmas morning, they ate breakfast and opened presents at home, before leaving to stay for two nights with their Linwood family. Lily would stay with Grandma and Grandad Kelly and sleep top to tail with Johnnie, and Rose and Danny would sleep over at The Dodds' house in Third Row. Mr and Mrs Dodd were having their Christmas dinner at Joe's this year, but they would all squeeze together into First Row later on for a Christmas night of games and a few drinks.

Rose unwrapped a book-shaped present that had been teasing her under the tree since it appeared a few days ago. Danny was thoughtful but he didn't usually choose a book for her because she had read so many, and she used the library every week. She'd already opened a box containing leather gloves, so this extra gift intrigued her.

A glimpse of orange told her it was a Penguin book, and then she saw the title, *Lady Chatterley's Lover*. This full edition had just been published after a court case about its content last month. It had flown off the shelves in hours because of the publicity the case had been given, but Danny had managed to get her one. 'Danny! This is wonderful, thank you.' She flew into his arms to give him a kiss.

'You'd better not take that to Linwood for bedtime reading or my mother will have palpitations.'

'You're right. I don't want to get into an argument about D. H. Lawrence and what should or shouldn't be in his novels. I love him, and for me he can do no wrong.' She carefully placed the book on her bookshelf. She would be poor company anyway if she took a book with her because she would want to slip away and read it.

Rose started packing yet another carrier bag with the paraphernalia she needed to stow in the boot of the car. 'Can we call in to Blackthorn Farm on the way to Linwood, Danny? I have a bag of apples for the ponies, and I'd like to wish the Fairbairns a Merry Christmas. I didn't see Daphne before I left yesterday.'

'That's fine, as long as we leave in a few minutes,' Danny agreed. 'We don't want to be late for Grace's turkey. She's overjoyed to be cooking a turkey instead of the usual chicken from Dad's allotment, so we'd better be early to enjoy it.'

Rose nodded, then swiftly got herself and Lily into their best coats. Grace was a brilliant cook, so anything she produced would be delicious.

They parked on the track leading to the farmhouse and Rose and Lily walked along to the field to feed the pit ponies apples, whilst Danny went in search of Ted Fairbairn who would be in one of the barns. There wasn't much time off on a farm, even for Christmas. The animals all needed to be fed and cared for, and the dairy herd still needed to be milked.

After the apples were demolished, Rose and Lily headed to the farmhouse. The top half of the kitchen door was open and Daphne Fairbairn was sitting at the large table, staring into a cup of tea.

Rose leaned over the bottom half of the door so Daphne could see her. 'Are you reading the tea leaves?'

Daphne jumped. 'You startled me, Rose. The tea leaves? No, I'm not looking into the future, I'm just deep in thought. I'm wondering what Jim's doing right now.'

She was red-eyed; she'd shed a tear or two. It was natural she'd miss her youngest. 'I'm sure he'll be having a wonderful time. He was going to Eric's brother's for the day wasn't he?'

Daphne nodded but seemed to be too choked to speak.

'Lily love, go to the barn and find your dad and Farmer Fairbairn. They might allow you to stroke the barn kittens, but try to keep your good coat clean.'

'I'll leave it here.' She threw off her coat, slung it over the door and ran off.

Daphne looked up. 'Young 'uns never feel the cold. Come in and I'll pour you a cup of tea.'

Rose let herself in and slipped into the chair beside Daphne. 'Don't fret. Jim wouldn't want you to be unhappy. He's coming back to England for a few weeks in the summer, isn't he?'

'He is, but he'll be playing in London and Liverpool and the like – I'll not see much of him. I'm being silly, I know, but today is the first time we've had nobody but ourselves at the Christmas table. There's Edward, missing in action, and I miss him every day. I can't help imagining the children he might have had who would be running all over this place. Our two girls live too far away to travel for the day. Maureen's a farmer's wife, and they can't leave the farm. Ann looks after her father-in-law who had a stroke, so... It's just me and Ted and a huge turkey.

What will we do once we've eaten? We'll have two hours to look at one another until the Queen's speech and another hour until evening milking.'

'I hadn't realised there'd just be the two of you,' Rose said as Daphne poured out her cup of tea.

'Don't get me wrong, we're as happy as fleas on the farm cat most of the time, but Christmas is about family isn't it?'

They sat for a moment while Rose tried to think of something cheery to say. She took a sip of tea and it came to her, a solution. 'I know! Why don't you drive over to Linwood straight after dinner and spend a couple of hours with our clan? We just chat or play a few games then listen to the Queen, but it'll be company – a change of scenery.'

Daphne forced a smile. 'We couldn't do that, it would be imposing.'

'We'd love to have you! Grace will be handing around mince pies and cake even though we've just had dinner, and you'd be more than welcome. Bring some turkey sandwiches along if it would make you feel better.'

Mrs Fairbairn squeezed her hand. 'You're a kind lass, thank you Rose. It would be nice to meet them before... Oh, what am I saying? Anyway, I doubt if Ted will even consider moving from his chair after dinner, but thanks so much for asking.'

Rose tried to follow the conversation. Meet them before what? When she thought about it, she doubted Ted would agree too. He was set in his ways was Ted.

'Meet them before what, Daphne?'

'I just got confused and lost my thread of thought, hinny. Enjoy your Christmas day.'

CHAPTER 15

*R*ose and Daphne were wrong about Ted.

After dinner Rose cleared the dishes while Grace filled the sink in the tiny scullery with hot sudsy water, and Lottie and Dennis from next door called around with Paul. All the children were having a noisy time of it when a knock came at the front door. Grace jerked her head up from the sink. 'Who's that, Rose? Mam and Dad aren't coming until five. Who would be calling at the front door on Christmas Day?'

All their relatives came through the backyard to the back door, it could only be Daphne and Ted. 'I think it's the Fairbairns.'

'The Fairbairns? The Fairbairns! You invited them here and didn't say? Oh Rose, I'd have cleaned up sooner.'

Rose laughed. 'Grace, the house is spotless, you have the best china out, and Dad and Danny are dressed in their Sunday best, so you haven't exactly been caught on the hop.'

'That's true,' Grace agreed.

They heard new voices and Rose was right. Danny was ushering the Fairbairns inside.

Rose took off her apron and went to greet them. Mr Fairbairn carried a covered tray, and Mrs Fairbairn carried a trifle. 'We didn't want to come empty-handed,' she explained. 'Please don't be offended, but there's nobody to eat these at the farm.'

After introductions were made, Lottie and Robbie popped back to their house next door to bring along two extra dining chairs. Rose smiled as Ted, Robbie, Danny and her dad became caught up in a debate about politics. For a change it wasn't Macmillan but the new United States president they were discussing. Ted thought Kennedy was a good chap but too young; Dad disagreed, and thought forty-three was experienced enough in life.

'I'm pleased the Catholics are getting a look in for once,' Dennis said. He wasn't a staunch Catholic, but sided with them when he thought it was called for.

Danny joined in with, 'Kennedy fought a good campaign, and the Democrats deserve a chance.'

Lottie took the youngsters upstairs and settled them with their toys. The main bedroom had the fire warming it as it always did on Christmas Day, and the three youngsters loved the novelty of playing in the upstairs room.

Grace and Daphne compared Christmas cake recipes and the cooking of poultry. As Daphne explained how she'd cooked her turkey, Rose yawned. Time for a short stroll or she would fall asleep.

Leaving Lottie and Grace to start another round of washing up, she took the Fairbairns for a stroll to the allotments. They marvelled at how much could be grown on the small plots. She showed them Dad's shed filled with canvases.

'Your father was saying he painted, but I had no idea he was so clever at it,' Ted said. 'Look at this!' He admired a painting of a group of pit ponies in a field on their summer break. 'This could be from our farm, couldn't it, Daphne?'

'It certainly could,' Daphne agreed.

'If you like, I'll ask Dad to paint your own pit ponies when the weather's better.'

Ted shook his head. 'Don't you put onto him, lass. Your father does a hard job without me eating into his free time.'

'But it's what he loves, Ted, just like you with your Ayrshire stock and Jim with his music. Painting is what he loves best.' Rose saw a flicker, a kind of understanding light up Ted's eyes.

'Speaking of which,' he checked his pocket watch. 'We had better be getting back soon to see to our beasts.'

'You'll just have time for a piece of Grace's Christmas cake and a cup of tea. The roads are empty today, so it'll only take half an hour door to door.'

Johnnie and Lily were still playing upstairs and Lottie and Dennis had taken Paul home, so there were just four of them left in the living room when the Fairbairns took their leave.

'Goodbye Ted, we'll see you soon no doubt,' Dad called as they drove off.

See them soon? Dad must've decided to paint at the farm, Rose thought.

'What a grand chap that Ted is,' Dad said, once the Fairbairns had driven away. 'I just can't imagine him firing you and being so hard on his son, can you, Grace?'

'He's nicer than I expected too,' Grace agreed.

'He hasn't had it easy. He lost his dream of having a son take on the farm after him and he looked for someone to blame,' Danny explained. 'We can all act the goat when we feel let down.'

'That's true.' Dad nodded and looked at Rose. 'I don't forget being a doylem and blaming our family troubles on you, Rose. I rue the day we fell out because I thought you had sided with your mother.'

Rose walked over to Dad's chair and planted a kiss on his forehead. 'That's all in the past, Dad.'

'Aye, it's the past – but the past has a habit of catching up with us, pet. I still think it might.'

'What do you mean by that, John?' Grace came in from the scullery carrying a tray with several sherry glasses on it.'

'I mean we may get a surprise visitor one day, and I hope we do. In fact, let's drink to that.'

They all raised their glasses as Dad said, 'To Joy's return!'

Then there was a knock on the back door, and they all started. Rose, for a second, thought they'd conjured her missing sister up. The door opened and Mrs Dodd appeared, followed by Mr Dodd. 'We're a bit early – Merry Christmas! I see you've got the sherry ready, our Grace. I'd love one… and a cup of tea, so get the kettle on, lass.'

CHAPTER 16

$\mathcal{R}$ose was only home above the bakery for a couple of days, because they were returning to Linwood for New Year's Eve. They lived far enough north to celebrate a new year just as enthusiastically as their Scottish neighbours over the border. On New Year's Eve there were parties and dances and the custom of 'first footing' after midnight. Visiting the neighbours to 'bring in' the new year was taken seriously in the rows.

It was good luck if the first foot over the doorstep was a dark-haired male carrying coal because this combination was known to ward off bad luck. A great deal of arranging went on in the rows to ensure the ginger and fair-headed males and all women stood back to help this good luck along.

Lots of knocking on doors went on just after midnight, and at every house the visitors were offered a new year's glass to toast the health, wealth and happiness of its inhabitants. Nobody was turned away, and the visits went on into the early hours.

On the Thursday in between Christmas and New Year Danny stood by the kitchen door and asked Rose a strange question;

strange for Danny, anyway. 'Does that smart suit you wore for our wedding still fit you, Rose?'

'I think it would, but why do you ask?'

'I'd like you to take the whole outfit to Linwood to wear again on New Year's Eve, for our wedding anniversary,' he explained.

Rose turned from the bench where she was peeling potatoes, put her arms around Danny's neck and kissed him. He wrapped his arms around her, and the kiss became a lingering one that would definitely have led to something if Lily hadn't been organising her new doll's house in the living room. When she broke away Rose said, 'Danny, I'm glad you remember the outfit, but a wool shift dress and matching jacket isn't the best choice for Burnside dance.'

'Take something for the dance too. I'd really like you to wear the dress in the afternoon.'

'Why? Are John and Grace having special visitors? Do you know something I don't?'

Danny laughed. 'You've hit the bull's-eye. Yes, I know something you don't, and I want you to take that smart outfit – and I'm not answering any more questions until New Year's Eve.'

Rose left her potato peeling to check out her bridal outfit. It was hanging at the back of her wardrobe in the cover it was bought in. She had worn it for her wedding six years ago, then for Johnnie and Lily's christening and for her brother Stanley's wedding, but it still thrilled her to look at it. It had been on sale at Hannah's of Gosforth and the material and workmanship were exquisite. The dark crimson dress was a plain shift, and the jacket was a swing style with unusual ornate buttons; it was a classic outfit and didn't look dated. The matching velvet bandeau hat set if off beautifully.

The dress zipped up easily. If anything Rose had lost a pound or two because of her energetic job on Blackthorn Farm. She'd leave the outfit on the outside of the wardrobe and the creases would drop out by Saturday afternoon. What did Danny know that she didn't?

'Oh, you too!' Grace exclaimed as she carried her outfit in to one First Row on Friday evening.

'What do you mean?' Rose asked.

'John has asked me to wear my wedding suit tomorrow, but he won't say why.'

'He's planned something with Danny, I'm sure of it! Maybe it's a special photograph? Why else would it be *these* outfits? I'll boil if I wear wool at Burnside dance on New Year's Eve.'

When Lily and Johnnie were settled for the night, Dad took out the sherry and the whisky and the best glasses. 'We have an announcement about tomorrow,' he chuckled, looking pleased with himself as he poured two sherries and two whiskies out.

'Spill the beans. We've guessed a visit to the photographer.' Rose was sure she was right.

'More than that, lassie, although a photographer is part of it.' Dad looked as smug as a wily gallowa who'd snaffled a pitman's bait. 'You tell them, Danny lad. It was your idea.'

Danny took a glass saying, 'Let's raise our glasses to us, the Dodds and Kellys first.'

They raised their glasses, then Grace chided him, 'Do get on with it, Danny. You've got Rose and me on tenterhooks!'

'Here's the plan. Tomorrow, New Year's Eve, is not just our sixth wedding anniversary – it is going to be a celebration to remember for the four of us. We missed each other's weddings, so we've arranged a special blessing to put that right. We're having a blessing at the chapel, then family photographs, then a bit of a party put on by Mam and Dad back at Third Row before we go off to the Burnside dance. It's all arranged, so you just have to be ready for eleven in the morning.'

Rose was speechless. Grace wasn't. 'Who's invited? Who's

doing the blessing? Mam'll need our best plates and cutlery or she won't have enough.'

Dad admitted, 'She took them yesterday while you were at the shops. I've been worried you'd notice them missing before we revealed the surprise.'

Grace dashed to the sideboard and opened it. Sure enough, all their best crockery was gone.

Danny took Rose into a tight embrace. 'Andrew is doing the blessing and Bella is playing the organ. Lottie and Dennis will be there. It'll be like last time, but in your own chapel instead of Gosforth.' Rose felt choked. What a beautiful surprise.

'Rose.' She turned at her dad's voice. 'Rose, I wanted to be able to walk you down the aisle. Would you like that?' Dad's eyes looked uncertain.

'Dad! I'd like nothing better.' She flew into his arms.

'And Grace,' Danny said, 'I'll be walking you down the aisle. I've cleared it with Dad.'

There hadn't been a New Year's Eve like it. Bella, her very first Sunday school teacher, was waiting at the door of the chapel with Andrew, her husband. He had married them six years ago when she wasn't speaking to Dad, and now he would bless the marriage and Dad would be present.

The chapel was decorated with holly, ivy and Christmas roses, and with the low winter sun appearing just on eleven, the stained glass window above the door showing Jesus as a shepherd with his flock shone a rainbow of light right down the aisle.

Bella took her place at the organ and the familiar tune of Wagner's 'Bridal Chorus' rang out as Dad escorted her down the aisle, followed by Danny and Grace. The men exchanged places when they reached Andrew and a blessing was given.

'We also have a gift of rings,' he said. It was hard to know who gasped loudest when Lily and Johnnie joined them with rings on smart velvet cushions. They sparkled in the candlelight. 'Eternity rings are given to seal your wedding vows, and to pledge your love for eternity,' Danny whispered.

Danny slipped a sparkling band onto her finger, and Rose couldn't see it for tears flooding her eyes and running down her cheeks. The organ piped out Mendelssohn's 'Wedding March'.

She walked back down the aisle, waving at Stanley and Brenda and gasping to see Helen and Matt with the Fairbairns; that explained Daphne's slip up about meeting her family. Jennifer held Lily's hand and she gave Rose a posy of winter violets as she passed them. Her eyes widened to see Frank Maxwell on the back pew with his father.

She had her man, her daughter, her family and friends around her; all she held dear. She had never been happier.

Still, a sadness clouded the moment. It wasn't her mother's early death, or her brother lost to diphtheria that saddened her; she could accept the grief that death brought to all families. It was the sister who was alive but didn't know she had a family who missed her. It was Joy missing out, yet again, that dampened her spirits.

In the small hours of the morning, Grace and Rose sat by the last embers of the fire. They were drinking tea, sitting in companionable silence and both admiring how their rings sparkled by the fire. Grace had three diamonds in a row on a gold band, and Rose had a gold band set with small diamonds and peridots, her birthstone.

Grace looked up at Rose. 'We have the best men in the world. I never dreamed such happiness could come to me, Rose.'

Rose nodded her head in agreement. 'I'll never forget today, and now we have family photographs! I can't wait to choose them for the album. 1961 will be a good year, it's had such a grand beginning.' The clock chimed two and Rose yawned. She stood up, ready for her bed. Danny had been there for an hour already.

'Your dad wasn't too pleased when Robbie knocked and walked in before Dennis or Danny. A fair-haired first foot, and empty-handed! He had to go back outside to find a piece of coal.' Grace carried the teacups to the scullery.

'Robbie was the worse for drink, Danny and Dennis should've pulled him back. Anyway, it's just a silly superstition.' They both shivered at the foot of the stairs. It was cold once you moved from the kitchen range.

'I hope you're right, hinny.' Grace kissed Rose on the cheek and they both crept upstairs, making sure they didn't tread on the creaky step third from the top.

CHAPTER 17

1961

*A*t the start of the year, the field in Seabottle was flattened and staked out for its new housing development; it was where Rose and Danny intended to buy their first property and they began to save even harder. Danny now ran two bakeries, so his hours were long and time flew by. They were going to choose their plot on the first day the sales office opened in July, and several times that spring they walked over to study the field intently.

They considered the view, the south facing gardens and the types of houses. They finally made their decision on an ideal plot, but they'd have to be first in the queue for it when the sales office opened.

It was the end of June and Rose hadn't seen her brother or Brenda, his wife, for weeks. The May bank holiday was when they last met up because working took up a lot of time and weekends were packed, with Lily's social life as well as their own. She really missed Brenda now their regular fortnightly meetings had gone by the wayside, so she was determined to meet her on Saturday. This was causing a bit of friction between her and Danny.

Danny, lying in bed with his hands behind his head, had a doleful look on his face and Rose knew why; he wanted her to go to the races. It was the Northumberland Plate, known locally as the pitmen's derby, at Gosforth Park on Saturday, but she had forgotten all about it. Rose felt torn as she sat at the dressing table brushing her hair. She liked the races, but she planned to meet Brenda in Morpeth on Saturday afternoon for tea and cake. Brenda's brief note to her on Monday had hinted at something she was excited about.

Rose, I'm shopping in Morpeth on Saturday. Try to meet up with me at the Clock Tower tea room for tea and cake at two. I've got surprising news. Brenda x

She turned to Danny, 'Sorry, love, I really am – but I haven't seen Brenda in weeks. Lily wasn't well last time we were due to meet, and you and I are going to look at the Seabottle housing development plans next Saturday to choose our plot. I don't want to ring her at work and put her off at this late stage. Besides, she mentioned important news.'

'I just can't believe you forgot the pitmen's derby, my favourite Saturday of the whole year, Rose. I wanted to take you and Lily like I did last year. She loves watching the horses.'

'I know, Danny. The date just slipped my mind while I was trying to guess Brenda's news. What do you think it could be?'

'A baby on the way, it's bound to be. This family is due to expand again – we haven't had a bairn since Johnnie arrived.'

He was echoing Rose's thoughts. 'Do you think so?' She padded over to the bed and he made room for her to fit into the crook of his arm. 'They've been married two years now. I could be an auntie soon!'

'I'll bet you a tenner to your ten shilling that is the news she wants to tell you.'

'I wouldn't bet on such things, Danny Dodd – it could bring bad luck. Anyway, if you're right I'll just have to look surprised.'

'Of course you must.' He laughed and mimicked Rose. '"Oh Brenda, well I never! You've taken me completely by surprise. I'll need a slice of Victoria sponge to revive me."'

Rose laughed and slapped his shoulder. 'Stop it! We might be totally wrong anyway.'

Danny turned and took her in his arms. 'You know, Rose, I've been thinking. It's high time we added to our own family.' He kissed her brow, and she raised her head to look into those inky blue eyes that always sparkled with laughter to check whether he was serious. He was.

'I love you, Danny, but I thought we'd agreed to wait until after we had moved.'

'I've been promoted, and we have our house deposit. We're choosing our plot next Saturday. That house will be up in no time, so we don't have to wait any longer, do we?' He kissed her brow.

While she was thinking of what to say, Danny changed tack. 'Rose, I could take Lily to the races and give you time with Brenda on your own. She'll bring me luck when I bet on The Plate. Is that all right with you?' Danny looked at her expectantly.

'There are such big crowds on Plate Day, Danny, and she can be a handful. Are you sure you'd keep a close eye on her?'

He pulled her closer to him and grinned. 'Of course I will!' Danny's lips found hers and soon she was lost in their warmth. His kisses and the desire they awoke in her meant she had to be careful, or that new addition would arrive before their new house had a roof.

. . .

Saturday dawned sunny and clear; Rose woke early but turned into Danny's warm arms and they lost all track of time, so they were running more than a bit late. Danny studied the horses running in the big race while Rose dressed Lily. She'd chosen a pretty blue dress with a bright yellow cardigan over the top, and a matching ribbon to keep her curls out of her eyes; that vivid splash of colour would make it easier for Danny to keep an eye on her.

'Who would you fancy if you were coming with us, Rose?' Danny handed her the list of horses who were running in the Northumberland Plate.

Rose glanced down the list. 'That one.' She took his pencil and circled Utrillo.

Danny laughed. 'I've spent an hour studying the form and you pick a horse out straight away. Why Utrillo?'

'Because Utrillo is an artist, self-taught like Dad, and I like his work.'

'Nothing to do with little Des Cullen, who used to ride Red God and Oxo out, riding him for Bill O'Gorman then?'

'Oh? Yes, of course… that as well.' She handed the paper back and planted a kiss on Danny's cheek. He'd been a bookie's runner in his youth and was the expert on studying the horse racing form. He looked handsome wearing his best racing cap, a beige and green check, with a tweed jacket and an open-necked white shirt.

She had a final word with Lily. 'Keep an eye on Daddy at all times. Look for his beige and green cap if you get parted, and if you ever do, stand still in one place until he finds you. He won't miss your yellow cardi.'

'Rose!' Danny frowned at her and she could sense his irritation.

'Sorry! I just wish I was going too.'

'Not my fault,' he mumbled.

'Danny, don't be like that.'

He sighed. 'Come here and give me a hug, then we'll both enjoy our day.' He tucked a strand of hair away before whispering in her ear.

'I know you worry, but I'll guard that bairn with my life. I love you.'

His assurances waylaid Rose's worries. 'I'll see you back at First Row after the races,' she said, kissing his cheek before picking up her bag. Danny was dropping her at the bus stop to catch the Morpeth bus and then going on to Gosforth Park for the races.

They'd arranged to meet up later at Linwood colliery rows because Lily was looking forward to staying at her Grandma and Grandad Dodd's overnight. Rose would enjoy going out for an hour or two with Danny and their friends, Lottie and Dennis, and then they'd stay over with her dad and Grace at First Row and enjoy a family Sunday.

CHAPTER 18

*A*fter a lovely afternoon filled with tea, cake and gossip, Rose caught the bus to Linwood colliery. She couldn't wait to tell Danny they had guessed correctly; she was going to be an auntie! Brenda looked a ghastly white colour when they met and couldn't face her cake, but she was overjoyed to be pregnant.

'We've been trying for ages,' she'd confided. 'Won't your Stanley make a great dad?'

Stanley was a strapping farmer of twenty-five now; two years younger than Brenda, but older than Rose when she had Lily. Still... Rose just couldn't imagine her little brother being a dad. Where had the years flown? Her other brother, Terry, was fifteen and doing well at King Edward VI school in Morpeth; she hoped that if Terry did well in his exams he would stay on into the sixth form.

Her mind floated back to Brenda's farm, thinking how lovely it would be to raise children in all that fresh air and space. When she got off the bus she was still lost in thought. It took a moment to register that Lottie and Dennis were standing there and they were waiting for her.

Lottie rushed towards her and clasped her in a bear hug, a groan escaped her lips and she was sobbing.

Rose's insides turned to ice. What was coming next? Why were they here?

'Rose, pet. There's been an accident.' Dennis's voice quivered and his eyes were all red and swollen. Dennis crying? Who?

'Dad? Lily?' she managed to ask through dry lips. Her eyes searched his for a clue of what was coming.

'No hinny, it's your Danny.'

Danny? 'My Danny?'

'He's been run over, Rose.' Lottie clinched both her hands until they hurt.

'Where is he? I have to see him.' Energy surged through Rose. She'd see him and make sure he soon mended.

'He's gone, Rose. He died.' Dennis's words almost made her laugh, but Dennis wouldn't joke like that.

She heard herself calling out, 'Danny!' and everything went black.

Rose woke with her head banging in her temples and a tight vice around the back of her neck. Her tongue was too big for her mouth, and she was too dry to swallow or lick her lips. Where was she?

A darkened room with the curtains closed, but she made out the shape of the wardrobe and chest of drawers. It was her old room at Dad's. Her pillow was soaked. Tears?

Then it all came back. Was it real? Had she lost him? She lay in the darkness but she couldn't think. The doctor... she'd been drugged, she couldn't raise her head. Her head swam and she was back in the isolation hospital when she was a girl... Christmas. She saw Danny tapping at her window with his cheeky grin and then cycling off into the mist. That grin had never changed.

She closed her eyes and saw his smile and remembered his

promise this morning before he disappeared into the mist again. Then she sank back into darkness.

Later that night Rose sat by the fire at her dad's with Grace. Dad had left them with a cup of tea laced with whisky each and gone up to bed. 'Is Lily okay with your mam?' Rose needed to see her soon but didn't want to upset the little girl any further by sobbing all over her. At the moment, she would.

'Yes, she was happy to stay with Grandma and Grandad Dodd tonight, with our Johnnie as planned. I don't think she's taken it all in properly, Rose – she's in shock too. I'm glad the bairns are sleeping over at Third Row, it's kept Mam and Dad from breaking down. Dad, well, he idolised Danny, didn't he? Tonight, once the bairns are asleep, I think Mam will fall to pieces too.'

'She will. She's lost a son.' Rose wasn't really thinking as she said this, and Grace's sob brought to mind that her comment wasn't quite true.

She remembered the night Danny admitted his suspicions that his big sister had him when she was in her teens, and not having a partner to stand by her handed him over to her mam. He'd heard plenty of whispers. It was the night Rose told him about Joy and what her own mam had done, and he had understood. As long as a bairn is loved... that was his opinion.

She grasped Grace's hand. 'I mean, you both have,' she whispered. 'Danny loved you so much, you know.'

Grace nodded. 'We need say no more.'

They sat in silence for a while. Rose revisited each minute of that morning and remembered those words he whispered in her ear to assure her 'I'll guard her with my life, Rose, I promise. I love her, and I love you.'

She had answered, 'I know you will, and I know you do.' Rose wrapped her hands around the cup and shivered, even though the fire glowed brightly. Oh, to turn the clock back and say she'd go with them.

'Do you know what happened, Grace?'

'We've heard bits. A couple of Danny's friends saw him and Lily and they told us about the day, but we only have Lily's story of how the accident happened. The police are talking to eyewitnesses though.' Grace drained her cup and took Rose's. 'I may as well drink this because you're not going to.'

Rose sat up and braced herself to hear what had happened. 'Tell me all you know.'

'Danny and Lily were seen having a lovely time. Danny carried her on his shoulders and was collecting some winnings when some men from Third Row chatted to him. After that, Dennis and Robbie bumped into him. He'd bagged the winner of the big race and he was saying Lily had brought him luck. He didn't have a pint with them because he had the bairn, and he was driving.'

'Utrillo won the big race then.' Rose smiled.

'I don't know about that, but Danny and Lily enjoyed their day at the races and the lads said he carried the bairn all over and kept her away from the drinking and cursing.'

'Where did he... where did the accident happen?' Rose gazed into the flames, leaping so strongly yet easily put out... like Danny.

'The police say he was travelling back on the A1 and pulled in at Wideopen shops – you know, just before the Reno cinema? He must've left Lily in the car for a minute, because when he came out she was in the middle of the road, and he sprinted and pushed her out of the way of a busload of racegoers on their way home.'

'Why was she in the road? Why did he leave her in the car? Why did this have to happen, Grace? Why?' A fresh surge of pain filled the emptiness. It was just as bad as the others. '*Why Danny?*' she raged.

Grace wiped tears away. 'I'm damned if I know. It wasn't the bairn's fault, it wasn't Danny's fault, it was just one of those things. Lily told me the bees had been bothering her all day because of her cardigan and ribbon. She'd taken her cardi off but it became chilly, so her dad buttoned it up on their way to the car. Anyway, when he opened the door to go to the shops, a bee must've got in and it frightened the bairn. She says it was in her hair so she swatted it off and opened the door, but it chased her. That's how she ran into the road.'

'It's my fault. My clever idea of putting her into that bleedin' yellow cardigan. How could I forget the flies and bees were attracted to it last summer? Oh Grace, it's my fault he's gone!'

Grace reached out and took Rose in her arms. 'There, there, hinny. Nobody is to blame.'

Rose knew different. She was the one who hadn't gone to the races; she put the gaudy cardigan on the bairn; she had badgered Danny until he had said he'd guard her with his life. She'd killed the love of her life.

CHAPTER 19

They had the funeral service in the chapel. The Dodds weren't churchgoers as such, but Danny had gone along now and then with Rose and he had been happy to see Lily start at their local Sunday School. Rose held Lily's hand and they walked up to the front with Grace, Terry and Johnnie to sit beside Mr and Mrs Dodd.

The doors were open and the chapel was filled with the heady fragrance of lilies and roses. As the organ started Rose looked behind to see her dad, Stanley, Dennis and Mr Dodd carrying Danny's coffin through the doors. Dappled colours from the stained glass window played on the brass of the coffin. Rose was taken back to the Sunday that Danny and Robbie shouted about going to war; their faces had been full of excitement and a rainbow of colours from that very window. Twenty years... twenty years and ten months. Danny! Tears flowed down her cheeks. He'd been cheeky, he'd been fun, he'd been loving; he'd been brave and he'd been hers. Her Danny. He'd been perfect for her, and she had been perfect for him.

What was she going to do now?

As they were leaving the chapel, Larry Elliot grasped Grace's hand. 'I'm so sorry, Grace,' he whispered, and tears coursed down his cheeks. It was a bit flaming late to be sorry. Rose flashed him a warning look and was about to lead Grace away, but Grace unlinked her arm from Rose and embraced Larry Elliot. How could she give him comfort after he'd been the one who left her to face her parents and hide Danny's birth from the rows?

Rose stalked off. Grace was far too soft.

Later, as they were having tea and sandwiches in the room above the Co-op, Rose couldn't help but question Grace. 'How could you give Larry a hug? His mother, Mary Elliot, told me he was the coward who left you in the lurch. Danny knew too.'

'We were just bairns, hinny. He was only sixteen and scared. He's missed out on a fine lad and I haven't. He gave me my greatest gift – Danny has been a light in my life, and I've never regretted having him.'

'You don't hate Larry then?'

'Hate him? I was soft on him for years, that's why I never came out and revealed who the dad was. I worried about folks guessing when Danny started to take on the looks of an Elliot. How can I hate my first love? And now look at me. Here's me with the best man in the rows and another bonnie laddie, and what has Larry ended up with? Moaning Kate, that's what.' She smiled. 'Don't fret about me, Rose. Twenty-nine wonderful years, even if I couldn't ever say he was mine.'

'He knew, Grace. He loved you.'

'Aye. We were close, we didn't need to spell it out.'

After the funeral, Rose returned to their flat above the baker's in Alnwick. How she wished she still had Danny here to talk about it; she ached to be in his arms and talk about the whole sorry mess. What would he say about Grace being so kind to Larry? Did he like the service?

She'd been staying at Linwood since the accident, but she

wanted to be back home so she could put Lily into her own bed and try to find a new kind of normal.

'Is Daddy in heaven and looking down on me right now, Mam?' Lily asked.

'He is, sweetheart. He's thinking it's time you closed your eyes.' Rose was turning into her own mother. Every bedtime conversation with her own mam had been answered with, it's time to close your eyes. Rose sat with Lily until she slept.

Their bedroom was as she left it on the day of the races; bed hastily made, Danny's clothes kicked into a corner – he could never find the washing basket – and her nightdress draped over the chair after Danny had removed it and persuaded her back into bed that morning.

They'd made love and it had made them late, but oh she was glad they had taken the time for lovemaking. They'd worshipped one another, never knowing it would be the last time.

By the door she'd left the carrier bag she'd been given by the police... Danny's race day clothes. She pulled them out. A speck or two of blood on his shirt.

'I'll scrub that out so it will be like new, Danny.' She took an intake of breath to protect herself from the fresh pain. There was no need; Danny wouldn't be wearing it again.

His jacket was in there, and his cap. She brought out the jacket and hugged it. She saw the package crushed in his pocket, and it became clear why he'd stopped at the shops. Mystery solved – a battered box of Roses. 'Roses for a Rose,' he'd always grin and tell her. He'd pulled over to buy her chocolates. Oh Danny, you silly beggar! I love you!

She lay on the bed, sobbing and hanging tightly onto his jacket until the room was in darkness. She must have fallen asleep. After lighting the bedside lamp she hung the jacket on the outside of the wardrobe. All that was left in the bag of belongings was his cap.

Rose knew Danny well. She knew what he kept in that cap.

She picked it up and inhaled deeply... Danny's hair cream, part of Danny's smell. Feeling along the peaked brim, she found the cut in the lining and reached inside. Yes, she was right; two rolls of cash. Danny always kept his wins safely tucked into his racing cap.

She took the rolls over to the dressing table, cleared her hairbrush and lipstick to one side, and began counting. Her heart pounded as she realised how much he had won. He'd bet on Utrillo, her choice, and Danny had experienced his best day at the races. After the biggest win of his life, he'd died bravely, knowing he had saved Lily. Danny Dodd would be grinning somewhere and calling that a bleeding good last day on earth.

'What about me, Danny? You've left me and I don't know what to do.' She'd been Danny Dodd's Rose; now who was she? She was Danny Dodd's widow. What else did life have in store for her?

CHAPTER 20

'We'll always make room for you here, lass.' Her dad was in the yard sketching Johnnie and Lily playing marbles by the gate. There was exactly a year between them, and they played happily together.

'It's a tight squeeze as it is with you and Grace and the two lads. I'll find somewhere not too far away so I can go back to work – that is, if Grace will watch Lily after school.'

'What about the Dodds' spare room? Grace and all the lads have left the nest now.'

'Dad! Me and Mrs Dodd? She's okay to visit but...'

'Aye, she'd take over with Lily and you'd quarrel. You haven't Grace's placid nature. The trouble is that all our houses are colliery except for Front Street where the shops are.'

Rose bristled a bit at Grace having a nicer nature, but he was right. 'You've given me an idea, Dad. I'll just pop over to Norris's. Shall I bring some ham and pease pudding back?'

'Grace likes to make her own ham and pease pudding, pet.'

Grace could do no wrong in her dad's eyes, and it still galled her at times. 'Dad, life is too short for boiling your own ham and making pease pudding – unless it's an occasion. I'll bring some back.'

She understood that she'd have to move. It was only common sense that she'd be asked to leave the Alnwick flat; they needed it for the manager who would replace Danny. She had managed to persuade the manager and his wife to keep on Meg Mason as a help in the house, so she wasn't leaving Meg in the lurch.

'How you can think about me when you have your own troubles I don't know, bonny lass,' Meg said as she hugged her farewell.

It still hurt, though. Her wonderful life with Danny was over, and she had to pack up their possessions and memories. Lily had settled into Seabottle primary school and had done well there, but now Rose would have to find somewhere else to live and put Lily's name down to start a new school in September.

Mr and Mrs Fairbairn offered her and Lily a room so she could keep Lily at school and continue to work at the farm, but the thought of seeing the new houses go up near the school, the house she was going to put a deposit on with Danny was too much… no, she wanted to be away from there, away from what could have been and in her own home with her grief. She wanted to be near her own folk and Danny's, and that meant stepping away from the job she loved and the house she couldn't have.

She never dreamed they'd be back at the rows one day, but if she wanted to find another job she'd have to be near to her family. That meant she needed to rent in Linwood or neighbouring Burnside, and as Dad said, the rows belonged to the National Coal Board and were solely for their miners. He'd reminded her that Front Street, with Norris's shop, Charlie's chippy and the double fronted shop that housed the barbers on one side and the hairdressers on the other, was a possibility. All of them had flats above so she decided to visit Mrs Norris to find out about renting one.

'Thanks for the tea, Mrs Norris. No, I'll not have a biscuit.' Rose was in the back storeroom sitting on a stool as Mrs Norris made up orders for Mr Norris to deliver.

'You were asking about the flats. The one above Charlie's is identical to ours, and you've been up there often enough. Two bedrooms, a big kitchen, a long scullery and steps down to the back yard and outside toilet. It's empty because Charlie shuts up shop and goes home to Burnside – but mind you, it'll stink to high heaven of fish 'n' chips, and so will your lovely new furnishings. The Lawsons might let you have the rooms above the barber's end – they lived there before they built their house onto the end of the street. The upstairs of the hairdresser's is used for stock, and there's a little cubby of a room for women who want their hair dye or perm done privately. Some of them pretend they're natural, you know. It would have to be the barber's side.'

'Will you put in a word, Mrs Norris? Ask the Lawsons first, because hair perm is better than chip fat, but I can't afford to be fussy.'

'I will, pet. We have one room here, you know, if you wouldn't mind sharing. Mr Norris and I, we wouldn't see you without a bed.'

'Thanks, Mrs Norris. It will be lovely to have you as a neighbour, but we do have a lot of stuff and need a bit of space to call home.'

Two days later Rose had the key to look at the flat above the Lawsons' shop. Mrs Norris had worked her charms on the couple because they weren't keen on letting it, but she'd assured them that Rose would be a good tenant. Rose had always had her hair trimmed by her mother before she'd gone to the hairdresser in Morpeth, so the Lawsons just knew her by the fact she was the pitman painter's daughter and Danny Dodd's widow.

Mr Lawson persuaded Mrs Lawson to agree because he knew the pitman painter and his lads who went in for their hair cuts, and he knew Danny from when he was a lad. They both felt sorry for her being left a widow but wanted to be sure she could pay, so Mrs Norris had offered to stand as a guarantor.

Rose thanked Mrs Norris. It vexed her, but she could see their point; she wasn't working.

She opened the back yard and found the toilet and wash house on one side of the yard, just as she expected. The concrete steps were dirty and the back door at the top of them was in need of a good coat of paint, but it unlocked smoothly. She turned the handle and stepped into a long scullery with a sink, a wooden bench and plenty of room for her new cooker and washer. The opening from the scullery into the main room had no door, just a limp old curtain across it, and pulling it back with the tips of her fingers, she walked into an airy square kitchen-cum-living area with a tiled open fireplace. Good, there was no range to black lead.

There were two windows looking out over the five rows, the pit wheel and the fields beyond. Across the street she could see into her dad's backyard and spied Lily and Johnnie, who were playing out. It was a great view of Linwood, and she couldn't get closer to First Row than this.

The door from the kitchen led to a narrow hallway, and to her relief the hairdresser's rooms and steps to the shops were blocked off. It looked like hardboard that Dad would use for his paintings, not soundproof, but it meant this living space was private.

A large bedroom with an alcove leading to a smaller room; this space would do for her and Lily. It was all filthy and hadn't been used in years, but she could see there was no damp and the dust and cobwebs were what her mam would've dismissed as 'top muck', nothing a good scrub couldn't shift. Yes, a scrubbing brush and mop, then some paint – maybe wallpaper to cover the bricks in the scullery – and she'd have to put down new lino.

She didn't know what they were charging yet. Mrs Norris had tried to find out, but she had to meet Mrs Lawson in person to agree terms.

'I've a feeling it depends on whether Mrs Lawson takes to you or not, hinny,' Mrs Norris sniffed. 'She's high and mighty at times – she's not Teasy-Weasy of London, but you'd think she was. Charges the earth for a perm.'

'It'll be good to have you as a neighbour, Mrs Norris.' She smiled, and it felt strange to stretch those muscles because she felt so sad all of the time. Perhaps being amongst old friends would help her to keep going. She had to keep going, for Lily's sake.

'Call me Elsie, please. You're a grown woman now.'

'All I need to do now is face Mrs Lawson and find out the rent.'

Mrs Lawson must have taken a shine to her, because she got the rooms for less than she was expecting. A bit of luck at last.

After a week of scrubbing, with the help of Lottie and Grace, and a week of painting and papering by her dad and Mr Dodd, the place smelled fresh and the windows sparkled.

'Grace can get a good shine on a window, can't she?' Dad asked.

Rose sighed. 'Yes, Dad, she can.' She had to agree with him, but she was sure no woman in the rows was ever praised as much as Grace; she couldn't remember her mam's cleaning ever being praised. Then again, after Mam he'd had to live with her efforts and fend for himself a lot for a few years, so no wonder he was grateful now.

Grace sewed curtains from a remnant they'd found in the

market in town. It was a bargain because the mustard with cream and black flowers was similar to an expensive Lucienne Days material she'd admired in Bainbridge's when she'd chosen her sofa. Before hanging them, Grace had given the windows the extra clean her dad was admiring.

A modern lino was laid right through the flat and it made all the difference; cream and gold flecked squares alternated with sage green and pistachio flecked squares, and the tiled pattern looked cheerful. She'd already brought her cream bedside rug and a large gold one for the fireside from Alnwick; the only handmade proggy mat would be at the back door in the scullery to stop dirt tracking through. Next week, when her furniture came in the Charlton's truck that Stanley was borrowing, the flat would take on the shape of home.

CHAPTER 21

wo days before her move back to Linwood colliery, Rose's birthday came around. For the first time, not a single soul remembered. Stanley was always hopeless, but even Dad must have missed the date because no card arrived in the post. She spent the day with Lily and kept herself busy by packing up the pieces of her life that she wanted to keep.

She excused Dad's memory lapse; he'd been on first shift all week and then spent hours painting upper three Front Street, and today he was fixing the rail in the backyard so the steps were safe for Lily to go up and down. There was too much going on to remember a silly birthday.

Rose told herself to be brave about reaching twenty-seven, already widowed, with her life packed into cardboard boxes. She checked the mat by the letterbox again. No, she hadn't got a single greeting.

After putting Lily to bed, she filled the bathtub with lots of water, added bubbles, sank into it, and then she howled... tears for being a widow, tears because she missed Danny, and tears because she couldn't see a future, but she had to be strong for Lily.

The torrent brought relief and got rid of the pressure of emotion that had been building up since Danny's funeral. She sank back into the tub, feeling exhausted but calmer, when the doorbell rang. Crikey! Anybody who knew her would know she was at home with Lily. She couldn't get out of the bath and let them see her in this pathetic state, could she?

It rang again. Dad and Grace didn't drive, so it *had* to be Stanley and Brenda calling because they'd remembered her birthday. She grabbed a towel and wrapped it around her; they'd understand how sad she was. She wrapped a smaller towel around her head as the doorbell rang again. 'All right, all right! I'm coming.' They'd wake Lily with that racket.

She opened the door and there was Frank Maxwell.

Frank was half-hidden by a gigantic bouquet of roses and a gift bag from Fenwick's of Newcastle.

'Frank!' She was open-mouthed and looked a mess, but she didn't care. Somebody had remembered. Hadn't Frank seen her being sick down an alley when they were in their teens? Hadn't he seen her when Lily was tiny, with hair like rats' tails and baby sick all down her dressing gown? Hadn't he always shown up in good times and in bad?

'I've called at a bad time, so I won't stay. I was in the area and just wanted to say happy birthday, Rose.'

She grabbed his hand. 'You will stay! It's always a bad time and I need adult conversation. Nobody else has remembered what day it is.'

Rose ushered Frank upstairs, remembering their first encounter when she was at school and she had fallen and cut her knee. Frank provided a handkerchief, and when he introduced himself, she'd realised he was Mr Maxwell the vet's son. They'd struck up a friendship and were both very taken with one another, but Frank's sister put paid to that.

When Frank went to Cambridge his sister Ruth intercepted their letters, so they lost touch for a long time. It was Rose's veterinary nursing job and a sick cat that reunited them, and they'd got their old friendship back but hadn't rekindled those romantic feelings of their youth. By then it was too late, because Danny had stolen her heart.

They opened the bottle of wine Frank had brought and toasted her birthday. Rose ate quite a few of the Belgian chocolates that were in the Fenwick's gift bag. 'It's so good to see you and talk about old times, Frank.'

'I know it's hard for you. I can't imagine... I'm here any time for you, Rose.'

'Thanks for that. Does Marjorie know you're here?' Marjorie, Frank's wife, had never been friendly towards Rose or Danny.

'Not exactly. We came north on Saturday for a week, and she gave me today off to catch up with old friends while she went shopping, then to the Coliseum with Ruth. I spent the afternoon in Morpeth and then made my way here on the off chance you would be home. I wasn't sure whether you'd want to see me or not. I didn't mention I might visit to Marjorie, because... well, I'm not sure she understands "male-female" friendships in the way Danny does... Oh God, I'm sorry, I mean *did*.'

Rose touched his hand, showing she understood. 'He didn't care for you at first! Remember the cat operation at Campbell's when you and I worked an all-nighter? Danny saw you leave the surgery the next morning and drove off in a huff. After that we didn't speak for a week or two, until he realised he had made an unfair assumption.' She paused before adding, 'I have to say this, Frank. I think Marjorie might be even *less* understanding about us being friends now that I'm a widow. I'll understand if you don't call around, I don't want to get you into trouble with your wife.'

'I think you could be right, Rose. She's sure I have a soft spot for you already and maybe she's right… but not in a romantic way.' Rose thought Frank looked a little flushed as he said that. He was used to her being forthright, but maybe this time she had embarrassed him.

He didn't stay long, and Rose walked downstairs with him. At the open door he kissed her cheek. 'You take care. I think the world of you, so whether Marjorie likes it or not, if you need help, I'm only ever a call away.'

Rose climbed back upstairs. A call away, a few hundred miles and a lifetime away. At one time in her teens she loved him as much, if not more, than Danny; but time and circumstance had changed those feelings. Now she was a widow, he was married, and Rose was sure Marjorie Maxwell wouldn't be keen on Frank seeing her on their rare trips north.

She picked up one of the chocolates he'd given her. It was nice that someone had remembered her birthday, but she'd give the world for her yearly box of Roses and to hear Danny's voice saying, 'Guess what? Roses for my Rose.'

CHAPTER 22

'I can't believe I forgot your birthday. My mind's been so taken up with making those steps safe for our Lily and you and getting that place in order, but it's no excuse. I remembered on Tuesday night, the minute my head touched the pillow, but it was too late to do owt about it by then.' Her dad scratched his head and looked sheepish.

'Don't fret, Dad, I know how much you've done.'

'Here, pet.' He pushed some notes into her pocket. 'That's not for the house. Go and get yourself some new things to wear. I'm sick of seeing you in that black frock.'

Rose kissed his cheek. 'It was new for the funeral.'

'Aye, and it's never been off your back except for a wash since then. Get something to cheer yourself up.'

Rose thought about what he'd said as she made her way over to Front Street. Dad was right, she'd worn the black shift dress with black stockings and ballet flats a lot. If it wasn't the dress, it was a pair of dark blue jeans and a black polo jumper. She couldn't face the trunk full of summer dresses she'd packed, because every one of them brought back a memory of being with

Danny. Anyway, they hung off her because she had no appetite and must've lost a few pounds.

The furniture was being heaved up the steps by Stanley and Dennis. They had wanted her out of the way, but she could always make them a cup of tea. Saying goodbye to her first home had been difficult, but now her furniture was being put in place Front Street felt a bit more like home.

Later that evening, after Lily was tucked up in the small room just off her bedroom, she sat on the sofa in front of the fire. She'd put candles in the grate because it was too warm for a fire and the room looked cosy in the flickering light, but it felt empty.

Rose usually curled up on this sofa with Danny. Everything was a memory. They'd gone into Newcastle and picked this modern Ercol sofa and its matching fireside chair with wooden legs and dark green cushions with care, because they were meant to last them a lifetime. They'd taken on weekly payments to Fenwick's; her dad didn't know that, he hated debt. Hadn't they been so proud when the furniture was finally all their own?

Tears, never far away, couldn't be held back any longer. 'Oh, Danny. It's going to be a long life without you. I hope you're watching over us and you're proud of how I'm keeping it together as best I can for Lily. I still can't take in that you're gone.'

Lily started at Linwood primary school during the first week of September. Johnnie, technically her uncle, started in reception and they put Lily up a year because she had done well at Seabottle school. She came home for lunch and was full of her morning. 'I have a lovely teacher, Mam. I'm really going to like it there!'

When Lily went off happily for the afternoon, Rose was left in the silent empty flat. The clock ticked, but Rose didn't want to put the radio on to drown its relentless counting of time without Danny.

Grief seeped its way into Rose's being. Sometimes it surged through her like a flood, but for most of the time it was just there, dampening her pleasure in life.

Next morning she decided she had to get out. This brooding was no good. After waving Lily off she put Dad's birthday money into her purse and walked to the main road to get a bus into Newcastle.

Wandering from store to store she perused the vivid skirts and blouses, but couldn't even find the enthusiasm to try them on. This black dress she had on, it suited her mood at the moment.

Lingering over a cup of tea in Fenwick's café, her thoughts drifted to Danny. How had she survived two whole months without him? Glancing at her watch, she realised she'd have to be quick, or she'd have to go home empty-handed. Lily would be home for lunch just after twelve.

She took a second tour of the department store and picked up a pair of black stretch slacks, a pair of black capri pants, a couple of fine knit black polo neck sweaters and a black sleeveless blouse. She looked for a sales assistant and a till without trying them on.

Her floral dresses and happy colours felt wrong on her just now, and she could understand how Dad had periods of using his dark sludgy paints whenever he was troubled. Earlier in the week, Lottie said she reminded her of Audrey Hepburn in *Funny Face* with all that black she was wearing. She'd enjoyed that film a couple of years ago with Danny.

As she was leaving the store, a pair of shoes caught her eye. Red shoes? Lottie would approve. She already had decent black shoes, so she tried on the red pair of ballet flats with a flat bow

on the front; a perfect fit, so she bought them. Ruby slippers –
Danny would've liked them, and now Dad couldn't say she'd
chosen *all* black.

The hours when Lily was at school dragged by. 'There is only so
much housework a woman can do without going mad, Grace. I
really want to earn my keep and keep our bit of savings for the
future, so I'm going to look for a job locally... that is, if you'll
watch Lily for an hour or so after school.'

'Aye, she's no bother. She can have a bit of dinner with
Johnnie and then play out until you're home.'

That settled it. Rose needed to face the world of work again.

CHAPTER 23

She had jumped at this job with Smedley and White, but was it a mistake? Rose glanced at her watch and her heart lifted; five o'clock at last, and she could go home. She'd never been a clock-watcher at Campbell's or at Blackthorn Farm, but working here was tedious. The two weeks she'd been employed had felt like an eternity.

Day after day she answered the phone, filed vets' notes, ordered stock, talked to clients and stood in her place at the reception desk watching the clock. The two older vets in this practice didn't hold with their assistant doing anything with the animals, and the youngest vet, who'd just joined the practice, had to toe the line. If only she'd known this before she started.

She seldom left the office or reception desk, and they didn't like her advising clients who came in. 'Mrs Dodd, please refrain from telling patients how easy it is to administer eye drops. Don't you realise that if they choose to return every day for a consultation, it benefits us?' Mr White looked indignant as a client left, smiling at her new skill.

'It's daylight robbery to charge daily though, isn't it?' She couldn't resist answering back. In the good old days when she was at Campbell's veterinary surgery, Roger, her boss, had encouraged her to do such services for free, and they kept their clients year after year.

'You'd better remember it's those consultations that pay your wages,' Mr Smedley reminded her.

She missed the camaraderie she had with Roger at Campbell's; work had been busy but rewarding. Helping to round up a herd of cattle for tuberculosis testing and standing by a colt as Roger injected him with an opioid before castrating him could be stressful, but it was always interesting. She'd been solely in charge of instruments and ensured they were boiled in the steriliser, but at White and Smedley's they didn't even give her that responsibility.

After leaving her job to have Lily, Rose had written down all she knew about assisting vets and Frank Maxwell had taken her work to show his father; it resulted in him helping her to publish a handbook for veterinary assistants. Rose and Frank had agreed the royalties should go towards funding treatment for pets whose owners couldn't afford it.

The Veterinary Assistant's Handbook by F Maxwell VetMB RCVS and R Kelly wasn't on the shelf of this practice, and when she mentioned it, without even saying she had a hand in it, Mr Smedley told her, 'Being a vet is men's work. In my opinion, female vets and female assistants shouldn't be contemplated.'

Rose had been speechless at the time, and now she wished she'd argued back and handed in her notice. Maybe working in Norris's shop, as she had before leaving school, would be more pleasant? Mrs Norris had offered her part-time work to fit around Lily's school day, and she wouldn't have to travel.

That evening Grace offered her a bowl of soup and a slice of a freshly baked stottie before she went home with Lily. 'You look peaky, pet. Are you eating at that job of yours?'

'I went to the park for some fresh air and ate a sandwich. Don't worry about me. I'm not sleeping very well and... and it's just got me thinking I might have jumped at the first job going.'

'What do you mean, hinny?' Grace sat down opposite her.

Breaking off a piece of bread, Rose explained. 'It's this job. The clients are great, but those two old fogeys aren't, and they don't like me talking to the clients or their pets much. They are members of the old guard, and a right pair to work for.'

'That's a shame... you could've been a vet yourself, your dad reckons.'

'Dad would say that!' Rose smiled. 'I just like working with animals, that's all, and I do have a way with them. Mr White had such a job with a lame dog today, and I know I could've helped him out – but no, it wouldn't have been my place to offer.' She took a bite of bread and sipped at her soup.

'That's his loss, I'd say,' Lily, who'd been reading, piped up.

Grace raised her eyebrows. 'Out of the mouths of bairns.'

Rose remembered being told off for 'cocking her lugs' many times when she was younger. 'I've told you about earwigging, Lily Dodd. Let me finish this soup then I'll get you home and ready for bed.' Rose felt better for talking about it instead of brooding.

There was a letter on their mat. The Yorkshire postmark and typed envelope told her it was from Frank, so she put it to one side to enjoy once Lily was settled for the night.

The clock chimed eight as Rose sat down with a cup of tea and reached for Frank's letter.

Dear Rose,

We're expecting a baby in April. It's marvellous news, but means that we're not likely to travel to Northumberland as often. Marjorie wants to be near her mother and doctor at all times, and who am I to argue?

I've followed the start of a new course for vet's assistants, supported by the Royal College of Veterinary Surgeons, with great interest. Have you read anything about it? It begins this year and I think it would be an ideal way for you to get a qualification. Unfortunately it is only being run at Berkshire Institute of Agriculture at the moment.

The year's fees are reasonable, although there are the exams to pay on top of that. The main drawback is that it's in Berkshire.

Maybe in the future a local college will take up the course. Send for Berkshire's brochure if you want to read more about it. Something for you to think about when Lily gets older?

Love, Frank.

Something to think about. Yes, that's all she could do – think and dream. The training was six months and then practical work; Smedley and White wouldn't want her to be hands on, anyway. It would be nice to look through the brochure for it though.

During their lunch break the next week Rose chatted about the new course to the young vet who was just out of training. She showed him the brochure she'd received, outlining the areas of study.

'It seems like a step in the right direction to me,' he said. 'It would take a lot of the everyday routine stuff off my hands, and I know that someone like you would be capable of lots of practical tasks.'

Mr Smedley, who chose that moment to collect his sandwiches from his cupboard in the kitchen, butted in. 'Absolute poppycock! I'm against it. It's a ridiculous scheme and I'm surprised at the Royal College of Veterinary Surgeons for having anything to do with it.'

'Why?' asked Rose.

'*Why?* Isn't it obvious? Veterinary medicine is a specialised profession, and young women like you should stick to what you *can* do.'

'And what exactly is that?' Rose felt her anger growing but tried to stay calm.

'Organising the office, making tea, and then going off to have babies. That's what.'

Rose stood up and her cheeks flamed as she spoke. 'I have never in my life met such a pair of old... old *dinosaurs* as you and Mr White. Women kept this country going during the war and helped to win it. We will not be put back into a place where out of touch men of your ilk are comfortable to keep us.'

'I think you should remember your place and watch your tone, Mrs Dodd.'

'No, I will not watch my tone. I've had enough of *my place* here. I'm resigning before I turn into a fossil too.'

'You're fired.'

'Didn't you hear me? I'm not fired because I resigned.' She grabbed her coat and bag and left the young vet looking white and open mouthed, and Mr White turning from puce to purple with rage.

CHAPTER 24

*R*ose got off the bus and walked over to Dad's allotment. Her heart lightened when she saw him bent over his spade digging up a row of new spuds. He lifted his head as she clicked open the gate.

'Hello, pet. Have you got a sharp lowse?'

Rose shrugged her shoulders; when a shift at the pit finished early it was a 'sharp lowse'. 'You could say that. I've walked out.'

'Pull up a cracket and I'll share a flask of tea with you. You can tell me all about it.'

After talking to Dad she wandered down by the burn to think through her options. She sat on the bank at the very place where she'd told Danny about her 'falling out' with her friend Lottie all those years ago. It had been the first time she realised that Danny Dodd had a thoughtful side and talked sense. When she was upset about Lottie being distant, he'd mentioned relationships could be for a reason, a season or forever, and she could only be herself. Oh Danny, I thought we'd be forever. Tears blurred her eyes and she wished with all her being that he was here to talk sense into her today.

But hadn't he given her the answer, right here all those years ago? He was with her, in her heart forever, and her Smedley and White season was well and truly over. Her sadness gave way to relief; she didn't have to button her lip or see them overcharge poor pet owners ever again. It would be nice to have a job like the one she had with Roger, but jobs and bosses like him were a rare find.

The next morning Rose went back into work to see whether she was expected to work her notice or whether she should take her pay packet and leave. She forced herself to open the door into Smedley and White's premises, and a couple carrying a box with a wailing cat tailgated her into the premises. 'We've been up all night with Smudge. He's been wailing and can't go to the loo.'

'Poor lad. Take a seat in the waiting room and I'll give you the first appointment.' She was about to ask if he'd eaten or drank any liquid and make a note, but remembered she wasn't to over-step her reception duties.

Mr Smedley entered the reception area. 'I hope you're feeling contrite, young lady.'

'I'm not, Mr Smedley. I'm feeling relieved that I've decided to resign. I'm here to find out if I must work my notice or whether I should take whatever wages are owing and go. I'd rather do that.' She met his eyes and caught his startled look.

'Oh.' He took off his glasses and made a slow job of cleaning them. 'In that case I think you should have the decency to work today and we will pay you your wages tonight. There's nobody else to take your place today so it would be very inconvenient.' He replaced his glasses, and as he made his way into the surgery he added, 'Show that young vet the ropes today. He'll have to fill in until we hire another girl.'

After five minutes with the vet, the couple came out with the woman in tears. 'Oh dear, is it bad news?' Rose handed her a tissue.

The man explained, 'It's his kidneys, and Mr Smedley thinks, at his age, we should…'

His wife wailed, 'He's only twelve, surely he could try something? I'm taking him home. I can't say goodbye yet.'

'But if he's in pain, love?' As the man said this the cat wailed loudly.

Rose couldn't help it. 'You could seek another opinion.'

'Could we?' The woman dried her eyes.

'I'm not saying the diagnosis would be different, but I can recommend Maxwell's. They have surgeries here in Ashington and in Morpeth. Mr Maxwell is brilliant with domestic animals.'

'It's worth a try.' The man picked up the box from the corner as Mr Smedley burst into the reception area.

'I heard that! You can leave right now. I'll post your wages and don't expect a decent reference.'

'They are entitled to a second opinion, Mr Smedley,' Rose answered, but he had turned and slammed the door.

'Oh dear, have we got you into hot water, pet?'

Rose smiled. 'No, you've done me a favour. I can leave right now and it's not a moment too soon.'

Dad and Grace were both home. From the window of her flat Rose could see Grace hanging some washing on the line in the yard and Dad opening the back gate with an armful of veg from his allotment. She checked the clock; it was an hour before Lily went there for lunch. She may as well go over and help Grace, because there was nothing else to do.

'Hi, I'm officially finished. I'll need to look for another job.'

'Sit down pet, I've just got a pot of tea masting. Your dad has something to say.'

'Aye, we talked about your work and about the college and we came to an agreement last night.' Dad looked very serious.

Rose frowned. 'An agreement about me?'

'We want to help you, hinny. We would like to keep Lily here for you and give you the chance to go to Berkshire. You said Danny and you had savings put by for the house, so could you manage to do the course with those?'

'Dad! Those savings are for Lily to go to college, not me.'

Grace handed her a cup of tea and said, 'The bairn is only seven. You have years to save for her – and anyway, she might not want to go.'

'Use your savings to better yourself, Rose – it makes sense. Go and do your course. You'll be back in no time.'

Rose sipped her tea. If only... It was a lovely idea, but could she really leave Lily for months? 'Thank you. I'll think about it.'

Lily and Johnnie came home for lunch. 'Would you stay for a bit with your grandma and grandad, pet, if your mam wanted to go back to school?' Grace placed cheese sandwiches and glasses of milk on the table for the two of them.

'Why would she want to go to school? It's awful, and you can't play.' Johnnie was finding it hard to sit still for a full school day.

'A school for grown-ups,' his dad explained.

'Like prison?' Johnnie's eyes widened.

'No!' Rose laughed. 'A school to learn about sick animals and caring for them.'

'You do that already, Mam.' Lily pushed away her milk and carefully wiped her mouth.

'It's just a thought, love. Nothing is decided, don't worry.'

After she'd tucked Lily into bed that night Rose sat down with a notebook to work out what it would cost to travel to Berkshire, pay the fees, take the exams and pay for lodgings. It would cost all of their hard-earned savings, but she would have letters to her name; Rose Dodd RANA. She would love that qualification, and Grace and Dad were a safe pair of hands. She sank onto the sofa to read the brochure again, although she knew it word for word. She closed her eyes and imagined setting off into a world of learning.

A cry from the bedroom brought her back to the present. She opened the bedroom door and heard sobs coming from Lily's bed in the alcove. 'What's wrong, sweetheart? I thought you were fast asleep.'

Lily sat up. 'I don't want you to go away, Mam. I don't want to just have Grandma and Grandad. I love them, but I've already lost Dad and I can't lose you too.'

Rose stroked Lily's hot little brow. 'Hush, hush. It was just an idea, Lily. Maybe it was a silly idea. I'm not going anywhere without you, you can be sure of that.'

'Promise?'

'I promise.' She sat with Lily until she fell asleep.

Lily was still restless in sleep as Rose crept out of the bedroom. She was annoyed with herself for giving her little girl a moment of worry. She tore up her calculations and the brochure. A qualification wasn't as important as her child's happiness.

CHAPTER 25

*L*ily still walked to First Row for lunch with Johnnie; it was as easy for Grace to make two lunches as one, and they'd decided to keep to the routine because Rose hoped to find a new job. She went over at lunchtime to have a cup of tea with Grace, and once the two bairns dashed off to school she set off for home to pull out her typewriter and update her curriculum vitae.

As she waited to cross the road, a smart silver car passed and turned into the back lane of First Row. Was that Mr Maxwell? She waited until he got out of the car and it certainly was.

'Mr Maxwell!' She waved to attract his attention.

'Ah, Rose.' He crossed the road. 'It's you I want to see. I was going to ask at First Row for your address.'

'I'm going home now – it's just across the road and above the hairdresser. There's no parking outside the flat, so do you want to leave the car and walk along with me?'

'I'll do that. There are one or two things I'd like to chat to you about, and after getting a new patient thanks to you, I thought now would be a good time.'

'How is Smudge?'

'Chronic kidney disease, but with medicine when he needs it and the right diet, I think he'll see another year or two. The couple who brought him in were grateful you helped them.'

Over a cup of tea Mr Maxwell talked about the new course at Berkshire. 'Young Frank mentioned you might be a suitable candidate, but I disagree. What would you learn that you hadn't read about or experienced already at Campbell's? I found out that they're using your handbook as one of their set texts.'

'Are they?' Rose's heart leapt at the thought that it would be put to good use. 'You mean *our* book though, don't you? Your qualifications got the book published.' Rose remembered pouring her heart, soul and all her knowledge about being a vet's assistant into her handbook, but it had taken a qualified vet to add footnotes to give it credibility and a publishing deal.

'I've been awarded a fellowship by the Royal College of Veterinary Surgeons due to the handbook and other papers I've written, so I'm extremely grateful to be involved, Rose. It seems that letters to your name can gather more letters.' He gave a wry smile.

'Well done, Mr Maxwell. I'd love letters to my name one day. It's an acknowledgement of hard work, isn't it?'

'Letters aren't everything, but they smooth the way in this field of work. Now, to get back to the book – remember when I asked after Danny's funeral, whether you still wanted the royalties to go towards treatment for animals with owners who couldn't afford the fees? You said yes, but is that still the case? I'd hate you and Lily to be struggling.' Mr Campbell put his cup down and looked around. 'Not that it looks like it. You've made a lovely home, Rose.'

'Thank you. We get by, and we have a little bit in the bank so we're comfortable. At least we will be when I find a new job.'

'You're leaving White and Smedley?'

'Didn't the couple tell you about the row with Mr Smedley when I recommended trying you for a second opinion? I've already left. I could never settle there,' Rose admitted.

'I can't say I'm surprised. Dreadful, the pair of them.' Mr Maxwell stood up and walked to the window. 'What an amazing view. Industry and countryside side by side – coal, crops and cows.'

'They're my exact thoughts when I look out. It's everything Dad paints in one sweeping canvas.' They stood for a moment drinking in the view, both lost in their thoughts.

As the sun dropped below the horizon, leaving the pit wheel a stark black against a glorious sky of peach and gold, Mr Maxwell turned towards her. 'I've been thinking over what you said, Rose. How about joining us at Maxwell's? You could be my senior vet's assistant and train our other assistants using the handbook. I'd see if other vets in the area wanted their assistants upskilled too. As well as training the assistants, you could revise the handbook and we could take photos to make it an illustrated edition. What do you say?'

Rose swallowed hard. What could she say?

'Do you need time to think it over?' Mr Maxwell asked.

'No, I don't need time, and yes, oh yes, I'd love to work for you.'

'Splendid! Come in on Monday and we'll talk wages and hours then.'

She walked Mr Maxwell to his car, waved him off, then rushed to relay her news to Dad and Grace.

'How many times have I said that when one door shuts another one opens?' Rose smiled as Grace used one of her many aphorisms. There was usually a grain of truth in them, though.

. . .

There was one fly in the ointment. On Monday when she went to discuss terms and to look around the Ashington practice, Ruth Maxwell was there. She sat behind the reception desk reading a magazine. Looking up, with a stony glare underneath the thick layer of make-up, she said, 'Hello, Rose. We're going to be colleagues, I hear.'

'Mr Maxwell didn't mention you were working here, Ruth. Are you a vet's assistant too?' Crikey, was she going to have to train Ruth with those red talons to take a dog's temperature?

'You must be joking.' Ruth shuddered. 'I'm office and reception only, and you're not senior to me. I'm Daddy's helpmate.'

Thank goodness for that. 'A smooth-running office is vital to the success of any business, Ruth,' she answered.

Ruth nodded and pointed to one of the closed doors. 'Dad's through there waiting for you,' she said, then went back to her magazine.

Rose decided she may as well try to be nice, but she'd certainly watch her back. She couldn't forget how Ruth had bullied her in her first year at school and then meddled between her and young Frank. Ruth Maxwell was a woman she didn't trust.

At the meeting with Mr Maxwell she learned the Royal College of Veterinary Surgeons could not have veterinary nurses because both the terms 'nurse' and 'veterinary' were protected by statute and charter. For now, the new qualification had to be termed Registered Animal Nursing Auxiliary to take this into account.

'We will call our revised handbook *The RANA Handbook*. What do you say to that?' Mr Maxwell asked.

'It's the same job, but if that's the current title, let's do it.' Rose couldn't wait to add photos and add new practices to the handbook.

She discovered her job at Maxwell's involved working at both the Ashington and Morpeth branch, and as she would be taking the assistants out to the farms and ferrying animals from Morpeth to Ashington, Mr Maxwell was providing her with a Morris Minor Traveller. She'd be driving again, working with animals, and she had a pay rise.

CHAPTER 26

'*W*hy does Rose Kelly get a car and not me? I'm your daughter and you said I would be a good helpmate and I haven't got my own car. I hate having to borrow Mum's to go anywhere.'

'Calm down, Ruth. The estate car belongs to the practice – it's for carrying animals and travelling to farms, and you do neither. If you ever want to use it, and have a good work reason, then you can.'

'It'll be filthy! I want a car of my own.'

'Then you'll have to start saving, my dear, otherwise it won't be your own.'

Rose stifled a smile. Ruth's face had been a picture of fury ever since she saw Rose pull up in the Morris Minor Traveller. She had gone to the Morpeth branch to pick up a lively spaniel bitch who was about to be spayed. Most operations were done at the bigger Ashington practice, nowadays.

Ruth stormed out of Mr Maxwell's room, glared at Rose and went behind the desk. The spaniel gave a low growl as Ruth passed; sparks of anger were making her nervous. 'Take that nasty thing through to Dad,' Ruth snapped, then turned her back on Rose.

Rose stood there; she just couldn't ignore Ruth's awful attitude. 'I heard you shouting through there and I could have been a client, Ruth. Arguments should wait until after hours, and name-calling the animals who ultimately pay your wages is totally unprofessional.'

Ruth rounded on her. 'Do *not* tell me how to behave! *You* are not senior to me, and that car is not yours either, so stop showing off as if it were.'

The dog started barking at Ruth's shouting and Mr Maxwell popped his head around the door. 'What's going on now?' he asked.

'Nothing, Dad.' Ruth started shuffling papers and trying to look busy.

Rose shook her head and followed Mr Maxwell into his surgery.

'Is Ruth still going on about the company car?' Mr Maxwell asked.

Rose shrugged. 'Something upset her, and I just told her that shouting wasn't professional.'

Mr Maxwell raised his eyebrows. 'It's a wonder we didn't get a full-on tantrum then. She is a spoiled woman, Rose. Her mother has spoiled her and now they argue all the time. I was persuaded to give her a job, but she's got no interest in the business, and how do I fire my own daughter? The annoying thing is we were going to get her a little run-around this Christmas. Now she'll sulk and moan until it takes the pleasure out of buying it.'

'You should let her know, Mr Maxwell. Tell her what your plan was, but say that unless she changes her attitude, you won't do it. How old is she? A grown woman and still manipulating people.'

Mr Maxwell scratched his head in a way that reminded her of

Frank. 'You talk sense, Rose, and maybe I should make a stand. But her mother won't hear of it. She ruins her.'

Rose worked a little later than she needed, but she didn't mind because the use of the car got her home quickly. It's too late to expect Ruth to change now, she thought, as she got into the car that had ignited Ruth's jealousy. As she drove home, Rose came to the conclusion that somebody should have made a stand years ago.

CHAPTER 27

*L*ater that evening Lily rifled through her bookshelf and pulled out a battered book of fairy tales. 'I'd like you to read me the Sleeping Beauty story tonight,' she said, placing the book on Rose's lap then clambering into bed.

For a six-year-old Lily was a good little reader, but she enjoyed a story at night and Rose enjoyed this bedtime ritual as much as her daughter. 'Don't you want another chapter of *The Lion, the Witch and the Wardrobe*?' The Narnia series hadn't been written when Rose was a girl and they'd left it on a cliffhanger the night before, so Rose was eager to crack on with that.

'No, I'm in the mood for a "happily ever after" story tonight.' Lily snuggled under the blankets and Rose read the familiar tale of *Sleeping Beauty*.

Afterwards, as Rose closed the book, Lily asked, 'Will you have a "happily ever after" mam?'

Rose frowned. 'What do you mean, pet?'

Lily turned solemn blue eyes towards her. 'Sleeping Beauty is awoken by a prince and lives happily ever after. Do you think a prince will come along one day to make you happy?'

Rose didn't know what to say. A picture, crystal clear, of her own mother saying, 'what will be will be' flashed through her memory. From that very book, they'd been reading *Cinderella and the Glass Slipper*.

She repeated the phrase. 'What will be will be. We can't see into the future, Lily. I thought I had my "happily ever after" until we lost your dad. Now... well, now I have a *mostly* happily ever after, but I am a bit sad at times. I'm just so glad to have you.' Rose reached across to hug Lily and gulped down the lump of grief that was blocking her throat.

'I want you to be very happy and find a prince for you, and a daddy for me. Can you do that, Mam?'

The tight lump was expanding to fill Rose's chest. Her daughter was missing her daddy, but what could she do? Nobody could replace Danny. 'It's time for sleep, Lily. We can't always have what we want. Just be glad you have me and two sets of grandparents to love you.' She brushed a kiss over her brow and walked swiftly out. Lily couldn't see her break down.

Leaning against the door she lifted her elbow to her eyes to stem the flow of tears and bit on her lip. 'Danny, Lily misses you, and I do too. I so miss you! How will we ever get over you?'

Rose sank onto the sofa and took in a few deep breaths. She could ride this wave of grief just like she'd ridden many others. What ifs, if onlys... they did no good. Her life with Danny had gone.

She still had the book of fairy tales in her hand. Turning to the front page she read 'To Elsie, Christmas 1906'. That was her mother's older sister. It was written in a grown-up cursive script, but underneath in rounder handwriting was, 'This book belongs to Ginnie aged 6, 1915'. Both her mother and aunt were long gone, lost to breast cancer like their mother before them. Rose shuddered. It seemed to be a family illness, so she checked her own breasts regularly and prayed she wouldn't leave Lily an orphan.

Below both of these faded inscriptions was her own claim to

the book in a darker blue. 'My favourite bedtime stories. Rose Virginia Kelly, aged 5'. She must ask Lily to add her name under the rest.

When she married Danny Dodd she had found her happily ever after, or so she'd thought. How cruel life could be.

Rose crept into Lily's room to return the book of fairy tales to the bookshelf and stood by Lily as she slept. Her hair fell in dark waves like Danny's; her mouth was like his too, quick to smile, but there the resemblance ended. She had the Kelly green eyes, Rose's dreamy nature, and often had her head in a book. 'Your daddy would be so proud of you,' she whispered as she quietly left Lily to her dreams.

Rose couldn't settle. She had created a new life for herself and Lily, but her heart hadn't caught up with her head; it still had a lot of healing to do. Remembering Mam and Aunt Elsie, she checked her breasts. No lumps, but they felt different – full and tender. No!

She rushed to the calendar that hung on the back of the kitchen door and scanned the weeks she'd survived without Danny. Four months, and so much had happened. But how had she missed this? Four months without a star on the calendar. Her periods were like clockwork. Was it grief?

Opening the wardrobe she examined her body in the long mirror on the inside of the door. She had lost weight and was thinner than in the summer, but was her belly more rounded? She felt sickly a couple of months ago but not often, and she'd put that down to not eating. The only tell-tale sign was her breasts, definitely more rounded. Was she imagining this? Her heart thumped. She should visit the doctor and ask for a test.

Lying in bed her thoughts scrambled all over, looking for another logical reason besides being pregnant. None. She didn't know whether she was happy at the chance of having Danny's baby or not; she just felt numb. Had she the strength to be a mother to another baby when she was feeling so low?

'Danny, you always wanted another. This child was conceived on the morning of the races, I'm sure of it. If I'm carrying your baby again, I'll be a good mother, I promise.'

*R*ose decided to give it just another week before finding out for sure. For now, expecting a baby wasn't real. When she handed a specimen in to the doctor she'd have to face a whole new change of plans, and she wasn't ready for that. She told nobody; not Grace, not Lottie, not Helen when they visited Blackthorn Farm in the Morris Minor and saw the pit ponies again on Saturday, not Brenda who was due to give birth this Christmas, and not her new boss, Mr Maxwell. What would he say when she had just started this wonderful new job?

Nobody guessed. She was thinner and looked peaky, but that was explained by her grief, and the thought of a baby didn't enter anyone's head.

The Monday after Ruth's row with Mr Maxwell, Rose suspected something was up. Mr Maxwell came downstairs late and then shut himself into his office, after giving Alice, the junior receptionist, instructions to call the young vet at the Morpeth branch and tell him to come over to take morning surgery, and to leave the rest of Mr Maxwell's day free because he had urgent business to attend to. Ruth didn't turn up at all, so Rose helped Alice to rearrange the day before going out on a visit.

It was almost twelve when she returned, and Alice informed her that Mr Maxwell hadn't called for his morning coffee or popped out to see how the practice was running.

'You go for your lunch now, Alice, and I'll look after the phones and the desk until you're back.'

Rose made Mr Maxwell a coffee – boiling hot milk, just as he liked it, with two sugars – and put a few ginger snaps on a plate. Should she ring and ask if he wanted his coffee now, or just knock and walk in? She decided to act as normally as possible. It wasn't unusual for her to knock then walk in with a cuppa, but today it felt strange.

As she entered Mr Maxwell looked up startled, as though he'd been lost in another world. There were papers strewn all across his desk and an ashtray full of cigarettes. When had Mr Maxwell started smoking again? 'I've brought you your coffee and some biscuits. It's late for elevenses, but we didn't want to disturb you.'

'Oh? Oh thanks, Rose. Just leave them here. I'm waiting for an important call.'

Rose knew she was being dismissed but had to ask. 'Is there anything amiss, Mr Maxwell? You seem to be…'

'I seem what, Rose?'

'You seem to be preoccupied, unsettled – not yourself.'

'Yes, I'm all of those things. I'll let you know what's going on when I know what's going on myself. And thanks for the coffee and holding the fort.'

Rose was none the wiser, but certain she'd find out if she needed to.

Everyone had gone. She'd told the young vet to return here first thing in the morning and was checking over his morning list when Mr Maxwell finally appeared. He looked tired and dishevelled, but he was smiling so it mustn't be bad news he was dealing with. 'Rose, do you have time for a chat before you leave?'

'Of course, Mr Maxwell. Shall I come through?'

'No. I've smoked a pack of cigarettes today and it smells like the top deck of a bus in there. Tell you what, let's walk along to The Collier's Arms – I fancy a pie and a pint. What do you say?'

'Yes, Mr Maxwell. I'll get my coat.' Well, what could she say? She was anxious to know what was going on, and she'd managed to refrain from eavesdropping at his office door all day.

They chose a table and Mr Maxwell went to the bar to order his pie and pint, and a lemonade for Rose. 'Nothing stronger?' he asked.

'Lemonade is fine.' Her hand went involuntarily to her tummy. She removed it immediately. She mustn't give the game away before she had a test.

From the back, Mr Maxwell was tall and broad-shouldered, with a mop of silver hair. He hadn't aged much since Rose first met him, and that had been... how long ago? The summer of '44, when she'd taken a lost injured pup to his practice – eighteen years ago. Her family had adopted Lucky, and he had been such a good companion.

Last summer he'd played chase with Lily in Dad's allotment, and with a wag of his stump of a tail he'd fallen into his last sleep in a puddle of sunlight with a ball between his front paws. Lucky was buried in his favourite spot in Dad's allotment. His luck in life had started with Mr Maxwell saving him. He was a kind man, and she enjoyed working for him. This, a drink after work, meant he had something important to say, she was sure.

'The barmaid is warming the pie and she'll bring it over.' Mr Maxwell rubbed at his eyes and shot Rose a tired smile. 'Thanks for running the practice today, Rose. I had a lot to do but knew I could rely on you, and I'm hoping my son Frank will be able to do the same in the future.'

'Frank? What do you mean?'

His pie came, interrupting their chat. 'This looks delicious. This isn't served up at home.' He took a mouthful and the pleasure on his face made Rose smile; she must ask Grace to bake him one of her meat and potato pies. He tucked into the food as Rose gazed around. She hadn't been into many pubs, but they always seemed cheery, chatty places, and it was clear that a few folk called in to wash away the woes of the day before going home.

Mr Maxwell pushed his plate to one side and took a sip of his pint. 'Where were we?' he asked.

'You mentioned Frank. Where does he come into your plan?

'Ah, yes. I think I'd better start at the beginning.'

It turned out that after Ruth's tantrum about a new car, her mother had joined in and defended her. Mr Maxwell had reached his limit and made a stand that weekend with the pair of them, and sparks ended up flying in all directions. He had taken a long drive and come to the decision that he would retire at the end of the year and pass on the practice to young Frank.

Mr Maxwell wanted to live in his small summer cottage by the sea in Alnmouth. 'It's near to the golf course, my favourite pub is along the road, and the terriers love the beach.' His face was alight as he spoke and Rose could sense his excitement over his retirement.

He explained how the Ashington house and the two practices would go to Frank. This left Mrs Maxwell and Ruth the sole use of the London apartment, and they were happy to spend their time in the capital near shops, restaurants, and what they called civilisation.

It seemed like the Maxwells were splitting up in all but name.

Rose thought it was a sad state of affairs to end a marriage in your sixties, but both might be happier. Mr Maxwell looked cheerier than she'd ever seen him.

'I'll fish and play golf at Alnmouth, and I'll do the odd lecture at the university. The new *RANA Handbook* is almost ready to be published. Isn't it so much better with illustrations?'

Rose nodded in agreement. They'd agreed to carry on raising money for animal charities with this new edition.

'I'll enjoy spending time promoting the handbook to veterinary practices. We did a good job with it, Rose.' He smiled and took a swig of his beer before continuing to outline his new life. 'I'll visit the countries that didn't interest Mrs Maxwell. She'll be free to shop and lunch in London, and I'll give her a decent allowance because she could never find work – but I think Ruth will have to learn to stand on her own two feet.'

Rose had to ask. 'Frank? Is he happy to move back north and take over?'

'He would be delighted to return to Northumberland if it wasn't for Marjorie. Did you know she's expecting?'

Rose nodded. Their babies would be due at the same time.

'She isn't keen on the move, and Frank is soft with that woman. But who am I to talk? I think they'll live above the practice but keep their current home in Yorkshire, so Marjorie won't feel too homesick.'

Rose twisted the stem of her glass. She wondered what these changes would mean for her.

Mr Maxwell must have read her mind. 'Frank wants you to continue the management and training of the assistants and to do exactly what you're doing now, so there's no need to worry about your role, Rose.'

Rose smiled. 'Thanks, Mr Maxwell.' She had mixed feelings about staying on at the practice but kept them to herself. She couldn't help feeling relieved that Ruth was leaving, but she was rather anxious about working with young Frank. They'd been friends, almost sweethearts, when they were younger. What would he be like as a boss? Besides that, there was the small matter that she might be pregnant too.

She really must get a test and let the Maxwells know her position.

CHAPTER 29

On Thursday evening Rose made a pot of tea and had just carried it into the living room to watch a TV game show where a contestant was intent on 'doubling her money' when there was a tap on the back door. She padded barefoot through to the scullery without putting on the light and called, 'Who is it?'

Rose unlocked the door to find Lottie standing there in her slippers with a cardigan clutched around her.

'What are you doing round here at this time of night?' Rose asked.

Lottie brushed past her. 'Let me in, it's blowing a northern gale out there.' Once she was inside, she laughed. 'This time of night?' she repeated. 'Listen to yourself, Rose. It's not even eight o'clock, you doylem. It's hardly curfew time for grown women.'

Rose smiled. 'You're right, Lottie. I'm just not used to anybody popping over after dark. What brings you here?'

'I need to say something. I thought of something after I saw you over at number one, and once I thought it, I just couldn't settle.'

'You look worried, Lottie? Is something wrong?'

'I don't know. Is there something going on? That's what I want to know.'

Rose wasn't sure what Lottie was getting at, so she offered her a cup of tea.

'Lovely,' Lottie answered.

'Splash of milk and two sugars, just how you like it,' Rose placed it in front of her before going to the cupboard to hunt out some digestive biscuits. Lottie had a sweet tooth.

'Okay, spit it out – you haven't come across just to say good-night,' Rose demanded as Lottie took a biscuit.

'You're right, I haven't. Don't get in a snip about this, but I have been watching you and I'm worried, and I don't know if I'm right or not. I'm your friend and I love you and I know you and I need to say something.'

Lottie's frown and flushed cheeks told Rose she was agitated about something and she started to feel flustered herself. 'Go on,' she invited.

Lottie put down her cup and counted on her thumb. 'I can't help noticing – one, you're always tired, two, you've lost your colour and you look pasty, three, you can't face Grace's bacon or sausage sandwiches, four, you're skinny but you're growing a bosom! I twigged this afternoon, and I'm sure you could be expecting.'

Rose sank back in the sofa. Lottie was more observant than she'd ever thought. 'You could be right, Lottie. I don't know and I'm frightened to find out.'

'I knew it!' Lottie reached over to hug her tightly. 'Oh Rose, it would be lovely if you were. Your Danny always wanted another, he told us so often enough.'

Rose relaxed into her friend's comforting hug. 'I know, but I'm on my own now and I've settled into a job that will keep me and Lily. It will mean more change and I'm not sure if I can face knowing yet. Do you understand?'

Lottie rubbed Rose's back, murmuring, 'What will be, will be.'

Suddenly she sat upright and jerked away from Rose. 'Bleedin' Nora! Rose, if you're pregnant you must be four months gone, or... or even more!'

'Eighteen weeks,' confirmed Rose.

'And you haven't been to the doctor?'

'Not yet.' Rose's eyes met Lottie's. 'You know how it is around here – once I go to the surgery the whole village will know.'

'I see what you mean. Nothing's a secret in Linwood.' Lottie dunked a digestive into her mug and looked thoughtful. 'I hoped I was expecting last year and I didn't want the rows to know, so I got a test from a doctor in Jesmond. It cost me, but at least I found out I wasn't without the whole of Linwood knowing we were trying for another.'

'You're trying?' Rose asked.

Lottie nodded. 'You'd think it was so easy with Paul that we'd have another no bother, but he wasn't an easy birth, and I don't know if it has affected things. I think I've lost two early on, but who can be sure?'

'You should have talked to me, Lottie.' It was Rose's turn to hug Lottie, who looked tearful.

'Hmm, just like you should've talked to me. Women keep secrets when they're hurtful, don't they?'

'We do.' Look at her own mother's birth secret. Rose couldn't agree more with Lottie's observation.

'Anyway, why I'm telling you now is because you could get a test from there and you'd know for sure, and I promise I'll keep your secret.'

'Thanks, Lottie.'

'But it won't be a secret much longer by the look of your chest,' Lottie remarked.

Rose had to laugh; it was true she was looking very full-cupped for her thinner frame. 'I'll have to find time to go to this doctor of yours. Do I take a sample to hand?'

'No, that's the best thing about going there. It's just two pills.

143

You take two little white pills, and if you have a period in a day or so, you aren't expecting, and if nothing happens, you are. Easy as that.'

'It's more private than handing a urine specimen to Noreen Wilkinson at the doctor's, I suppose, but I'm not sure about taking pills. They have them to stop you becoming pregnant too. Can you get them at the clinic?' Rose said.

'You can, but I wouldn't use those! My church wouldn't allow it, but it won't mind these ones. Tell you what, I know the clinic so I'll go and ask for you. They'll give the pills over no bother because I've registered before, and then you can take them whenever you feel ready.'

'Lottie, you're a true friend. Thank you. What do I owe you?'

'I'll let you know the cost once I've been. Rose, I hope you *are* expecting Danny's bairn and have a brother or sister for Lily. There are family benefits now and your dad and Grace will support you, as well as the Dodds. That little bairn will be so wanted! Don't worry about being widowed, you're living in Linwood and we look after our own.'

'Thanks, Lottie – I'm glad you know. I'm glad you've guessed, but I just want a few more days to take it all in. I'll do that test at the weekend.'

'Okay, I'll pop around to the clinic tomorrow.'

They clasped one another and Rose felt a weight drop from her shoulders. One of Grace's favourite sayings sprung to mind: a trouble shared is a trouble halved.

She slept well that night.

Lottie popped around with the tablets the next night. 'Take them. The sooner you do, the sooner you know,' she urged.

Rose put the tablets in the sideboard drawer. 'I'll take them tonight and I promise I'll let you know the result as soon as I can.'

When Lottie left, Rose looked at the tablets. The two ingredients showed they were hormone based and the instructions were just as Lottie had said: take two and wait to see if you menstruate.

Rose was all for advances in science if they were needed, and thought the hormone-based contraceptive pill that the NHS was giving out was a good idea so parents could choose the size of their families. If only her own mother had that option. Something niggled; did she want to put hormones in her body if she was carrying a baby? Did she really need two little pills to tell her she was pregnant?

The usual way was to wait until there was no possibility you weren't pregnant or to take a urine test where they injected your urine into a rabbit. Rose wasn't keen because it involved the autopsy of a rabbit, so she hadn't bothered with Lily. She just knew as soon as she missed that she was pregnant.

'Be honest, Rose – you know already. You know you've never missed three periods in your life,' scolded a little voice in her head. She pushed the pills to the back of the drawer. If she took them, it would be to prove her own instincts were wrong. She didn't need them to know she was carrying Danny's child.

On Sunday morning, when Lily and Johnnie were at Sunday school, she told Grace. She was delighted and ran around after Rose all day. Dad heard when he came in from his allotment. He just nodded and said, 'Children are a gift to cherish. Danny will be happy wherever he is.'

Lottie came round in the afternoon and kindly offered to spread the word around Linwood. Rose smiled as Lottie debated whether to tell her mam or her sister Eileen first.

She got into work early on Monday and phoned Helen and Brenda to relay the news, and after their congratulations she felt more ready to face Mr Maxwell and tell him she was pregnant.

Mr Maxwell was more upset than she had imagined. 'This is

wonderful for you, Rose. I congratulate you and wish you well,' he told her, but his face didn't match his words.

'What's bothering you, Mr Maxwell? I'll leave the practice in good order.'

'I'm sure you will, but I can't help worrying about Frank's takeover without you to support him with the office, the clients and the staff. Marjorie is digging her heels in about the move. Maybe I should put off my retirement for a while.'

'I could work until February and stay in the back-office, Mr Maxwell. I'd like to work for as long as I'm able. I'd rather work than sit knitting a matinee jacket.'

Mr Maxwell smiled. 'It seems strange we have come so far since the war, yet a pregnant woman is meant to keep out of sight,' he mused.

'It does to me too! I mean, the cattle and the mares just get on with it and have no problems, but women are meant to fade into the background. I'm all for working wives and mothers... if they'd like to, that is. It's about choice.'

'You're right, Rose. We'll arrange for you to work as long as you want to – you will be marvellous at settling Frank into the post. If you want to carry on after the baby is born, and Grace Kelly is willing to look after the baby, then you can work afterwards too. I'm sure Frank will agree. We have always been forward thinking in this practice.'

'Thank you, Mr Maxwell.'

Rose thought about Mr Maxwell's words all day. Work 'til the last month and then go back after a few months? It certainly wasn't the norm, but it wasn't the norm to be a widow in your twenties either. She knew Grace would jump in quick as a flash to look after Danny's baby. How would she feel leaving him with his grandmother every day? It was one thing arranging such a thing before the baby was born, but afterwards she might feel differently.

She was going to wait until she showed, but decided to tell Lily about the baby that night before she heard it from someone else. 'I don't mind if it's a boy or a girl. It will be lovely to have someone to share my room with,' Lily confided.

Rose looked around Lily's room, little more than an alcove leading off Rose's bedroom; it would be a squash, but hadn't she shared with her brothers with a curtain rail to divide a small space into two parts? It was no good dreaming of the roomy house in Seabottle with the south-facing garden because she'd lost that dream along with Danny. This was her life now, and she had to make the best of it.

CHAPTER 30

*I*t was December already. The days had been full of preparing for the changeover and Mr Maxwell's retirement, and suddenly the second of December had rolled around and tonight was the leaving party.

Rose changed into a navy dress that was a couple of inches above her knee, so she teamed it with matching navy stockings; shorter dresses were becoming quite the fashion now, and this loose style suited her changing shape. She hastily twisted her shoulder length hair into a French plait and then she sat at her dressing table to apply foundation and mascara. She finished with a slick of new nude lipstick and checked how she looked in the long mirror on the inside of her wardrobe door.

To the front she was her slim self, but standing to the side there was a bit of a bump; it wasn't too noticeable yet because the A-line dress skimmed over her curves. She slipped on her red ballet pumps as Lily wandered into the bedroom.

'You look pretty, Mam. Can I try some lipstick?'

Rose added a dab of lipstick to Lily's pout, saying, 'It's time to take you over to Grandma and Grandad for the night. Have you got everything you need?'

'Just these.' Lily dragged a bag of books and stuffed toys across to the door. 'You're staying one night, not a week,' Rose exclaimed as she picked up the heavy load.

'No Mam. You're not to carry heavy things.' Lily took the bag from her.

Rose smiled and picked up her car keys. 'Maybe you'll learn not to pack so much if you have to carry the bag yourself.'

With Lily deposited at number one, she set off for Ashington. She was looking forward to the evening, especially seeing Frank; he was here this weekend for Frank Senior's leaving celebration without the family, but they were all moving to Ashington in January.

The 'do' was going to be attended by everyone from the Morpeth and Ashington branches, and Mr Maxwell had arranged to have it in the best room of The Collier's Arms. He had arranged a buffet and a free bar, and all staff, past and present, were invited. Most had accepted because they wanted to give Mr Maxwell a good send-off; they'd all put into a whip round and raised enough to replace his familiar battered golf bag with a smart new one.

Rose thought it was wonderful that her boss was so well-liked and respected. It was a shame his wife and his daughter Ruth weren't going to make the effort to travel from London. Frank had made sure they were comfortably set up, and it was this practice – his life's work – that had generously provided for them.

Vera, who had been his personal assistant and receptionist for years, was a surprise guest. Although Vera left the practice and moved to the coast a few years previously, young Frank kept in touch with her, and she was easily persuaded to come. Rose hardly recognised her. She wore her hair waved, making it look less severe, and the jade dress she wore in place of her plain grey work garments flattered her; she looked years younger.

'You look wonderful, Vera!' Rose exclaimed.

'Thank you, I'm enjoying my life. I worried about leaving Frank at Maxwell's, but I wanted to do charity work with the PDSA – and I've taken up golf at Tynemouth Golf Club so I have a better social life too.'

'Mr Maxwell is looking forward to playing more golf when he moves to Alnmouth.' The idea popped into Rose's head and was spoken before she could think better of it. 'You two should play together sometimes! Now he's living a quieter life he'll need some company, Vera.'

Vera's eyes widened. 'He's moving to the cottage? That rural life won't suit Mrs Maxwell.'

Rose took Vera's arm and lead her to a quiet corner. 'I think it suits her very well. They've discussed their future and they're amicable about living it apart, Vera. Mrs Maxwell and Ruth have settled for the London flat, Frank is moving into the Ashington house, and Mr Maxwell is happy to retire to the holiday cottage by the golf course and make it his permanent home.'

'Well, I never would have thought it. He'll have peace at last.' Vera's flushed face couldn't conceal her pleasure.

'We both know how he deserves better, and he could do with his friends around him once he gives up work. I hope you'll be a friend to him. Don't be shy, Vera. You know he's always valued you and never found anyone like you.' Vera would be a wonderful companion to Mr Maxwell, and divorce was more common nowadays, so if anything more came of it, there could be a future for the pair of them. They would both be what, approaching sixty? They had a good few years ahead of them and were perfect for each other.

Mr Maxwell came to join them. 'Vera, what a surprise! How lovely to see you here. We have a lot of catching up to do.'

'You certainly do!' Rose smiled and left them to it.

'What are you grinning at?' asked Frank, who was pushing his way to the crowded bar.

'Bring me a lemonade and I'll tell you.' Her grin widened as she looked in the direction of Mr Maxwell and Vera.

'Ah! You're thinking in fairy tales again aren't you, Rose?'

'They happen sometimes.' She perched on a chair. 'I'll wait here for you and keep this seat spare.' She patted the one beside her.

When Frank returned with her drink he said, 'It's cheering to see so many familiar faces.' Then he lowered his voice. 'Remember all those years ago when we were teens and I said Vera would've made Dad a better wife?'

'I do.' Rose remembered it clearly.

'I still think that. My mother just thinks of herself and how things look to people who really don't matter – she doesn't care about Dad. It's sad.'

'When we're in love we don't always choose wisely, and then we can be stuck with a partner for life. I've read about it in so many romances,' Rose said. 'I've seen it happen a few times in the rows too,' she added.

'I heartily agree with you on that.' Frank stared solemnly into his pint.

'Frank? You and Marjorie? You're okay, aren't you?'

His smile seemed forced. 'We *were*. I thought we were fine, until this chance to move north upset the apple cart. Marjorie's plans for me to be persuaded to join her brother's practice, so we'll live near her family, have been scuppered. She loves the idea of a husband with two practices, but not *where* they are. I only hope she settles here.'

Rose patted his arm. 'So do I.'

'What about you?' Frank asked, changing the subject. 'Dad's given me strict instructions not to overwork you and I wasn't sure whether to congratulate you in public yet or not. A baby is going to be a real comfort to you, isn't it?'

'Yes, it is. I was planning on telling the staff before Christmas, so just a week or two longer – if they haven't guessed already.'

'You're slim, and everyone is wearing those loose frocks nowadays. You can't tell with Marjorie either. You're both due around the same time.'

'Yes. We're lucky it's not the year of the pencil skirt,' she said.

'The *what*?'

Rose laughed. 'I'm just talking fashion.'

Frank's smile faded and a serious look darkened his eyes. 'Rose, I need to say this once because I know you'll hate a fuss, but my rules are: Just do what you can physically manage, no risk-taking, rest whenever you need to, take antenatal appointments whenever you need to, and your leave of absence is for as long as you want after that baby is born. Your job will be waiting because we do need you at the practice, but that baby must come first.' Rose burst into tears and Frank put his arm around her. 'What is it? What have I said?'

'You're being nice, and I'm pregnant so I'm all hormonal,' she sobbed.

Pam, the head receptionist from Morpeth who was chatting nearby to one of the veterinary assistants, turned her way. 'Are you alright, Rose?' Pam mouthed. Rose gulped and nodded.

She blew her nose. 'What's the point in waiting? I think I'd better tell the staff on Monday or they'll be making wild guesses about why I'm weeping all over you. Pam looks concerned.'

'Good idea.' Frank looked over and gave Pam a wink, then said, 'Come on, let's circulate.'

As Rose got up fom her chair, Pam was straight over. 'Are you sure you're alright, Rose? That new boss of ours hasn't been upsetting you already, has he?'

'No, Pam, I'm fine.' She linked the receptionist's arm and walked her over to an empty spot by the fireplace. 'Frank and I have been friends since we were at school and we'll work together just fine, so you have no worries there. My tears were because my emotions are all over the place. There is one thing I do want to tell you though, something you can help me with on Monday.'

It was settled. On Monday, Pam would get around all of the Morpeth staff to let them know that Rose was not only widowed but pregnant and due to deliver around Easter, and she wanted nobody to fuss around her. Rose would do the same with the Ashington practice.

Monday came and, as she requested, folk didn't fuss, but heavy objects were grabbed out of reach and cups of tea were frequently made for her. She had the best job with a wonderful workforce, and working meant she could lay aside her grief for a few hours of the day.

CHAPTER 31

NEW YEAR, 1962

*L*inwood colliery's Christmas preparations went ahead, but Danny's absence left a gaping hole in their family as well as her heart. Rose tried to stay cheerful for Lily's sake, but the constant pretence exhausted her, and she lost count of the times she slipped into the bedroom to lie down and shed a few tears, as each Christmas tradition brought back memories of last year.

'Dad says we have to put the star on the tree first, remember?'

Rose's eyes brimmed with tears. She did remember… and she remembered that huge tree he had lugged up the stairs last Christmas. They should have been celebrating Christmas in their new home in Seabottle by now. *Danny, I wish we'd had more time.*

Brenda gave birth to a boy on Christmas Eve. She was happy for her old school friend, and for her brother. Stanley had already asked her if they should change their choice of Daniel if it was a boy, because she might want the name for her own baby.

'No, Stanley. Danny would be thrilled that you and Brenda chose to name his nephew after him. Keep to your plan.' Having said that, she had no idea of what she was going to name their child. She just wanted a healthy birth first of all.

. . .

On New Year's Eve, First Row was full of noise and laughter. Rose twisted at her eternity ring; the symbol of Danny's love sparkled radiantly and comforted her. It was tighter because of her pregnancy, but for now she could still wear it with her wedding band. How glad she was that they'd repeated their vows to one another a year ago on this very day. She'd never have guessed what the coming year would bring.

Time dragged as she waited until the clock chimed twelve. Afterwards, she could leave everyone to wander the rows and welcome the new year into one another's houses. She longed to return to her own flat across the road.

Dad walked her home, carrying a sleeping Lily over his shoulder and bringing Dennis from next door who had a large lump of coal in his hand.

'You need a decent first foot, a tall dark-haired man carrying coal,' Dad said.

'I hope I'm a lucky first foot for you this year, hinny. You could do with a bit of luck,' Dennis said as she unlocked the door.

'I'm not sure I believe in superstitions, but if it makes you two happy...' She stepped aside to let them in.

Dennis entered first and Dad carried Lily into her bedroom as Dennis strode over to open the living room window and let the old year out. 'I wish Robbie didn't believe so much. He blames himself, you know.'

'For what?' Rose was puzzled.

'He blames himself for bringing bad luck on to your family when he barged into number one and became the first foot last year, instead of a dark-haired fellow like me or Danny. Remember how he walked in just after midnight? Fair-haired he was *and* empty-handed, then look what happened to your Danny.'

'That's just daft, he wasn't responsible,' Rose exclaimed.

'Try telling him that. He's not been out tonight, you know.

One of the lads reminded him about it and it upset him – him and Danny were close. It's not just the first foot mistake – he saw him that day at the races and thinks if they'd talked a minute more, it mightn't have happened.'

Rose had harboured wild thoughts like that herself; Robbie wasn't the only poor beggar who was plagued with the 'if onlys'.

Dennis placed the coal on the hearth and stood back.

In return, she handed him a tot of whisky, another tradition.

Dad came in from Lily's room, picked up the tot waiting for him and gave Dennis the nod to raise his glass and make a toast.

'Here's to love and laughter and happily ever after,' Dennis said, then drank his tot in one.

'Here's to good health in 1962,' Dad added.

Rose hugged them both and saw them out of the door before closing it and leaning her back against it to howl. Her heart, scalded with grief, was sore and filled with pent-up rage at the world.

'Danny, how can I have love and laughter without you? You were my happily ever after.' She threw herself onto the bed and cried for what could never be.

She thought about Robbie, Danny's lifelong friend, and how he felt responsible for bringing them bad luck. How could she put that right? She gave herself up to the release of sobbing, but at the same time she knew she could never let herself cry like this again. She told herself, 'I have a child to care for and another on the way, and I have to provide for them. I might not have love or laughter, but I have two good reasons to carry on.'

Rose was glad to get back to work on Tuesday. She would work throughout January and February to make sure Frank was settled, and then she'd pass the reins and the car keys into the capable hands of Pam. She'd talked it over with Frank, and they'd agreed this was the best plan.

'I know you'll make sure both practices run smoothly, Pam,' she assured her stand in on the day she left. 'You'll need the car to get between the two, and your hours might be more flexible because you'll have some emergencies to contend with.'

Pam took the keys, saying, 'I've just passed my test so I can use the car, and I've driven the Morpeth to Ashington route a dozen times so I know it well. I'll take good care of the car and all of the vets, Rose. The only thing I refuse to do is touch the animals – I'm a people organiser, and I have to admit most animals make me nervous.'

Pam was cool, confident, and always immaculately turned out, with never a hair out of place; she had been known to pop in a curler or two over her tea break to keep her hair just so. With her ready smile, she was popular with their clients. Rose was fond of her, but she had to admit she was pleased about her reluctance to be 'hands on' with the pets. The animal side was Rose's speciality, and she wanted her job back in a few months' time.

CHAPTER 32

The week after Rose took leave from the practice, Helen picked her up from Linwood to take her to Blackthorn Farm for a few days. Lily stayed with her grandparents because it was a school week, but she'd be joining them all on Friday after school. The Fairbairns had invited her 'for a proper rest', and Rose was looking forward to seeing her old friends, human and four-legged.

'It's just like old times,' Helen said as they sat at her kitchen table drinking tea.

Rose smiled. Yes, at times like this she almost forgot. Yet always, at the back of her mind, like a sore tooth she couldn't help prodding at, was the pain that Danny wasn't going to be at home waiting for her.

After her tea, Rose stood to take her leave of Helen. 'I'll stretch my legs by taking a walk to the farm. I'll have to stop by the ponies on the way.'

'Take these apples.' Helen handed her a bag of windfalls. 'Matt will bring your case to the farmhouse later.'

Rose set off for the ponies' field, but halfway there she took a right turn and found herself heading towards the new Seabottle housing development. She walked over to the plot she'd carefully chosen with Danny. Their plot on the corner with the south facing garden had curtains at the windows; it was occupied. Her heart pounded. The new owners were in.

From a distance, she looked at her other future; the one where Lily would have a garden and they'd both be looking forward to their long-awaited second child in a house they owned. 'Danny, I couldn't get the house. A mother on her own can't get a mortgage. It's built just how we imagined, and they've got the garden lawned, with a swing. It was the right plot to choose. I'm so glad about the baby, though – you were right about that too, about not waiting. Lily won't be an only child.'

She turned away when the back door opened and a woman came out with a basket of washing for the line. She held back her tears. That wasn't her future now, and there was no time for tears. She was here to rest and make sure she had a healthy baby. Her last gift to Danny.

Spike and Sampson cheered her up with their snorting and whinnying as she approached. Soon she had five ponies nudging at her for apples, and weeks of tension left her body as she buried her head into the familiar smell of their necks and looked them over with a practiced eye to check they were all healthy. 'I've missed you lot,' she murmured, 'I shouldn't have left it so long.'

'You've taken your time in getting here!' Daphne greeted her. She was at the door, ready with a hug and a telling off. 'I was about to send out a search party because Helen called to say you were on your way over an hour ago.'

'Sorry. I stopped off to see the ponies,' Rose explained.

Daphne stood back but kept her hands on both of Rose's shoulders as she scrutinised her. 'I knew exactly where you'd be, and that was where I was going to send Ted when he came in. Are the ponies all in good enough health for you?'

'They're in great shape, unlike me,' Rose answered.

'You look well, lass. You could have a bit more meat on your bones, but after all you've been though these past few months, you look champion!'

Champion was high praise indeed from Daphne. Rose was then plied with Border tart and warm cheese scones. 'It's delicious, but you'll be making dinner in an hour.' Rose tucked into a buttery scone.

'Yes, dinner won't be long – and you'll make room for that too.' Daphne opened the oven to check on dinner, and the delicious smell of beef wafted across to tease her. Rose sat back and relaxed into being pampered for a day or two.

The days passed in a haze of reading, good food and chatter with Helen and Daphne. Ted took pride in parading her past the repairs and improvements to the farm, and he showed off his Ayrshires with pride. 'I'm hoping for a win at the county fair this spring. What's your opinion, Rose?'

'I think this could be your year, Ted... with that one over there.' She pointed to a bonny heifer.

'That one? I wasn't thinking of her, Rose. Why would you pick her? Point out her winning features.'

Rose was only too happy to do this, thinking how lovely it was to be back on a farm.

A frosty Wednesday morning brought the Fairbairns a blue letter with red, white and blue piping around the edges; an airmail from Germany.

Daphne tore it open and let out a shriek. 'Oh! Oh my goodness, I need to sit down.' She opened the back door into the yard and called, 'Ted!' before sinking onto a kitchen stool.

'What's wrong?' Ted rushed from the barn and Rose felt her baby lurch and kick in anticipation of what was in the letter.

'It's our Jim, our bairn. He's coming to visit us. He's coming on Thursday,' Daphne explained.

'That's tomorrow! It's Thursday the morrow, lass.' Ted rubbed the stubble on his chin.

Rose had never seen two happier people in her life. Ted hugged Daphne and there was a glint of tears in his eyes as he said gruffly, 'About bleedin' time he got back here and visited his mother! He can help me to repair the small barn roof and make himself useful while he's here. That's if his hands haven't grown too soft.'

'You'll not nag my boy, Ted Fairbairn. I won't have it!' Daphne raised her voice and looked ready for a fight.

Ted seemed unperturbed and winked at Rose. 'Won't I? If I don't get on his back, he'll think he's on the wrong farm.'

'I'm so happy for you both,' Rose said. 'I'll cut my visit short so you can prepare. I'm sure Helen will drive me back later.'

'You'll do no such thing. We have plenty of room, and Lily is looking forward to coming here for the weekend. Jim will be glad of the extra company. We'll invite Matt and Helen over on Friday night and have a bit of a party,' Ted said.

Rose understood the startled look Daphne gave her; Ted wanting a bit of a party meant he must be delighted at his boy's return. 'Right then, a prodigal son to prepare for and a bit of a party means we need to start baking.' Rose got to her feet. 'I've rested enough. I can't bake but I can chop and peel – so come on, Daphne, let's get cracking!'

. . .

After Jim's arrival the week whizzed by. Lily arrived after school on Friday; she travelled on the bus with Grace, who stayed for a cup of tea but left before dark and before the party started. Jim's mates had been told they were welcome and there was a lovely atmosphere in the farmhouse.

'I've never felt this happy since before we lost Edward,' Daphne confessed. 'A farmhouse full of people to cook for, and young folk and laughter. You never know how things will turn out, do you?'

'No, you don't,' Rose answered, and couldn't help patting her belly as she said it.

Daphne laughed and she joined in. This visit had been a real tonic for her.

Large fluffy flakes of snow fell on Saturday and transformed the farm into a silent glistening landscape of white against a silver-grey sky. Rose and Lily spent the day sledging with the Wilsons, before heading home for ham and pease pudding supper at the farmhouse. The snow was lying thick as darkness fell and Ted suggested they build a snowman in the yard. 'It's dark, Ted,' Daphne tried to stall him.

'We have yard lights, and the wind has died down. You women get the hot chocolate prepared, and Jim, Lily and I will make the biggest snowman this farmyard has seen.'

'Can I? Can I, Mam?' begged Lily.

Rose shrugged her shoulders. 'They're your feet that'll be cold.'

Out they went.

Lily came running in for a hat and scarf, then an old staff, and finally one of Ted's father's clay pipes. 'I've never seen a better snowman. Have you, Mam?' Lily called through the window. Her eyes sparkled.

Looking at her daughter dancing around the snowman with red-appled cheeks, Rose felt a lump gather in her throat; this pregnancy had her feeling as soft as clarts. A bit of snow, Lily, Ted and Jim all looking happy, and Daphne pouring hot chocolate; the scene was going to have her in tears.

Danny, I've been happy today, was her last thought before she dropped off to sleep that night.

CHAPTER 33

*R*ose and Jim took a walk over to visit the pit ponies after eating Daphne's enormous lunch on Sunday. Lily was having one last visit to the Wilsons' to play with Jennifer, and Matt had already collected their bags to put into the Land Rover.

'I've really enjoyed the week back here with your parents. I feel like I've had a proper holiday, and I'm ready to go home and prepare for this little'un.' Rose patted the belly that had expanded over the week.

Jim linked her arm to help her over an icy patch. 'I was dreading the return, but it's been a revelation. Much better than I could have hoped really. Dad seems a changed man – well, changed towards *me*. I keep kicking myself in case I'm dreaming.'

'He was heartbroken when you left, you know. He raged on and cursed you of course, that's Ted, but he was in shock. He learned to accept you for who you are, and it was a tough lesson.'

'Yes, for us both. I was homesick at first, but the excitement of the music kept me in Germany. It's a hand to mouth existence, and you have to want to play badly and hope for a bit of luck to stay.'

'If you keep playing, your break will come. Look at those Liverpool lads you were telling me about who are going to make a record, imagine that. They might knock The Shadows off their perch.'

'Aye.' Jim nodded excitedly. 'They might.'

They reached the ponies and Jim was quiet for a while. Rose had the feeling he wanted to say something, so she petted the ponies, fed them carrots and waited.

'I won't get a record deal over there, Rose. I haven't told anyone yet, but I'm going to pack up after our gig next week and travel to London'

'Is there a good music scene there?' Rose asked.

'There is, but I'm going there to find work. Any work that's not farming and will pay good money so I can play at night. I haven't the money to stay with the group.'

'But you've been with The Jems through thick and thin. Why leave now?'

'It'll be hard, but I've no choice. I had to pawn my guitar to fly over here, and the money Mam has slipped me will get it back, but after that I'm on rice and beans. The others have come home this week to raise some cash. Eric sold his motorbike yesterday and the other two have scraped a few hundred together from selling stuff and borrowing, but can you imagine me asking Dad for a loan? We're just speaking again now so I just couldn't bring myself.'

'I didn't realise it would be so tough,' Rose said.

'Neither did I. I'm going to do the gig, buy a ticket to London and look for proper employment, but don't you let on to anyone that I'm on my own there – I don't want Mam to worry and I want them to think I'm doing okay. It's one thing being a failure to myself, but I can't be one to my dad again.'

Rose mulled over what he had told her while they finished feeding the ponies their carrots then walked back past the Ayrshires.

'I think Dad could win the show with that one.' Jim pointed out the cow that Rose had favoured.

'I said that! Wait 'til I tell Ted you've got a good eye for a winner!'

Jim smiled. 'Something must've rubbed off on me. I wish Edward was still here – for Dad, to pass on the farm. I'll give London a good try, and if I'm still nowhere in a year or so, I might come back with my tail between my legs and try to settle here. With farming I know what to do, but I just don't love it.'

Rose hated seeing Jim so dejected. 'You'll do no such thing! Stop thinking like that Jim. Fight for what you want – fight to get your music heard and fight to stay in the band. Tell them you don't have the cash but you're their best singer.'

Jim laughed. 'Where do you get all your spirit from?'

Their walk had taken them to the barn where Jim had first played for her. Rose went inside and sat on one of the bails. 'Jim, when I was a girl, I wanted to be a vet. I'd passed to go to grammar school and I was good at science, and you know I love looking after animals. I put it aside because my mother died, and I didn't fight to get that dream back.

'I got my exams and decided to work with animals, but I settled for less. I didn't fight to get into college and do the veterinary course. My dad would've backed me up, but I settled. I told myself I was doing it to look after Dad and Terry, but in truth I put the dream to one side.

'I'm happy and I don't regret anything I have done, but I do regret what I didn't do, and that was to try my hardest to put letters after my name and become a registered vet. I know how to treat sick animals, I read up on the latest research, but I haven't a qualification.

'Look at you! You don't need to settle. You're free to go after your dream, so don't stop at the first hurdle.'

Jim nodded, then pointed to the gaping hole in the small barn roof that was letting in shafts of sunlight. 'I'll offer to fix that with Dad on Monday. It's not a job for an old chap like him.'

Rose nodded. 'That would mean the world to him.'

As they walked back Jim took her arm again. 'Rose, I listened. I took in all you were saying. I'll talk to the lads, but I know I need to contribute more than my voice. We need new equipment to compete with other groups, and I haven't a pair of shoes with a decent sole at the moment.'

Rose said her goodbyes and joined Lily at the cottage. 'Time to go home, Lily,' she said, expecting an argument.

Lily jumped up saying, 'Yes, time to go and see Grandma and Grandad. I've missed them. Grandma said when we get home we'll be getting the crib out. Can we, Mam?'

'Yes.' Rose smiled.

'See, Jennifer.' Lily turned to the older girl. 'I told you I'll soon have a brother or sister. I'm not going to be an only child ever again.'

Rose tossed and turned that night. She was thinking of Jim's words.

She had the house deposit money in a bank account just sitting there. A widowed woman couldn't get a mortgage. It would help Lily though college. She also had Danny's winnings from the races that were still in the lining of his cap, and she kept that in a suitcase under her bed. She was keeping it in case of a rainy day, but she didn't need a dinghy *and* a raft.

Lily wouldn't need the bank savings for years so that would be enough to save her from a flood like Noah's, never mind a rainy day. She could give Danny's winnings to Jim as an investment. He could pay her back with interest when he made money; if he didn't, then she had lost her investment.

With her mind made up, she slept soundly.

. . .

In the morning, after waving Lily off to school, Rose took the cap from the suitcase and removed the roll of money that was tucked under the lining. Danny won this money with a flutter on the horses, and she was sure he'd like to see her take a gamble on Jim. She tucked it into her handbag and headed for the bus stop and the Seabottle bus, hoping nobody stopped her to ask where she was going. This investment would be just between her and Jim.

'What did you forget? Helen asked when she slipped into the back door of the cottage. 'Nothing, but I want you to help me out.'

'Anything,' Helen said.

'Find Jim and ask him to come over to do a job – fix your washing line or something. I need to see him on his own. Tell him it's urgent and then just leave us for a few minutes.'

Helen gave her a long look. 'Should I know more details? Have you two struck up a romance?'

Rose burst out laughing. 'Helen, what a question! He's a few years younger than me and I'm about to pop.'

'Stranger matches have been made.' Helen looked flushed. 'Okay, I'll not ask any more, but don't you dare tell him I thought that.'

Rose stopped laughing. 'Don't worry, I won't repeat it to a soul,' she said, then Helen went off on her errand.

A few minutes later Jim came around the back and she opened the door to him.

'Rose! What's going on? Helen came over to the barn acting like she was Jenny Sparks the spy. She told me to come here to fix a washing line, but she was winking at the same time. Now she's slipped away.'

'I asked her to get you here under false pretences and she's completed the mission, so come in.' She closed the door and pushed the envelope in his hand.

'What's this?'

'I want to invest some savings. I won't need it until Lily is due to go to college, so you have years to pay me back. I want to invest in you and your music, Jim.'

Jim looked at her, then at the envelope, and put it on the table. 'I can't... I couldn't.'

'It would make me happy if you did. You can pay me back with interest. I might make my fortune. Why not?'

'Do you mean it? Do you really believe in me that much?'

'I do.'

He hugged her and sobbed.

Helen came into the kitchen as the two of them were hugging and sobbing. Jim released Rose from the hug and she wiped her eyes, blaming her pregnancy hormones for her emotion.

'What's your excuse?' Helen asked Jim.

'Hay fever.' He grinned and picked up the envelope. 'Thanks, Rose. I'd better get back to the roof. I'll write to tell you how it's going.'

Rose nodded.

Helen closed the back door after Jim left. 'What was in that envelope? I'm making a pot of tea and buttering a teacake, and while I do I hope you're going to come clean with me, Rose Dodd.'

Rose told Helen about Danny's winnings and what she'd done with them. She asked her to keep it to herself.

'You're kind, Rose, but you're not a fool. Jim will pay you back whether he makes it or not. Your belief in him has been the making of the lad. He'll not let you down.'

'Fancy you thinking we had a fancy for each other,' Rose teased.

'He is quite good-looking now with his long hair though, isn't he?' Helen said.

'I can't say I've noticed,' Rose answered, 'but I hope the music fans do. It'll help to sell records.'

CHAPTER 34

*J*ust like his sister, six and a half years earlier, this baby seemed eager to make an early appearance. The kicks were fearsome, and she imagined a boy, a miniature Danny Dodd. Wouldn't that be a miracle?

The week before the baby was due, Rose spent her days making up the crib, boiling and hanging out the nappies she had kept since Lily was a baby, hand-washing the pile of woollens knitted by Grace and several other women in the rows, and packing a bag with toiletries, slippers and two new nighties. No sooner had she folded the freshly aired nappies into a neat pile, placed the bag by her bedroom door and breathed a sigh of relief at being ready at last, than her back pain began.

Should she lie down or let Grace know? She waddled over to talk to Grace, but let out a squeal as she entered the yard of number one. Her waters, they broke in one long gush! She spied Lottie's face peering over the wall.

'Grace, come quickly!' Lottie yelled, and Grace got her into the house as Lottie sped round into the yard.

Grace sent Lottie over to Rose's to collect her packed bag, and Dad, in bed from his night shift, was woken up.

'John, get up! Rose is in labour. You need to run along to the phone box and call an ambulance.'

Rose was having her delivery at the Princess Mary Maternity Hospital in Jesmond, and the frequency of her labour pains told her she would be lucky to get there before this baby arrived.

She insisted on walking to the ambulance and was waved off by a group of women from the rows; in Linwood some news travelled faster than nits in a schoolyard. She would have smiled and waved back, but another contraction made her sit down and grip her escort's hand.

'This one's in a hurry, Mrs Dodd, but don't you worry – if we have to stop, I've done this before.'

'I'll try to hang on,' she said through gritted teeth.

But she couldn't; Rose had the urge to push. The baby wouldn't wait.

She squeezed the man's hand and heard him telling the driver to pull in. This was really happening!

Robert Dodd wriggled his way into the world in the back of the ambulance and screamed at the top of his lungs as he was handed to her. He had a shock of dark hair already, his sturdy limbs kicked, and how those healthy lungs wailed. 'Danny, I wish you could be here to see what our love has created,' Rose wished as she looked at her little miracle.

Her helper seemed to know what he was doing with the afterbirth, and she saw the relief in his face as he examined it and it was whole; she was like that after helping to deliver a calf, relieved it was a success.

As she cradled her son, the ambulanceman asked the driver to carry on.

'There's no need to rush now.'

'Thank you. You did a wonderful job.'

He grinned at Rose. 'This is a story to tell him when he's older.'

'I will. I'll tell him he wouldn't wait. How far off are we?' Rose asked.

'Not far from Jesmond now, Mrs Dodd. You can tell your little lad he was born just by the Reno cinema in Wideopen.'

The name yanked at Rose's heart and she drew in a sharp breath. The Reno? Danny's boy was born at the side of the A1, right where his dad had died nine months ago. Danny, were you with us? she wondered. Was she being fanciful, or was it a coincidence?

Rose decided to name her son Robbie after Danny's pal since childhood. She couldn't ease the man's guilt about bringing bad luck to the family by being a giftless, fair-haired first footer, but she had thought of a way to show him she didn't blame him or believe such superstitious nonsense.

Two days later, Robbie arrived at the hospital with flowers and a fishing rod, and she asked him to be godfather. She placed young Robbie into his arms, and the young man's face lightened. 'I'll be the best godfather ever, young Robbie. We'll fish and I'll take you foraging for mushrooms and blackberries and the like where me and your dad went as lads.'

Robbie Dodd didn't have a father, but he would never be short of love.

CHAPTER 35

*W*omen in the rows had always worked when extra money was needed, but they usually fitted any job around their men's shifts and their bairns' school times, so the jobs were a few hours cleaning, seasonal farm work, or part-time shop work. Even in the sixties that was the way of it, and Rose knew she had raised a few eyebrows in handing Robbie over to Grace that summer and returning to her full-time job at the vet's practice.

'What with your work car and you say they want you to have a telephone installed in your flat before you return, you're having a career like you wanted, but don't you miss having time with the little'un?' Lottie asked. She'd popped over to Rose's for an hour after the children were in bed.

Rose sensed a hint of disapproval. Lottie was trying for a second child and had no intention of working while Dennis, a pit electrician, made good money. She wouldn't play the single mother card because it wasn't the only reason she worked.

Who cared what other people thought, as long as the arrangement suited her and Grace and her children were happy?

'I enjoy my time with Robbie at night and at the weekends but

I don't mind leaving him with his grandma so she can dote on him while I visit a lame pony or help to deliver some pups. We both do what we're good at, and I don't see why it's anybody else's business.' She smiled, but she wanted to finish the discussion.

'Okay, that's me told.' Lottie took no offence and changed the subject to her favourite one. 'I wanted to tell you, I'm a few days late. Do you think I could have those tablets, the ones you didn't take to see if I'm pregnant or not?'

'Why don't you give it a week or so and then you'll know anyway?' Rose wasn't keen on taking pills unless they were necessary, and that's why she hadn't taken the ones Lottie had given her.

'It takes the wondering out of it, that's why. I'll wait another week, but I'll take them home tonight anyway so I've got them to hand.'

Rose gave her the pills before she left. She had a feeling that Lottie, ever impatient, would take them before the week was out.

On Sunday morning, while the house was empty of little ears because they'd all been sent off to Sunday school, Lottie came into the kitchen of number one looking glum. 'I'm not pregnant,' she muttered. Paul, so easy to conceive, was almost nine, so she had waited a long time for a second baby, and Rose was lost for words. 'Grace, get the kettle on, and I'll pop over to Norris's for teacakes.'

'You'll do no such thing. I can have a batch of girdle scones made in the time it takes you to go along and buy them. It's a Sunday, so those teacakes will be yesterday's.'

'That doesn't matter if we're toasting them,' Rose said.

'It matters to me, and this poor lass needs the comfort of good homemade food.'

Lottie sat back and soaked up the sympathy. At least sharing her disappointment with Grace and me over a girdle scone and a cup of tea will perk her up, thought Rose.

As she was settling Robbie for the night, Rose pondered on how Lottie was taking such a long time to conceive again. Wasn't it strange how babies weren't always born to the ones who wanted them most? It seemed so unfair.

That had been her mother's opinion when she had taken fairness into her own hands and given one of her twins to Dorothy Fletcher. Rose accepted it had happened; it had been seventeen years ago now, and Joy would be a young woman. She accepted it and she understood her mother's reasoning, but she still didn't agree with it. She looked down at Robbie. How could her mother separate a baby like this one from his twin?

What would her brother Terence think when he found out he had a sister? He didn't know, and Dad didn't think he should be told about his twin until he had finished his studies and matured. Rose was glad it wasn't her choice. Her choice not to tell Dad had been hard enough, and caused no end of trouble between them. She only hoped that when the day came Terry took it better than Dad had all those years ago.

CHAPTER 36

1963

*I*t was a gusty May morning and Rose battled with her flapping unbuttoned coat as she unlocked the door to the Woodhorn Road surgery. Stooping to pick up the post, she made her way to the reception area. She started work two days here, then the other three days at Morpeth, but as the day unfolded she could end up at either practice, or even a farm up by Otterburn. She'd been back to work for ten action-packed months; the days flew by and she loved the variety.

This practice in Ashington was mainly for domestic animals and its waiting room was always packed with a variety of creatures and clients by the time surgery started, whereas the Morpeth practice was quieter but offered a different challenge. The practice in Morpeth had to deal with bigger beasts, who had muckier illnesses and lived down clarty tracks.

She loved both, but preferred the farm work around Morpeth where she was out and about as the senior vet's sidekick. Pam organised their workload as well as the young vet's and a veterinary assistant's list, and she managed the clerical side of things. Rose had finished training a new assistant for Ashington, so she was just needed to cover the two weekdays when staff had their day off. Saturday was her day with her own bairns, and she looked forward to it.

Frank, as head of the practice, was based in Ashington, where the animal hospital and operating theatre was stocked with the most modern equipment. He was a wonder with domestic animals and the most intricate surgery. Rose was in awe of his skills when she saw the frail little creatures he worked on and how he healed them. With Frank she had swiftly picked up their old friendship and camaraderie, and they enjoyed working together, as well as being a good team in the theatre.

She looked at the list as she switched the kettle on, but sounds of an angry wife carried downstairs and distracted her. They were at it again; or rather Marjorie was at it because there was no reply to her raised voice.

A door banged. Rose flinched. The sound of footsteps thudding down the stairs was followed by a demand. 'Rose, hurry upstairs and get my case while I put Deborah in the car.'

Rose said nothing as she watched Marjorie place the toddler in the fancy pram in the hallway and wheel her to the car. The pram's wheels went into the boot and the body went on the back seat, so Marjorie could take it wherever she wanted. Rose was making do with the pram she used for Lily. It had been passed on to her by Lottie from Paul's baby days; Lottie would have it back whenever she had another.

Prams lasted for generations in the rows. She did admire this one of Deborah's, but if she had drawn money out of her savings and bought one for Robbie, Grace would have been reluctant to use it and would have fretted about getting it dirty, and folk from the rows would say she was 'up herself'.

'Why are you still standing there? I asked for my case.'

Rose was startled by the tone. Marjorie Maxwell was taking her temper out on her now.

She was about to go upstairs and obey the curt order when something sparked in her brain; the something that told her enough was enough and to stand up for herself. She turned back to face Marjorie.

'Excuse me? Were you *asking* or *ordering* me to help you with your case?'

'I'm *telling* you. I'm in a hurry and you're not helping!'

'That's right, I'm not helping. My job here is to open the practice and prepare it for a morning surgery that starts in fifteen minutes. I'm employed by the practice, and I'm not taking orders to carry cases for you or for anybody else.'

'How dare you speak to me like that?'

'How dare you give me orders?' Rose regretted rising to the bait, but she just couldn't hold her tongue at times.

Frank appeared. 'Oh no, not you two now!' He had Marjorie's case. 'Here, I've got your luggage. I'll put it in the boot.'

Marjorie sniffed and turned her back on Rose. 'Frank, you need to speak to that woman for talking to your wife with disrespect.' As she walked off behind Frank, Marjorie started on him again. 'What time can you be back in Yorkshire on Friday? We have an invitation...'

Rose took a deep breath and calmed herself. Marjorie Maxwell might row with Frank and make his life a misery, but she was not going to give her orders.

Frank came back in and watched as she pulled out the files of the animals on the morning list. 'She's tootling off to Yorkshire again. She's only been here three days. Three days! She doesn't give it a chance, and it's not worth hiring the help she wants if she's not going to be here.' Rose put the files down and turned towards Frank. His eyes were strained.

He chewed at his bottom lip; he always did when he was worried. 'She was in Yorkshire with her parents all winter right through the big freeze, I could understand that. Then she didn't want to travel because of flooding so she put off coming here, but it's almost summer now and she hasn't been in this house for a full week all year.

'I don't know how this will end, Rose, I really don't. I want to see more of Deborah and Marjorie, so do I just give up the practice to please her? Would that be letting Dad down? I told her I'd be taking over and we would have to move here one day. We discussed it before we got married, but she hoped I'd change my mind and settle in Yorkshire. We can't find a compromise.'

Rose wasn't sure what to answer. Luckily she didn't need to, because the door opened and two of the staff came in. Another hectic day was about to begin.

CHAPTER 37

*T*here wasn't a moment to give Frank's problems another thought until she was driving home. She thought over the morning's incident and couldn't help but compare Marjorie and her self-centred ways to Frank's mother. He had certainly chosen someone hoity-toity and very like his mother. Not that *they* liked one another much; they were too alike.

After returning to work she had felt useful; even more than that, she had felt fulfilled, and being busy helped to ease the pain of losing Danny. She hoped Frank didn't sacrifice the practice or she could be out of a job again. One thing was sure, she was keeping right out of the marriage difficulties. Didn't she have enough to contend with?

As she approached home, her thoughts settled on her own situation. She'd handed Robbie into Grace's care at four months and everything was working well. Grace and little Robbie were happy. So was she, except… except, if she was honest, she thought Grace spoilt him. Robbie was coming up to fourteen months, and would be walking if Grace didn't carry him everywhere and feed him all the cake and biscuits he wanted, so he was a bonnie but chubby little cherub.

Grace hadn't been soft like that with her son, Johnnie, nor with Lily either; but it seemed that this baby had captured her heart and could do no wrong. How could she say anything when Grace was so good about minding the children, and wouldn't Robbie walk when he was ready? She'd have to bite her tongue with Grace, but maybe she'd have a word with Dad.

As she walked into number one, Robbie came shuffling up to her on his bottom – he didn't crawl – with a big beam on his face and a buttered jammy crust in his hand.

'What are you having just before your tea? She picked him up and nuzzled the sweet buttery smell of him. 'Here, Mammy.' Robbie tried to feed the soggy crust into Rose's mouth and she laughed.

Grace wiped floury hands on her apron, saying, 'No bairns go hungry in this house. He didn't eat all his soup at lunchtime. Did you my little soldier?' She scooped Robbie from Rose, saying, 'I'll just give him a beaker of milk and then I'll get the dinner on.'

The back door opened and Lily rushed in and wrapped her arms around her. 'Hi, Mam. Can I go back out to play for just half an hour before tea? They've got the long skipping rope out in Third Row.'

'You may, but don't have me out looking for you.' She sat down and watched Robbie bottom-shuffling after Grace to the scullery. Rose contributed to the grocery jar every week and they all ate together at number one every work night; it was easier all round, but it meant she only had Robbie to herself for an hour before bed and at the weekend. No wonder he preferred to follow Grace and her endless supply of goodies.

'This is what you wanted, Rose Kelly,' she told herself, before calling through to the scullery, 'Grace, I'm just popping to the allotment to meet Dad. I'll take Robbie in the pram. Is there anything I can bring back?'

'No, pet, but just leave the bairn here with me – he had a walk in his pram earlier. Didn't we go to the Co-op, bonny lad?'

Rose shrugged on her coat and left. It was easier not to argue, but she would talk to Dad about Grace.

She might have guessed Dad would take Grace's side. Didn't he always? As they walked back from the allotment he made his opinion clear. 'Grace has the bairn all week and he's a happy, bonnie laddie. He'll run that baby fat off him as soon as he's on his feet. Stanley was that build if you remember, and we couldn't fill him. He's got Danny's looks, but he's not going to be that wiry build.

'If I were you, I'd be glad of Grace's help. Aye, she spoils him, but that's not a crime – and when he gets a year or two older he'll be running away from her cuddles. It sounds like you're wanting to keep *all* the bonnie marbles in this game, our Rose.'

She looked at him and kicked at a stone on the path. 'Point taken, Dad.'

She knew what he meant; she was being self-centred and wanted everything – her job, her children looked after, and her ways of bringing them up being followed. It was true and her main gripe was one she hadn't mentioned; the shiny marble she really wanted was to be Robbie's favourite, just as she was Lily's, and that's what was eating away at her most.

'Dad, I'm being selfish. Don't say anything about this to Grace.'

Dad linked her arm. 'I'm the soul of discretion and have no intention of breathing a word, hinny.'

When they crossed over to the flat after their dinner, Rose found a letter from Germany lying on the mat. She opened it.

. . .

29th April 1963

> *Dear Rose,*
>
> *Just a few lines to let you know we're doing okay and I haven't had to pawn my guitar again. We are becoming well-known and the work hasn't dried up all year. My German isn't improving, just a few phrases, but we won't be here much longer as the music scene in England is looking better for groups like us.*
>
> *Remember those lads from Liverpool I told you about, The Beatles? The ones who made a change in their line-up and had a record out last October? You must listen out for their new LP. They're becoming really well known and playing Newcastle Majestic in June. Imagine that!*
>
> *If the Tyneside Sound does half as well as the Mersey Sound, we'll be happy. I am so glad I stuck with The Jems and I'll never forget your help. Here's a picture a fan took of us playing at the Star club.*
>
> *Yours sincerely,*
>
> *Jim*

He seemed in good spirits – a fan indeed! Rose studied the black and white photo of four long-haired lads on stage. There was Jim singing into a mic with a crowd of girls looking up at him, and she smiled to think he was making a go of this chance. All The Jems needed was a break and they might make records too.

Maybe it was a coincidence and Dad didn't breathe a word, or maybe he hinted gently, because after their talk Grace stopped handing Robbie snacks if it was near to teatime, and she carried him less to encourage him to walk.

By June he was toddling all over and spoiling Johnnie and Lily's games. 'Me too, me too,' he'd say as he waddled after them.

'I think I've been babying him a bit,' Grace confided to her. 'It's a wonder you didn't point it out because my mother did – she can't help interfering. It's because he's the last baby we'll have in the family for a while, and it's so lovely when they're at the stage when they need you.'

Rose hugged Grace. Some days she loved her stepmother and other days she was infuriated by her, but she knew Grace's heart was huge and her love for her grandchildren was boundless. Weren't they all blessed to have her?

CHAPTER 38

*J*im's next letter brought more good news.

June 1963

   Dear Rose,

   We're recording a single this week! We have a manager. He was in a successful Tyneside band himself but he's managing other groups now and he has great plans for us. He wants us to record one of my own songs because it goes down well in the clubs as the last slow dance.

   'Break-up Blues' it's called. It's a twelve-riff blues I wrote after I had to leave my guitar in the pawn shop last year. It's about breaking up then being reunited. I was writing about my guitar, she's my girl of the song, but it sounds raw and real, so Charlie our manager says.

   The B side will be our old dance number that I've played you many a time, 'The Best Day of The Week'. When it's released you'll have to look out for it in Arthur's record store in Morpeth. They always have a wide selection of new artists.

   We have gigs in London and in Birmingham later in the year and

Charlie (manager) is trying to get us a Newcastle spot around December so we can all be home this Christmas. That'd be champion! Don't mention it to Mam and get her hopes up though.

Life is great and you know I have you to thank, so thank you Rose!

Love Jim x

Lily loved music and was thrilled to know somebody who was in a band. Rose promised her they'd buy The Jems' single.

She looked out for it being released, and sure enough a poster appeared in Arthur's record shop window in July. Rose went in to ask for it.

'The Jems' single? It's selling well because they're a local group,' the girl behind the counter explained. 'Do you want to go over to a booth to listen?' She pointed to the line of sound-proofed alcoves with headphones inside them on the side wall.

'No, just wrap it. How much is it?'

'Six and thruppence.' The girl nodded towards a poster on the wall. 'Isn't Jim Fairbairn handsome? They all went to school round here, you know.'

'I do know.' Rose smiled. 'Tell you what, I'll take two.' She handed the girl a pound note and waited for her change.

'That's seven and six change. Enjoy The Jems.'

Rose crossed over to the paper shop and scanned the *Melody Maker* and the *New Musical Express* to see if there was a mention of The Jems in either. There was a column in both, so she took them to the till. Jim Fairbairn was costing her a small fortune today.

After work she picked Lily up but left Robbie with Grace. 'We're paying a quick visit to Blackthorn Farm,' she explained.

'Great! Can I call on Jennifer?' Lily asked.

'Yes, we'll not stay long, but I have a present for Daphne.'

'What brings you here at this time, lassie?' Daphne was washing up and listening to the radio.

'I have a surprise! Turn that radio off and we'll play something different.' Rose handed Daphne the packet containing The Jems' single.

'Oh my goodness – he's done it, just like he said! He's made a record, our Jim – fancy that.'

'Let's play it then. You have a radiogram in the sitting room, don't you?'

Daphne nodded. 'I do, but I've never used it, Rose. I just know how the radio works.'

'It's easy. I'll show you.'

Lily had run off to tell Jennifer about Jim's record, so they both came running in with Helen on their tails. 'You have the single?' she puffed.

Rose waved it at her and all five of them crowded around as she put the black disc on the turntable. The arm lifted and the stylus touched the vinyl, then boom! Guitar and drums came blasting out, and Jim's clear voice sang out about the best day of the week.

'Oh, I've put the B side on,' Rose exclaimed.

Jennifer and Lily were dancing to the song as she explained to Daphne about A sides being the main song and the B side being a way of filling the other side of the disc.

'So we get two songs?' Daphne asked.

'Yes, "Break-up Blues" is the other.'

After listening to both, Daphne and the girls decided the B side was lively and best, but Helen and Rose loved Jim's haunting voice singing of heartbreak.

'You'd really think he lost a big love, wouldn't you? He sounds so sincere,' Helen said when they'd listened a second time.

Rose checked that Daphne was still in the kitchen making a pot of tea. 'He told me he had pawned his guitar and was heart-broken without her,' Rose whispered. 'Remember when I made the investment?'

Helen laughed. 'Of course, I remember you using Danny's winnings. You might have backed a winner with Jim.'

It was as they read the snippets in the music papers over a cup of tea and a slice of cake that Daphne decided to start a scrapbook. 'I'll collect things too and bring them here, and we'll stick them in when we visit,' Lily suggested.

After that, Lily was forever on the lookout for mentions or photos of The Jems, and due to their manger creating news stories about them, they were often in the music and local papers.

Rose and Daphne received letters from Jim about *Juke Box Jury*, a popular TV show that Lily watched avidly every week; Charlie had got the single onto the show. New releases were played and discussed and declared a hit or a miss. The show ran on a Saturday night and was watched by all the younger folk in the nation, or so it seemed, because there was always discussion among them about the new releases that aired on the show.

As Lily and Rose watched, Rose could see Lily had her fingers crossed on both hands. 'Make it a hit!' her daughter called to the television. It scored fours and fives and was declared a hit. After that the *Melody Maker* charts showed The Jems rising to number sixteen in the pop charts.

Rose handed the paper over to Lily to cut out the chart.

'Imagine them getting to number one!' Lily said.

The single began to fall after that, but the group was now well-known and Jim phoned her from Germany, so he must have some cash.

'We've got the Majestic Ballroom in Newcastle, Rose,' he shouted and inserted coins at an alarming rate. 'We're home for Christmas!'

. . .

Rose loved Friday nights when she could relax with her two bairns and didn't need to worry about a hectic early start the next morning. They often had fish and chips from Charlie's, then once Robbie was in bed she would watch TV for half an hour with Lily, and that suited them all fine.

It was a chilly autumn night and Rose could feel a draught coming from under the back door when she lifted the long sausage dog draught excluder that Grace had made her. She moved it to stop it getting soaked; her son had been on a stool 'helping' with the washing up before bedtime, but had flooded the floor so she needed to give it a quick mop.

Once Robbie was in his pyjamas, Lily offered to read to him. He loved this idea and Rose was happy to leave them to it, because she wanted to finish cleaning up in time to sit down with Lily and watch *Take your Pick* at seven o'clock.

Rose could hear the murmuring of Lily reading Robbie's bedtime story and the TV playing in the living room as she speedily dried up the suds so she could replace the draught excluder and keep out the cold. The only heating was the fire in the living room, but once the thick scullery curtain in the doorway was closed, they'd be cosy.

The TV in the living room was already turned on to a northern news show, *Scene at 6.30*. Rose half-listened to the normal chatty stuff being presented by Mike Scott. Just as she was putting the mop and bucket away, she heard a change in his tone. 'We are getting reports that shots have been fired at President Kennedy's motorcade in Dallas.'

A lump of ice formed in the pit of her stomach. Had she heard correctly? Rose rushed to the TV to turn on to the BBC.

Nothing.

She turned back to the other channel for the game show and kept the TV low so Lily could watch, but she shivered by the radio in the scullery, waiting for an announcement.

'Aren't you going to watch, Mam?' Lily called. 'You like this.'

'I will in a moment, sweetheart. I just want to catch some news.'

A radio bulletin confirmed it.

The United States President has been shot, but there's no news yet of his condition. It happened as he was riding with his wife in an open car through the streets of Dallas, Texas. Several shots rang out and President Kennedy collapsed into the arms of his wife. An eyewitness described seeing blood on the President's head. Another passenger, the Governor of Texas, was also shot down. The President has been rushed to hospital, but there's still no word of his condition.

She turned off the radio and went into the warmth and sat by Lily. 'Someone has shot President Kennedy. That's what I was listening for.'

'He's a good president, isn't he? Why?' Lily asked, just as Michael Miles's show was interrupted for a newsflash to confirm the shooting.

Lily knew the end of the show signalled her bedtime. Rose filled her a hot water bottle to take to bed, and as her daughter was climbing under the covers she checked on Robbie, who was fast asleep and clutching a toy gun. Rose gently prised it from his grip before turning to tuck Lily in. 'I'll pray very hard for the President, Mam,' she whispered.

'So will I, pet. Goodnight.'

She placed the toy gun in the sideboard out of sight, feeling glad that such weapons were hard to come by in this country. Robbie had plenty of toys so wouldn't miss the gun. Tonight she would pray for the president and for his wife and two children, that they may be kept safe in this dangerous world where hatred flared and real guns maimed.

A hospital soap, *Emergency Ward 10* had started when Rose returned to the TV. She sat down to watch, but it was abruptly pulled at 7.40 p.m. with confirmation that Kennedy was dead.

Rose shivered; a numbness stopped her tears. Shock, disbelief – she had felt like this before. Sudden death was hard to accept.

His poor wife. Rose knew what it was like to have her husband snatched from her, but she hadn't witnessed the horror of it, hadn't been soaked in his blood like Jackie Kennedy. She turned off the TV. What a tragedy. What a loss to the world.

Rose tossed and turned in bed. She wanted to escape her thoughts through sleep, but it evaded her. Tonight's news brought back the grief that had almost swallowed her over two years ago. By some miracle, she'd carried on.

By some miracle? The word lingered in her head. She hadn't prayed since losing Danny. She felt too angry. She'd promised Lily she'd pray tonight, so she would pray for Jackie Kennedy and her children, and she'd ask for something too. She wanted guidance or a purpose to her own life.

'Give me a purpose to carry on besides being a mother. Show me how I can do some good in the world, to make a difference. You've taken Danny, can you give me a good reason to be here without him?'

CHAPTER 39

1964

*R*ose was sure she was being watched. She could feel eyes on her as she walked from the Woodhorn Road surgery and unlocked her car on her way to visit Peg, the Turnbulls' sheepdog, in Hepscott. She whisked around but there was nobody in sight except for a shop assistant from Briggs the Jewellers crossing the street, and somebody in the driver's seat of that light blue car parked further up the road.

She'd noticed the car a couple of times and made a mental note; it was a Hillman Minx but she didn't know who drove it. She glanced as she passed by, but the driver stooped to pick something up from the footwell so she was none the wiser about who they were.

It wasn't the first time she'd felt watched. When she'd popped out for a few groceries in her lunch break earlier in the week, she had the distinct feeling she was being followed. It hadn't unnerved her, she was more curious than anything; who would want to keep track of her? However, today she felt a bit rattled.

Rose set her mind on the task ahead of her. She was going to check on Peg and see if she was ready to deliver her pups in the next day or so. The Turnbulls would manage the litter's delivery fine, but she'd promised to drop off some enriched puppy milk in case there was a runt in the litter who needed extra feeding. The enriched milk was a new product and Maxwell's had a few free samples, so they may as well go to Peg's pups.

When she parked outside the vet's surgery later in the afternoon, the light blue car had gone. She was puzzling over her feeling of being watched as she took off her coat and Frank came into reception. 'Is something wrong with Peg?'

'Peg? No, she's as fit as ever. Why do you ask?'

'Because you're frowning. You look perplexed.'

Rose hesitated; should she tell Frank? Would he laugh off her misgivings? 'I'm baffled because I keep getting the feeling I'm being watched. Don't laugh.'

Frank sat in a waiting room chair and patted the one next to him. 'Sit down, you have to tell me more. What's given you that impression?'

Rose told him about the occasions she'd sensed she was being watched and asked if he knew who the light blue Minx car belonged to.

'I don't. Ruth has changed cars recently and I wouldn't put it past her to snoop about for no good reason, but she hardly ever visits me or Dad. Anyway, it can't be her because she's off on an autumn holiday to Scotland.'

'Are you sure she's there?' Rose asked.

Frank laughed. 'You have the same suspicions as me! Yes, I'm sure she's there. She took Mum and sent me a postcard.'

'That leaves me without a suspect then.'

On Friday Lily came running out of number one's yard and up to her as she parked her car. 'Hi Mam, are we having a chippy tea or having some of Grace's ham soup?'

'Whatever you prefer, sweetheart. I don't mind.' Rose was glad it was the weekend and she'd have a full day with Lily the next day. She planned to visit Helen and her family; Lily loved to go there, and they could spend an hour with the pit ponies too.

'Let's go to our own place and have fish and chips from Charlie's,' Lily decided.

'Let's pop in to tell Grace our plan, and then I'll go home to set the table and make a pot of tea while you join the queue at Charlie's.'

'A woman said hello to me today when I was playing in the school yard,' Lily told her as they walked towards number one.

Rose squeezed Lily's hand and stopped them both in their tracks. 'What woman? Someone we don't know?'

'I didn't know her. She called me over. "Lily!" she called, and when I turned she waved me over. "Are you Lily Kelly?" she asked, and I shook my head and told her I was Lily Dodd, but I was Rose Kelly's daughter. You know some of your school friends still call you Rose Kelly. She put her hand through the bars and said, "Pleased to meet you." I shook her hand and asked, "Should I know you?" She laughed and said, "Not yet, but we'll meet again one day."

"What's your name?" I asked and she didn't answer, she just asked where we lived and I said, "I don't give my address to strangers who I don't know and who won't tell me *their* name."'

'You were right not to give out your address.' Rose's mind was reeling. Was this anything to do with her watcher? She didn't want Lily being followed too. 'I wonder how she knew who you were?' Rose asked.

'I wondered that too, so I investigated just like Nancy Drew. She'd asked two older girls in Johnnie's class to point out the Kellys, and they pointed to Johnnie then to me.'

Rose took Lily inside. Grace had heard this tale already and hadn't any idea who the woman could be. Lily and Johnnie went out to play for half an hour before the chippy opened and Rose spoke up as soon as the door closed behind them. 'It could be Joy. It has to be Joy looking for her family.'

'How can that be when she's in Australia?' Grace asked.

'She could have come back! I've felt eyes on me a couple of times in the past few days. Maybe she's checking us out before she decides whether to meet us or not.'

John Kelly came in from his shift and declared Rose's suspicion was nonsense. 'The lassie is just eighteen, same age as Terence. She wouldn't travel this far on her own, and Dorothy Fletcher wouldn't want her meeting us if she did. I think you're barking up the wrong tree because you want it to be so, our Rose.'

'Maybe.' Rose wasn't convinced. It had to be Ruth Maxwell, up to no good, or Joy Fletcher, wondering how to approach the family who had given her away. Ruth was on holiday, so she hoped against hope it was Joy. Imagine if her little sister had travelled back to her place of birth to find her family. Hadn't they wished for this?

As they ate their fish and chips, Lily mentioned the lady again. 'I think I *could* be like Nancy Drew in the stories, Mam. I keep searching my brain for more clues. That lady was wearing a long beige coat and had her hair tied in a fancy way in a scarf, Mam. I couldn't tell if she was dark or fair.'

'Can you remember anything else?' Rose asked, casually. 'Was there a car parked there?'

'Like she was a kidnapper?' Lily's widened eyes showed excitement more than fear.

'No, I just wondered if she had driven here, that's all. Now tell me what you'd like to do tomorrow.' She changed the subject because she didn't want to make Lily anxious.

At bedtime Rose read a chapter from *James and the Giant Peach* and was trying to do the voice of Aunt Striker. Lily giggled.

'What's so funny?' Rose asked. 'I'm being a mean aunt so I'm nothing to laugh about.'

'Your voices are all the same. Grandad's better at voices… Dad did good voices too. At least I think he did, I've sort of forgotten.'

Rose put the book aside and stroked the stray locks of hair from Lily's forehead before kissing it. Swallowing a concrete lump of grief, she managed, 'He was good at voices, sweetheart. He was one of the best.'

Rose was far away in thought when Lily brought her back to the present.

'I've remembered another clue. It popped into my head. That lady, Mam, the one you've been guessing about – she talked in a sort of funny voice. It wasn't like us and it wasn't posh like on the news either. She talked a bit like she was in a film.'

'Do you mean American? Like *Wagon Train*?'

'A bit… but not quite. She's from somewhere different though.'

That somewhere was Australia, Rose was sure of it.

When Rose took her new information over to number one the next day, Dad and Grace still weren't convinced. 'There are hundreds of accents, and you're clutching at a very soggy straw, hinny.' John Kelly looked up from his sketch of a pit pony pulling an underground load and rolled the charcoal between his fingers.

Grace nodded her agreement as she knitted socks on four needles. 'Surely we would have heard from the mother if she was going to put in an appearance?' Rose had to admit that Grace was right; Dorothy Fletcher would have let them know.

She hunted in the drawer that held the Bible and birth certificates for the last letter from Dorothy Fletcher. She searched for the bit she wanted.

'Listen to this, Dad – "*Lately, I have considered that Joy will have no close family after her father and I die; I expect my own parents will be laid to rest by then. That is why I am writing, to keep in touch. I have made up my mind to reveal the truth to Joy in my will, or after Mr Fletcher's death, whichever comes first. I hope it is not for many years yet, and if she ever needs to find you I hope you will make room for her in your warm-hearted family."* See? Maybe something happened. It's possible that Joy knows about us.'

'I hardly dare hope you're right. I'd like nothing better.'

Rose hugged her dad. 'We'll just have to see what she does next.'

A week later, Dad handed her a battered envelope with a foreign stamp. 'It's addressed to you. The postmark is from last month. It's been re-directed from Linwood, New York, would you believe.'

Rose tore open the envelope and raced through its contents before handing it to Dad. 'That's it, mystery solved. It *is* Joy who is watching us and deciding whether to meet us or not.' She didn't say I told you so, but hadn't she known it all along?

'Read it out John. What does it say?' Grace looked pale, whereas her dad was as excited as she felt.

September 3rd 1964

Dear Rose,

I'm writing about Joy. She has disappeared with her savings, and I am worried for her safety. She is headstrong and only eighteen. I don't know if she remains here in Australia or if she is travelling to England. It is all my doing. My husband, Neville, died in a mining accident and that left me feeling low. I feared that Joy would be left without any family at all.

I decided to break the news about her birth. I had always intended to reveal the truth one day. Rose, you have no idea how she reacted! She was so distraught. She blamed me for stealing her and she couldn't face the fact that she hadn't been Neville's daughter. She wouldn't look at me or speak to me for days and then she packed her bags and left in the middle of the night.

I contacted the police, but they weren't much help and they thought she would return in a week or so.

However, she hasn't returned or written, and her college course has started. Now I'm not sure whether she is living in the city or she has headed back to England.

If she looks you up, will you please let me know? She has my parents' address, but I don't know whether she'll go there or not. They will be so shocked to hear how I came to have her! I can't bring myself to write to them about it.

I am ill with grief and now this worry about Joy, and I know you may not have any sympathy for me because of what I did, but I have always had Joy's interests at heart.

Kindest regards

Dorothy Fletcher

'It's a disaster for Dorothy Fletcher, but isn't this wonderful news for us? We have a chance to reunite.' Her dad hugged her and Rose, speechless for once, could just nod.

Grace tilted her head and gave them both a long look. Rose was right in thinking one of Grace's aphorisms was heading their way.

Taking the letter, folding it and putting it carefully in the envelope, Grace said, 'Don't count your buckets of coal before they're safely in your shed. I just hope she's as willing to let bygones be bygones as you two are. We just don't know, do we?'

CHAPTER 40

*F*or the next couple of weeks Rose kept a lookout for the light blue Hillman, but her follower seemed to have gone to ground. Surely Joy hadn't come all this way to take a look then vanish? Rose didn't think she could bear it. She told herself it would be hard to introduce yourself to a family who hadn't seemed to want you. They would have to be patient and give Joy time to approach them.

Early on Thursday morning, Rose was about to wheel Robbie across to First Row – Lily had run on ahead of them – when she bumped into Mrs Lawson opening up her hairdressers. 'I'm opening early this morning as it feels chilly and it's a Thursday. I like the place to be warm for my pensioners,' she explained.

It clicked with Rose that today was the day when the pensioners got a special deal for a shampoo and set. She looked across at her car, parked outside number one ready for her to go to work. 'Frost the first week of November! I hope we don't get freezing and floods like last winter. I'm sure the car will be frozen up again, even though I put newspapers on the windscreen last night.'

'Yes, lassie, today's a cold one.' Mrs Lawson was bringing out her street sign to announce her pensioners' special.

'I'm glad I've run into you, Mrs Lawson. I wanted to see if you could fit Lily in for a trim this Saturday. Her fringe is like a Shetland pony's, and she won't sit still if I come near her with scissors.'

'Of course. Bring her in about ten.' Mrs Lawson went to her desk and scribbled Lily's name in her large black appointment book. 'By the way, I've been meaning to tell you, I had a client asking after you earlier this week.'

'Oh?' Rose groaned inwardly, Mrs Lawson was a good gossip, and she didn't want to be late for work. She glanced at her watch thinking she would be running late if she got caught up in a long chat.

Mrs Lawson caught the movement and Rose flushed when she said, 'I won't keep you, lass. I know you're a worker like myself. It was just the daughter of a past under-manager came into the salon and asked after you Kellys. He moved when she was a baby, but she came back to Linwood to see where she was born.'

Rose felt blood rushing to her ears and thought she would faint. 'What was her name?' She knew her name, but how was Joy introducing herself?

Mrs Lawson switched on the electric fire and bustled about in the sink area sorting out perming curlers as she spoke to Rose. 'Fletcher, Joy Fletcher she's called. I vaguely remember her mother, but she had her hair done in Jesmond, not in my salon. Your mother was quite friendly with her for a time – well, they'd both lost a laddie to the strangling angel hadn't they? I told Joy that. It was a terrible year, the last year of the war. A pretty girl, she is. You'll *never* guess who she could be the sister of.' Mrs Lawson paused, looking for a reaction from Rose.

Rose couldn't swallow. *Don't say Terry. Don't say our Terry.*

Rose's heart thumped almost into her throat. 'Who is she like?' she managed to ask, and her voice came out high and strangled.

'She looks just like that film star, the sultry one... you know who I mean. She has the same look and the same hair. Lovely hair she has, and a natural blonde too. It needed a good two inches cut off it in my opinion, but she just wanted a wash, dry and updo. What on earth is the actress's name? It's on the tip of my tongue.'

Rose sighed and managed to breathe properly as Mrs Lawson searched for a name.

'I've got it! She's the double of that French actress Bridget what's-her-name.'

'Brigitte Bardot?' Rose asked as relief washed over her.

'That's her. Long hair all over the place and a striking face. Wouldn't let me put it up into one of my French rolls but had it loosely tied into a bun, and then she tied a scarf around it herself.'

Robbie squirmed in his pram. After she dropped him off at First Row she'd have the car to defrost and she needed to open the practice in half an hour, but she couldn't leave without knowing everything.

'You said she mentioned me?'

'Yes. Her mother had talked about you Kellys and mentioned she got on well with your mother. It turns out they moved to Australia when Joy was ten. Very chatty she was.'

Rose stepped inside and grabbed a seat. 'What else did she say?'

'Told me all about her life in Australia. She's just a slip of a lass to be travelling here on her own, but she wanted to see where she was born. She mentioned her mother and yours had been expecting together – your Terry is the same age, isn't he? I told her about Terry starting at the university. She asked about the whole family and asked where your mother and her brother, Douglas, would be buried. I told her she couldn't miss the cemetery if she kept to the road out towards Burnside.'

Rose gulped. Her mouth was too dry to speak, her teeth stuck to her lips. 'You told her about us?'

'Yes, about your dad remarrying and all of you. She said she might call in on you and I said you were a friendly family and wouldn't mind at all. I mentioned you had the flat above here, so don't be surprised if you get a caller.'

Mrs Lawson finished with the curlers and said, 'I have to go in the back now to sort out my towels.'

Rose stood up. 'Sorry to keep you. I have to dash or I'm going to be late opening up.'

'You drive carefully on those frosty roads,' Mrs Lawson called as Rose wheeled Robbie away at speed.

Grace met her at the gate. 'You're late, Rose. Lily has been here fifteen minutes – are you all right?'

Rose nodded. 'I'll tell you tonight, I have to dash. Take Robbie straight in because it's cold.' Her hands trembled as she removed frozen sheets of newspaper from the windscreen then turned on the ignition. Oh my goodness, it really was happening, Joy knew the truth and she had found them.

Her sister knew where she lived and worked, and where her dad lived, so whether they met or not was in Joy's hands. Rose could think of nothing else. Thoughts spun and tussled with one another. She'll be nervous; she's discovered she was given away. She's just found out about her birth family so she's reticent about introducing herself. We mustn't frighten her off. What if she hasn't liked what she's seen of us? She might just disappear.

Rose struggled with her thoughts all day and was glad to close at five o'clock. She was parking outside First Row as usual when she saw the blue Minx across the road by the shops on Front Street. Her heart thumping, she crossed over and walked towards the car, but as she drew closer she was disappointed to see it was empty. She looked in the back seat; no clues there. She walked around to the driver's side and peered in.

'Are you looking for me?' A figure stepped out of the shop doorway and Rose turned around. She was face to face with her sister.

CHAPTER 41

The last time Rose saw Joy she was a little girl, about the same age as Lily was now. She'd secretly watched her playing in a school yard, knowing who she was but unable to speak to her. She hardly recognised the young woman in front of her and would have passed her in the street.

'Hello, Joy. I've been waiting for a chance to see you for a long time.' Rose held out her hand.

Joy looked at the proffered hand but kept hers stuffed in her pockets. 'From where I'm standing, you haven't seemed keen to meet me.'

The voice was cold, and Rose lowered her hand. 'I've had a letter from Dorothy. I'm sure learning about your birth was a shock. Do you want to come up into my flat, to chat or do you want to go across and meet the rest of us Kellys?'

'I'm not sure I want to do either.' The same cold voice.

'We've all been longing to meet you,' Rose assured her.

'Longing… longing? That's funny.' Joy gave a forced laugh and stared at Rose. Her eyes darkened – was it with anger? – as she said, 'My mother told me that you've all known about me for years. I've come to see the family who could give me away, to see what sort of rabble I come from.'

Rose swallowed back a sob. Her sister was hurt, that was all; she didn't mean any of this. She had come to find them. 'Come upstairs and we can talk. Maybe I can explain.'

Joy gave a slight nod. 'I can't wait to hear how you explain this away.' Her tone was sarcastic, but she followed Rose around into the yard and up the stairs to her flat.

'It's a cosy little place you have here, right opposite your father. I bet you're his golden girl, aren't you? His only daughter.' Lily's voice was taunting as she looked around Rose's home.

Rose swallowed hard as she switched on the kettle. She had imagined hugs and tears when they met. How wrong she'd been. This wasn't going to be an easy reunion. 'Take a seat and I'll tell you everything you want to know.'

Joy took off her coat and flung it over a chair, but she paced the floor. 'I want to know why me? Why was I the giveaway girl, the twin who was rejected? How could my own mother keep her son and give me away? She's not here to tell me, so you'll have to do.'

How many times had Rose told this story? She'd heard the reasons from her mother's own lips and was the best one to tell it, but it broke her heart every time. She'd explained it to Dad when he found out and witnessed his rage, confided in Danny and been held in his arms and comforted, and now she had to tell her sister. This sister was someone she'd fretted over for years. 'Before I start, it was Mam and Mam alone who made the decision, and Dad and I have thought about you and what you were doing on every birthday, every Christmas Day, and many a day in between. We have waited for this day and you're welcome, so don't think you're unwanted. Can I give you a hug?'

Joy stepped back. 'No. I came for answers, not for a welcome or your approval.'

'Okay. Take a seat at least, and I'll pour us some tea.'

'I drink coffee, two sugars.'

Rose tried to control her tears and her breathing as she made two drinks with shaking hands. This was a nightmare. Could she ever put it right? Joy was as fair as Terence, and she had Dad's eyes, but with her clothes, her accent, and her confident manner, nobody would take her for a Kelly. She seemed like a stranger to Rose, and she'd always imagined there would be an instant bond.

She handed Joy a mug of coffee, walked over to close the curtains and hoped Lily wouldn't notice her car was parked outside First Row and come running across to find her. She locked the back door, just in case. If anyone popped over and found it locked, they'd knock but they wouldn't get in.

At last, she sat on the sofa and gave Joy her full attention. 'I first found out I had a sister when I was fourteen. The Fletchers moved soon after you were born, and I bumped into Mrs Fletcher when she was shopping in Morpeth. You were in a pushchair, and when I looked at you, I knew. At the age of three, you were identical to my brother Terence.'

Joy butted in. '*Our* brother, Terence.'

'Yes, our brother,' Rose agreed. Blimey, this was hard. 'Mrs Fletcher knew from my face that I was suspicious when I asked your exact birthdate, and she made an excuse to dash off with you. I was physically sick at the thought of what might have happened.'

'This is *my* story, not yours. Never mind being sick – I want to know why. What did *our sainted* mother say when you asked her about discarding me?'

Joy's eyes bored into her and Rose was dismayed at the hatred she thought she saw there. 'Mam gave Mrs Fletcher the *gift* of you. You weren't discarded, Joy. She told me what she had done and why and swore me to secrecy. I loved her. I didn't agree with her, but I kept her secret.'

Rose tried to retell the story her mother had told her as accurately as possible. Joy deserved the truth, and she didn't know what Dorothy Fletcher had already told her. 'Mam's family have a history of breast cancer. Our great-grandmother on our mother's side died young and our grandmother became ill when Mam was eight. She was diagnosed with cancer in her breast and was determined to bring up Mam and her brothers and sisters, so she underwent a radical treatment. Mam remembered her coming home after the removal of her breast and chest muscles and being unable to use her right arm. She didn't mind the pain or the loss of the use of her arm, because she'd be able to see her children grow up and marry. She didn't though. The cancer spread and she died the next year. Mam was left with a fear of doctors and dentists interfering with her and avoided them at all costs. Dad reckoned it was a proper phobia.

'We lost Auntie Elsie, Mam's older sister, to cancer of the breast when I was a baby and Mam was expecting again. Mam decided she would finish her family after the boys arrived because she didn't want to leave young ones or give me, the eldest, the job of raising children and staying at home. Auntie Elsie had raised Mam and her brothers and had no life of her own.

'Just before Mam found out she was expecting you, she found a lump.' Rose paused and swallowed hard. 'She didn't need a doctor to tell her it was the disease that had plagued her family. She was frightened of treatment. It hadn't worked on her mother and there was her phobia around doctors. She didn't tell a soul.' Tears ran down Rose's cheeks. It was hard relaying this story and reliving her mother's fears, the fears that had probably killed her.

'How did this make her give me away?' Joy was dry-eyed and clearly wanted her to go on.

'When she found out she was expecting and suspected it was

twins again, she was worried she'd be too ill to manage and would have to depend upon me. She didn't want me to leave school to look after two babies.' Rose's eyes filled with yet more tears. 'I would have. I loved Mam and would do anything for her, but Mam had a different plan. She was friendly with Dorothy ever since the diphtheria epidemic when they both lost a son. Dorothy confided she had miscarried a much-wanted baby, and Mam decided one baby to a loving home desperate for a child would lessen the burden.'

Joy stood up and walked to the window. Drawing back the curtains and looking out onto Linwood rows, she said, 'So I was born over there, and I was the burden. The burden that her precious firstborn shouldn't have to care for.'

'It wasn't like that, Joy. Maybe I used the wrong words. Mam wanted a good life for you as well as me. Your mother, Dorothy, had miscarried again after losing her son, and she was longing for a child to love. She asked for a girl if Mam gave birth to one, or it could have been Terence.' Rose walked to the window and touched Joy's shoulder. 'They were doing what they thought was best. I think they were wrong, and so does Dad, but they were doing this with love.'

Joy shrugged her off and turned to face her. 'Dorothy chose a girl?'

Rose nodded. 'You were very much wanted.'

'How did they hide it?'

'People knew Dorothy was expecting, so after the miscarriage, she kept up the pretence, said she'd been expecting twins and lost one – it happens. She paid a private doctor in Jesmond to book her into a clinic there and forge the birth. Mr Fletcher had no idea. The doctor came and collected you after you were delivered by Mam's neighbour. You were born at her house, number two, and taken to the clinic through the night. When Dad came home from his shift, he had a son, and nobody was any the wiser until I saw you.'

'Maybe I was lucky to be the giveaway. Imagine being brought up in that sooty little house and not having horses to ride or fresh air to breathe. Imagine being too poor to travel.' She stopped and looked Rose up and down. 'Oh, I'm forgetting, you don't have to imagine. You have lived that life, haven't you? You're still living it.'

Rose tried to curb the spark of anger she felt. Her sister was hurt and wanted to hurt back. 'Yes, I am.'

'I loved my dad. He was clever and we were such great friends. When he died, part of me did too. I'm not sorry I'm a Fletcher, but I am sorry that Dad died. He didn't deserve it, and I wish it had been the one over there – the one who couldn't feed or clothe me.'

The spark flared again, and Rose couldn't help herself. 'That's enough! Don't you dare stand here and say something like that. You don't know that man. You don't know how he's grieved for you, but he hasn't gone after you because he knew you were settled and happy in the family you'd been raised in. You have had a good upbringing, but you haven't learned either manners or compassion, Joy Fletcher. I can tell you now, that with your uppity attitude and callous treatment of people's feelings, you aren't a Kelly – and you're nothing like the Fletchers either, who were good people. Douglas Fletcher was a lovely lad and Mam thought you'd be brought up to be the same. She'd turn in her grave to hear you today.'

'You're showing your true colours now.' Joy's pretty mouth hardened as she spat out, 'You can tell the rest of that… that pack I'm not meeting them. I have no wish to. I'm well rid of you lot.'

'Are you going back to Dorothy?' Rose asked.

'It's not your business, but no, I'm not. She can do without me for a while for keeping such secrets from me and telling such tales. I'm staying with my grandparents. They don't know any of this. Just imagine their shock if they knew their only living grandchild came from your stock.' She laughed and walked to the door. 'I've seen enough, and I haven't liked it. I don't need a sister, thank you.' She unlocked the back door and her footsteps faded away.

Rose didn't go after her. What else was there to say? What could she say to Dad? Should she tell him or not? It would break his heart.

CHAPTER 42

*R*ose walked into First Row an hour later than normal, but she hadn't been missed.

'Working late, pet? The kids have had their tea and yours is in the oven.' Grace stooped to take out a plate of stew that Rose knew she wouldn't be able to swallow.

'Sorry, Grace. I've had an upset stomach all day. Could I just collect my two and go? I'll have some tea and toast when they're in bed.'

She wouldn't tell them about today; she'd wait to see if Joy had a change of heart. Why hurt good people?

Silence. Rose watched and waited all the next day, but there were no more sightings of Joy.

On Saturday, while Lily went across to First Row to show her newly-trimmed fringe off to Grace, Rose wrapped Robbie up and wheeled his pram over to the cemetery to talk to Mam. She had no flowers; it wasn't the season for many, and her favourite

Christmas roses weren't out yet. She'd popped a trowel and a couple of dusters into the base of the pram to tidy up the grave. She hadn't been there since September but chatted to Mam in her head, just like she still chatted to Danny.

As she approached, she could see a splash of bright colour. She thought someone had taken flowers, but when she got nearer, she gasped. The red spray she had mistaken for flowers became clear. BITCH was daubed right across Mam's headstone. What could she do? How would she get this off?

She grabbed the extra blanket folded at Robbie's feet and draped it over the offending message. Had anyone seen it? She rubbed at a corner with one of the cloths she'd brought, but the paint was dry and wouldn't budge.

'It's all right, hinny. I've brought the right cleaner and some brushes to get rid of the paint. I'll have it as good as new in no time.'

Rose whirled around to find Dad standing there, laden with a bucket and brushes on his wheelbarrow. 'I sometimes come along on a morning to talk to our David, so I found this bonny mess earlier on. I have just the stuff to put it right, so you take the little'un home and least said soonest mended, eh?'

Rose flew into her dad's arms. 'Dad, it's her! It's Joy! I wasn't going to say, but she came and she's awful. How could she do this?'

Dad patted her back. 'The Kelly temper, hinny. Remember how I raged at you for siding with your mother and we didn't speak for a while. She's raging and she's given vent to it. She isn't mentioned as a daughter on the headstone, so it could be she snapped when she saw that. We can try to understand, make allowances, can't we?'

Rose didn't think she could. 'She's mean, Dad. I don't like her.'

'I don't think she likes herself to do this. When you're as old as me, Rose, you'll understand that people act in funny ways when they're hurt. Your Mam did a lamentable thing when she separated that lassie from her blood family. I still think she made a mistake, but I don't think she deserves *this*.' He shook his head.

'She made a mistake, but she was a good woman was Ginnie. I'll make sure the grave is put right, and look...' He pointed to the barrow. 'I've brought a few sprigs of winter heather from the allotment. Leave it to me. I didn't want you to see this, and I'm sorry you did.'

Rose kissed Dad on the cheek before turning to wheel Robbie back towards the gates. Dad could excuse Joy for doing this, but she couldn't. Hadn't she explained what Mam had gone through? Did her sister have no compassion?

Dad returned an hour later, and Grace sent Johnnie and Lily over to the welfare to play on the swings so they could talk it over without little ears listening.

'I want you to step back from this, Rose.' Dad sounded firm. 'If the lassie contacts you again, point her to me. You were nowt but a bairn yourself when you had to keep her presence a secret, and it isn't your job to make amends for your mother.'

'I don't care if I don't see her again. She's nothing like our Terence. She doesn't feel like a Kelly.'

'She is a Kelly, and will forever be one whatever you feel, Rose. I'd like her to know why I didn't chase after her. It wasn't for our family's benefit but for hers, and she needs to know that. She's had an upbringing full of opportunity. It's just a shame that she's been indulged and she's headstrong, but I suspect she's had a mother and father who wanted her so much they gave way to her too often and too easily.'

'She's at the grandparents now, you say?' Grace looked up from darning an elbow of Johnnie's school jumper.

'She said so, but they know nothing of any of this. They just know she has argued with her mother and come to them. She doesn't want them to know her story.'

'She'd better keep in line in future then.' Dad looked stern. 'Any more foul play like the one we found today, and I'll be talking to her grandparents.'

'She didn't say where they lived.'

'Folk with money living near the borders aren't hard to locate. Dorothy Fletcher's maiden name was Goodchild, so I'll find them when I need to. I just want to make sure the lassie is looked after while she is over here.'

Dad might want to find Joy's whereabouts, but Rose had had her fill of her. What would he make of her and her manner?

Dad changed the subject to share a rumour that was sweeping through the rows. 'While the two little'uns are out, I might as well tell you there's talk about closing Linwood pit. I know there's been talk before, but this time it seems more likely. We're working in seams very near to Burnside and they are the bigger mine of the two, so if one has to close, it'll be us.'

'What'll you do, John?' Grace asked. 'Will you transfer?'

'If another pit will have me until I reach sixty-five, I'll have to, hinny. We have Johnnie to get through school, and seeing as Terry has just started his studies in Manchester, he'll need us for another year or two. His tuition is free and his accommodation grant is generous, but the lad still needs a bit of help. One coal seam is the same as any other to me.'

Rose could see it made sense to close Linwood. It wouldn't be the first small mine to be sacrificed because it wasn't making a big enough profit. Times were changing. Coal was the main source of power in the country but Linwood, like many smaller mines, didn't have the latest equipment and couldn't be as cost-effective as others. Ponies were being replaced by machinery, and miners had to move with the times.

CHAPTER 43

*J*im sent Rose good news and a photograph in a brief
letter.

November 1964

   Dear Rose,

   *Hope all is going well with you, Lily and Robbie. I've enclosed our
latest signed picture for her because I hear she's making a scrapbook
with Mam.*

   *The picture I've sent will be on our album cover. Yes! We're making
an LP, a long player with ten tracks on it. There will be some old blues
numbers mixed with some of our own songs. The title of the album is
Rough Diamonds and our next single is 'Rough Diamond Blues'. Look
out for it in the new year.*

   *We're planning a 1965 tour of Europe including some venues near
home so we'll get to see our friends and families.*

   Love Jim x

. . .

Lily was delighted with the photo. 'Can I put all of Jim's letters in the scrapbook too, Mam?'

Rose thought about it. 'No, Rose. Letters are for one person, and don't ask Jim's Mam either. She'll treasure his letters.'

'I meant yours. You don't, you just leave them in any drawer.'

'They're still private.' Rose didn't want any clues about her lending Jim money to surface, and in many letters he thanked her for giving him his chance.

A cloud of gloom settled over Linwood. Discussions of pit closures hung in the air and it seemed every possible scenario included Linwood being on that closure list. Most men would move to other pits in the area. Would that mean their families would eventually move away from Linwood to be nearer the men's work? If that happened, the village would never be as vibrant again.

'If they keep Burnside I'll be happy to walk along there for a shift. Our rescue teams work closely together, and I'll have plenty of marras to work along.'

Dad was upbeat about his future as long as Burnside stayed open, but that option wasn't assured.

'You might have to travel as far as Ashington, John. If you do you'll have to get a bike for the nightshift and a bus for the day.'

'If I get a bike, I'll be using it for every shift, hinny, to make it pay for itself. I don't fancy cycling along there in the winter months, but if it's all that's on the cards for me then I'll do it.'

In the end it turned out that Burnside was given a reprieve and John was transferred to the neighbouring pit, along with all of the Linwood miners who wanted to move. The village gave a collective sigh of relief and the 'tute had a coronation day atmosphere on the Saturday after it was announced.

John Kelly hadn't gone to the 'tute on the Saturday. He took Robbie and Johnnie to dig up some veg and help him mix paints in his allotment shed. 'I'd rather celebrate by finishing off my painting, pet.' He kissed Grace on the cheek and set off with the lads.

When Rose, Grace and Lily called in to the Dodds later that afternoon, the men were all sitting around the kitchen table with a few sandwiches and pasties to soak up the afternoon's beer.

Grace's dad had already retired the previous year and her brother Joe, the one closest to Danny, had always worked at Burnside; so when Billy, who was in his forties, heard his transfer was successful, he was delighted. 'The only thing that mars this day is my bonny Star,' he said. 'They're not taking the Linwood ponies because they have plenty, and they're using machinery more and more, so I'll lose my loyal marra.'

'What'll happen to him, Uncle Billy?' Lily asked. 'Will he go to a good home like our ponies at Blackthorn Farm?'

Billy shrugged his shoulders. 'Who's to say? It's up to the National Coal Board.'

Joe nodded in agreement. 'Aye, you're right, Billy.' He turned to Lily. 'Old Sparkie – the one I told you about, Lily, the one who saved my life when there was a fall of stone – he went to Batey's Farm just along the road. I saw him regular 'til he passed, but there'll be too many for Batey's Farm to handle. Star might have to go further afield.'

Lily's face clouded with dismay, but Rose reassured her. 'He'll be looked after, pet, there's no worry on that score. There are rules about the treatment of the pit ponies.'

Billy joined in. 'Aye, they canna go for slaughter and they're not to be ridden, so if they're not wanted, like the Linwood stable, then they'll be retired from work.'

'That's good.' Lily's face lightened in relief.

Billy bit into a pasty and chewed for a while before saying, 'The trouble is *where* they'll go. There isn't a retired pit pony centre here in the north of England. I think the nearest is miles away in Lancashire or thereabouts.'

'Why is that the case?' Lily frowned.

'Never needed one here, I suppose.' Billy scratched his head and Rose smiled; he wasn't used to Lily's incessant questions. 'We usually farm them out one or two at a time like Joe said to the neighbouring farms, but this lot might have to go so far away that we can't visit them.'

'That's not fair, Uncle Billy!'

I know, hinny. I canna bear the thought of not seeing Star every now and then. He's fond of a sugar sandwich on a Friday, and he'll not get that when he's far from home.'

'Mam, can you have a word with Farmer Fairbairn? Ask him to take Star for Uncle Billy?'

Rose knew Ted Fairbairn couldn't help out. Yes, he took a retired pony every few years and could sometimes have half a dozen, but those gallowas he already kept could live into their thirties so his space was limited. 'I'll look into places locally,' she offered.

'All of us drivers have scoured the area for weeks, hinny. We'd like nothing better than to keep the gallowas nearby and to keep in touch with them. They'll miss the work, and the crack will our ponies. They're not ready for lazing and having nowt to do and being split up from their little cliques.' Billy shook his head and an air of gloom settled over the table.

Rose took Lily and Robbie home but brooded on the pit pony situation all evening. Her dad was sorted and the men could easily travel to Burnside so the village wasn't in any jeopardy, but surely these working animals deserved some consideration?

Her research the next day showed Billy had been right and the nearest large centre for pit ponies covered the Yorkshire and Lancashire coalfields. Their ponies would be cared for if they went there, but they'd be miles from their old workmates. Why should they be?

She decided to write to anyone interested to discuss solutions. After all, there would be more mine closures in the area and more ponies arriving above ground and in need of re-homing. Machinery was taking over from ponies, so why hadn't someone planned for this?

As she got into bed, she said a quick thank you prayer. 'I asked for a challenge to come my way, the chance to do some good, and I've got it. Thank you, Amen.'

'I hope your letters make a difference, Rose, but the fact is the ponies have served their purpose, and like a retired miner it's the scrapheap for them.' Her dad wasn't convinced about her plan.

'A retired miner gets a certificate, a pension and the chance of an aged miners' cottage, Dad, so the ponies should get a retired ponies' rest home.'

John looked up from stretching a canvas across a frame. 'Aye, but there's a long wait for the cottages, pet. If I put my name down now, I'd be lucky to get one when I'm seventy. Like most things in mining, there's good ideas but not enough to go around.'

Rose sighed. 'Well, I'm fighting for the ponies and their rights. Somebody has to!'

'A lot would like to help but they don't have your way with words, pet.' Dad took up his hammer to tack the canvas down.

'That's just it, Dad, you're right! I'm going to start a petition. I have the words, but I need names behind me. Will you be first to sign?'

'I will, hinny. It's a champion idea.'

*A*fter a winter's walk through Plessey woods, Rose parked the car in its space outside number one and Lily insisted on calling in to Grandma and Grandad before they went home. 'Grandma likes to see us, and she might have made a cake for us to try,' Lily explained as Rose picked up Robbie and gathered together their paraphernalia in the back seat.

'Five minutes then,' she warned. 'Grandma sees you often enough and might like an afternoon to herself.' It was hard to keep them away and Grace never seemed to mind, so Rose lugged her bag, Robbie, and his pram into the yard.

'Hello, my treasure!' Grace swooped to take Robbie out of her arms, and Rose sank into a chair by the fire as Lily and Johnnie raced upstairs on some game-related mission.

At times it was lovely to have an extra pair of hands to take the children, but Rose did worry that they'd rather be here than at their own flat. It wasn't really a family home, that flat; maybe, one day. She caught herself going into the dark cloud of 'what ifs' and 'if onlys' and jollied herself out of it. 'Where's Dad? Is he painting at the allotment?'

Grace had given Robbie a buttered crust with jam on, and he

was after following the older two upstairs. 'Not until you've finished your crust, young man.' Grace placed him on the mat by the fire before answering Rose. 'No, he went out for the afternoon.'

'What do you mean "out"? Out of Linwood? Where to?'

Grace took a breath; she looked hesitant. 'He's been meaning to tell you, but I suppose it's left to me. He's found out where Joy is staying, and he's seen her once or twice.'

'What?' Rose raised her eyebrows. She couldn't believe what she was hearing.

'He's meeting Joy. He found out where the Goodchilds lived, near Warkworth, and he visited and introduced himself as a friend of Neville Fletcher's. Explained he'd painted their grandson Douglas because Neville liked his art, so he told the truth.

'He can pass himself off to anyone when he wants to, your dad. He said he wanted to know how the Fletchers' daughter was faring because Dorothy had written to us and was worried about her whereabouts.

'That got him into the house, and he met Joy. She didn't blow his cover and he didn't let on about her shenanigans around here. They went for a walk and got on well. He liked her, Rose. He said she was a spirited lass and had been given a free rein, but she was a joy to be with.'

Rose rubbed at her ears to get rid of the loud pounding in her head. That girl had been so mean to her. She obviously had another side, the side she'd shown to Dad. Bile rose in her throat. Dad liked her, but hadn't seen how mean she'd been when they met. 'He's looking at her with rose-tinted specs, Grace. She was mean about us all.'

Grace sat down. 'Listen, hinny, she's angry at her birth mother for doing what she did. Surely you can understand that? She's angry at Dorothy too for keeping such a secret. When she met your dad, they got on. She likes him, and she knows he wasn't part of the exchange. She wants to meet her twin. That's natural, isn't it?'

'She wants to meet Terry? But *he* doesn't even know!'

'It's high time all this was out in the open. Dad is going to explain and then take him to meet Joy when he's back for the Christmas holiday next week. He wants to put it right with them both. He's got a lunch at a lovely pub in Warkworth planned.'

'Oh.' Rose sat silently. She had to ask. 'Has she changed her mind about seeing me again?'

The pity on Grace's face said it all. 'She knows you sided with your mother, and she knows you kept her secret from your dad. It was a hard choice for you, such a young lassie, but it's one that's distanced you from your sister. It's her dad and brothers she wants to get to know.'

Rose felt numb. She stood up. 'I'm going home now, Grace.' She didn't want to meet Dad after his jaunt out with his new-found daughter. Picking Robbie up, she called up the stairs for Lily.

'Can I stay another hour, Mam? I'll be home before dark.'

'No, you can't. I want you to come home now – no arguing.'

'Don't be upset, lass.' Grace held out her arms.

Rose gave her a brief hug. This wasn't Grace's doing. Rose left the house, her mind buzzing with troubled thoughts. She was being pushed out. Everyone was going to be reunited with Joy but her, and she'd pined for years for her sister.

Rose kept herself busy throughout the Christmas season because the March timeline for Linwood's closure was drawing near. She gave many hours to her letters and her petition gained signatures as people started to take notice of her fight for the ponies to stay in Northumberland.

A full-page article in the *Evening Chronicle* drew attention to their plight, and she was interviewed for *The One O'Clock Show*, a local Tyne Tees daytime programme. As her fight became well-known locally, she always carried a petition paper with her because she was recognised and approached when she was out and about.

The publicity resulted in more donations, so with the help of Mr Maxwell and Vera, Rose found out how to set up a charity. Vera put her PDSA experience to use and offered to run 'Pit Pony Champions'. Rose and Mr Maxwell agreed that future royalties from their new illustrated *RANA Handbook* would be used to start building up the charity's funds, and a reprieve for the Linwood ponies seemed to be closer.

Terry came home for Christmas and helped Rose with the letters. He offered to take her petition for the NCB back to university and add to her signatures.

He had his day out with Dad and Joy and, although she was longing to, Rose didn't ask know how he felt. Terry didn't bring it up either. He was enjoying his engineering course and living in Manchester and was happy to talk about that, but he didn't mention having a twin sister at all. Had Joy asked him not to mention her?

The knowledge that Joy was ignoring her gnawed away at Rose, and she had nobody who understood. She almost confided in Frank, but he had enough worries of his own with Marjorie wanting to spend all her time in Yorkshire. His wife still hadn't settled, and it looked less and less likely she would.

CHAPTER 45

*J*t was early in January that Batey's Farm, who always kept a couple of retired ponies, offered their large field that lay behind the Miner's Welfare Park and the Working Men's Institute to the charity.

'We rely on this community to buy our eggs and milk and help with the tatie picking, so we want to help with this. That back field is seldom used. We wouldn't sell it off, it might be building land one day, but we can lease it. You can have the first year free, and I wouldn't charge over the odds after that,' Farmer Batey offered.

A plan took shape. They had found a suitable field, but they would need to erect a paddock for when they needed to limit grazing or to give the rest of the field time to recover. On top of that, it would take lots of volunteer hours to ensure the ponies were provided for and kept healthy.

They'd have to build a shelter at the far end to provide shade in summer and a warm dry refuge in winter. They needed willing workers to check on the animals, to monitor their grazing and feed, and to ensure they had fresh water. An added duty was regular field cleaning with checks for any hazards or poisonous plants. A regular outgoing would be a farrier to trim their feet, and the vet for health checks and floating the ponies' teeth.

Rose was sure there were willing volunteers to do these duties, but they needed to be organised and trained.

Dad showed her where to start. 'You need to call a meeting, hinny. We'll ask Bert Simpson, Lottie's dad – he's the union rep and he'll rally the men to attend. The bairns can write and deliver invitations to all the houses in the rows.'

The meeting to form the Linwood Pit Pony Champions supporters' group was arranged for Saturday, January the thirtieth, and they aimed to have a decent attendance.

The week before their meeting Churchill, the Prime Minister who lead the country through the Second World War, had his eighth stroke and died. He lay in state for several days, and the day of the funeral service was the Saturday of the meeting.

On the night the Working Men's Institute was as packed as it was on a Derby day, and although a number of miners weren't supporters of the statesman, others were ready to celebrate his leadership qualities during a dark time. Whether for or against the great man, his passing seemed to have awoken the miners' Dunkirk spirit, because they all stayed to attend the meeting.

'Look at the turnout, Dad,' she whispered. 'I feel nervous to talk to them all.'

'Get yourself up there, lassie. They're just waiting for you to tell them how to help.'

She stood on stage, took a large swallow, and in her loudest voice, asked, 'Do you want to save Linwood's ponies from travelling south and away from the folk they've worked for?'

Loud 'Ayes' and a multitude of hands waved in front of her.

'We look after our own, and these ponies have been loyal marras,' shouted Tom Smith, a horse-keeper who was taking redundancy because he was near retiring age.

Rose breathed a sigh of relief. They were behind her and

some were willing to help. 'Who can fix fencing and make a shelter for the ponies?' she asked.

A smattering of hands were raised.

Bert stood up. 'Come on, we've more joiners than this, and we'll need diggers too. Where are you coalface workers who are used to hewing great lumps of coal? Digging a few foundations will be nothing to you. Many hands make light work – we'll crack this in a few days.' Dozens of extra volunteers raised their hands.

Rose went on. 'Who understands the gallowas and is willing to check them over every day?'

'Aye, we can do that, Rose.' Tom Smith stood up and pointed to two other retired horse-keepers either side of him.

Rose's next question, 'Who is willing to help the horse-keepers if they train you?', was met with a good show of hands, and a few children waving frantically. Pony care was going to be popular.

'Anybody can pick up dung, but who is willing to do it to keep the ponies' field clean?' At this, her dad stood up.

'I'll do that, Rose, and I'm sure all the other allotment holders will want to join in, won't you?' There was a loud chorus of ayes. 'There's goodness in that dung, so if we all take a turn to wheel it along to the allotments, we can start a communal manure heap.'

Mr Dodd agreed. 'Good idea, John. I'll provide my spare barrow and the manure will help to grow our taties.' He asked, 'Who is in favour of starting a communal manure heap?' There was a second loud chorus of ayes, and by the end of the meeting almost every house in the rows had a part to play.

The joiners and craftsmen of Linwood and Burnside gave Rose a list of the materials needed to build a shelter in the corner of the field, fix the fencing and to create a paddock near the shelter. When it arrived, the work would begin.

A great relief was The National Coal Board coming on board at the eleventh hour and agreeing to pay the charity for the ponies' keep. They would have had to do this wherever they were stabled, so Rose had written to say it was only right for them to contribute.

There would be twenty ponies, and the three retired horse-keepers who offered ten hours a week could each be given a small weekly wage, but the rest of the care was made up from their rota of volunteers.

Rose and Lily had offered two hours on a Sunday, and when he heard about the rota Frank offered to do a monthly hoof and tooth check with Rose on the first Sunday of the month.

After the materials were paid for, Vera updated the charity's accounts and announced to Rose that Linwood Pit Pony Centre could run for a full year, and they'd have time to raise money for future years.

Rose handed Vera a box of chocolates. 'Thanks for your help, Vera. There's still plenty to do, but at least we have time on our side.'

'*Y*oung Jim Fairbairn has made the nationals! What a kerfuffle about his new record.' Dad was waving the paper at her when she called around for a chat. 'They have banned it from the radio.'

'Why is it banned, Dad?'

'Little ears. Tell you later.' Dad signalled that Lily was listening in.

'Lily, why don't you go out and call on one of your friends along the row,' Rose suggested.

'I want to hear about what happened to Jim's song. It'll go in the scrapbook.'

'Go out and play and I'll see what can go in your scrapbook,' Rose insisted.

Lily shrugged and left by the back door. Rose followed her to check she wasn't listening behind it, as she would have done at nine years old.

Dad handed her the paper, already open at page four.

'*Stormy Weather for The Jems*,' the headline announced.

Rose scanned though the article. '*Jems' song banned by radio for* lyrics. "We are rough diamonds but we've been misunderstood!" says The Jems' singer, Jim Fairbairn.

The article explained their predicament, and underneath there was a picture of a moody-looking foursome under a large umbrella.

After scanning to the end, Rose burst out laughing and read the details more carefully.

"The Jems' new single "Rough Diamond Blues" caused a storm over the airwaves this week. It was banned yesterday because of a flurry of complaints about the song's lyrics.

It is thought that many complaints came from members of a newly-founded association formed by viewers and listeners who are against the excessive use of bad language on the air waves, although the association has not confirmed this.

The association's purpose is to challenge the BBC's lack of account-ability in this area and recently it has locked horns with the corporation several times.

In this case, the offending lyrics were Jim Fairbairn's pledge that he would 'Rid this whore from my heart any which way I can.'

The Jems' manager, Charlie Chapman, explained that the listeners who complained about referring to a woman in such a way had misun-derstood Jim's words. 'He is singing about a thick mist wrapped around his heart,' Charlie explained. 'The word Jim sings is "haar" – it's pronounced exactly like whore but it's a northern word for foggy weather.'

The line is followed by 'there's a fret round the soul of this rough-cut man' and a sea fret is a haze coming inland from the sea, so it seems like the listeners were mistaken. With this misunderstanding cleared up, The Jems' single will be back on the air and climbing the charts in no time.'

'It's a funny tale, but I hope it doesn't stop the single and the album selling, Dad.'

John took the paper back. 'Any publicity is good publicity when you want to be famous, pet. People will listen in and their record will sell even better. Look at the commotion about that D. H. Lawrence book. When it eventually reached the shops, it was bought by folk who'd never read a book in their lives.'

'That's true.' Rose remembered how hard it had been to come by a copy of *Lady Chatterley's Lover* once its ban had been lifted. Danny found her a copy for Christmas that year though. Oh, how she missed him. He'd have laughed at this.

Dad's prediction was right. The single was talked about and bought and raced up the charts. Jim called her. 'Have you seen where we are?'

'Last time I looked you were trying to kick Cilla off her number one slot.'

'We're climbing nearer and we're getting airtime in the States too. We're booked for the rest of the year, Rose. We've bleedin' well made it.'

'Enjoy it, Jim, you deserve it.'

'I'll pay you back, Rose... with interest! I'll never thank you enough.'

'It wasn't really a gamble. I knew you were a winner.'

'Bye, Rose. I've got to go...'

He'd gone.

The smile didn't leave Rose's face all night. Danny's winnings had done some good, and they weren't lost; she hoped Danny knew that. She went to her bedside and took the photo from her top drawer. It hurt too much to keep it out all the time, but when she was happy like tonight she could look at the photo of the two of them smiling and looking into each other's eyes and be happy for those good times.

CHAPTER 47

*R*ose walked to Dad's allotment, enjoying the clear
March morning. Her job was to pick some carrots
and sprouts for their dinner while Lily and Johnnie were at
Sunday school and Grace was bustling about in her Sunday
cooking frenzy. The basting of the meat, the mixing of the Yorkshire pudding batter and the making of a pudding with apples
was all going on in a steamy fug, and Rose was glad of the
fresh air.

He had built a bonfire and was sitting on a cracket watching
the flames.

'Aren't you painting today, Dad?'

'I'm having a bit of thinking time, hinny. Come and pull that
spare cracket up for a minute. We haven't passed more than the
time of day all week.'

Rose pulled up the stool and sat watching the flames. Her dad
would talk when he was ready.

'I went to Warkworth yesterday. I was due to meet Joy by the
church and we were going to have a walk, but she didn't appear. I
worried. I wasn't sure whether to leave or to go to the grandparents' house. They still don't know we're kin – Joy doesn't want to

tell them, so who am I to argue with that? Anyway, I decided I'd give them a knock, say I was passing and ask after Joy.

'When the grandfather came to the door, he invited me in. "Come in, come in, Mr Kelly," he says. It turns out they haven't told Dorothy that Joy is there with them. Joy wouldn't have it and they didn't want to upset her, and now Joy has gone off. She's been gone over a week. He was hoping I might know of her whereabouts.'

'Has she gone home to Australia? Did she have money to travel back?'

'Nowt so simple, hinny.' Dad threw a few more sticks on the fire and Rose waited. He wouldn't be hurried.

He stared into the flames a while, then said, 'It turns out she's been seeing the chap who does their garden. He's a gardener at the big house beside them but keeps the Goodchilds' garden tidy too in his spare time. Joy took to helping him and they have both gone off together. It's created a stir in Warkworth, let me tell you.'

'Have they eloped?' Rose asked.

'No, Rose.' Dad shook his head, then said in a low voice, 'He has a *wife!* She's the live-in housekeeper at the big house. Joy and him, they've gone off, but they'll not be able to marry.'

'Oh, Dad!'

'Aye. I could kill him, I could.'

'He didn't kidnap her, Dad! We're not in the Dark Ages. It seems unfair on his wife, but they must have fallen in love and decided to be together.'

'She's far too young to know her own mind. She's nowt but a bairn, not nineteen until next week. This will be another birthday I'll miss.'

Rose stayed quiet. She had married Danny at twenty, and at nineteen they knew they were deeply in love. Joy knew her own mind, she was sure. 'Dad, when they're settled, she might write and let you know where she is.'

'I hope so. I'll go there and knock his block off. He's twice her age, Rose. Mr Goodchild says he's well into his thirties.'

'Do you think she's run off with a father figure?'

'She had a good father in Neville Fletcher, she's got her grandfather and she's got me, as much use as I am. What does she want to waste her life on a married man like that for?'

Rose said nothing. She knew her dad was upset, but she just couldn't see Joy as the victim here. She had gone off with somebody else's husband, and she knew what she was doing. Joy Fletcher got what Joy Fletcher wanted.

At last the day came for the gallowas to be brought up from the mine. Rose loved the buoyant atmosphere in the village. Each pony had to be hoisted by a sling, which was nerve-wracking for both them and their work marra who helped, but once at the top all of the rows were out to welcome them as they stumbled into the daylight.

They were led to the field next to the welfare and walked around the whole area until they seemed settled. One at a time, they were let loose. Some made for the shade of the shelter, some stood still by their marra waiting for an instruction, and others trotted over to the fence to be offered apples and carrots by the lads and lassies who called for them.

Most of the pit ponies had a short name, because this was quicker to shout in an emergency, and they were all swift to respond to it.

'Blaze, over here!'

'Tom, come for a carrot.'

'Star, have some apple,' a small voice piped.

Star came forward and nuzzled the apple slice from Deborah Maxwell's hand. Frank had brought Deborah along and she was holding her hand flat towards a velvety nose as Lily had shown her.

'You must be so delighted to see this day, Rose,' Frank said.

'I am, Frank,' Rose admitted. 'But I'm not done yet.'

'What do you mean?'

'We need to plan for when the other pit ponies come to the top. There'll be other closures before long, and what then? The Pit Pony Champions charity will have its work cut out to find a centre for all of them.'

Frank put his arm around her and gave her an affectionate squeeze. 'You're the most remarkable woman I know.'

Rose looked up to see pride shining in his eyes. She could sense something else too. Frank kept it well-hidden, but he loved her. It had to stay that way. She thought the world of him; she wouldn't say it was love – because he was married and she couldn't disregard that, even if it wasn't a happy union – but her feelings for Frank ran deep. If he thought she was remarkable, that just made her day.

CHAPTER 48

*A*t nine o'clock one evening, there was a tapping on Rose's door.

'Who is it?'

'It's me, Joy. Can I come in?'

Rose opened the door to see her sister standing there. 'Come in, come in.'

'Thanks, Rose. I know I don't deserve a second chance with you, but I have nobody else to turn to. I need help.'

'What is it?' Immediately, all her past resentment left her. Her little sister needed her, and if she could help, she would do it, gladly.

'I suppose you know I ran off with Bobby?'

'Yes, Dad told me.'

'We've set up home in a little terraced house, and he's got some casual gardening work and farm work so we should be as happy as can be, but ... but ... I've found out I'm pregnant, Rose! I'm expecting and that wasn't part of the plan.' Joy sank onto the sofa, sobbing.

Rose put the kettle on. Her mind was racing; her sister was

expecting but unmarried, and the man was already married so he couldn't marry her anyway. This was a sorry mess.

She handed Joy a mug of coffee. 'Two sugars. I remember how you like it.'

Joy shuddered. 'I can't face it. Can I have tea?'

She turned back towards the scullery and Joy followed her. 'What does the father say about all this?' Rose asked.

'That's the trouble.' Joy burst into a fresh bout of tears.

'What has he done?' Rose took Joy in her arms. 'He hasn't left you, has he?' she whispered.

'No, no!' Joy sobbed, 'he's delighted. He thinks it's wonderful, and now I'm trapped.'

Rose's arms fell to her side. 'You're trapped? What do you mean?' There were fresh sobs from Joy. 'I'll get our tea and you can take your time and tell me from the beginning.'

As Rose sipped her tea, Joy explained. 'Bobby and his wife had been married fourteen years and had no children. She blamed Bobby, and he thought it could be because they hardly ever had intercourse – she wasn't keen on that side of things. She blamed him for being infertile and said he'd ruined her chance of being a mother.

'When we got together, he was so unloved. He fell for me, and I must admit I found him attractive. It was far too quiet and dull around Warkworth, and when I asked him to leave with me, he agreed.

'I thought his wife was right and he wouldn't make me pregnant either, but I was wrong. I should have been more careful. Of course he wants a child, but I'm just too young. I don't want to settle down. I wanted an adventure, not this responsibility.'

Rose took a breath. She really did find it hard to understand this silly girl. She'd encouraged the man to leave his wife and now she didn't want him or his child. 'What now then?' she asked.

Joy sighed. 'I'm going to stay with him. He'll love us and provide for us, but I'll need a sister and family when I've had this baby. I won't manage on my own! Will you be there for me? Will you tell Dad? Will he forgive me for disappearing? I want to get to know the Kellys.'

'What about your grandparents? What about Dorothy? Are you going to tell them?'

'No! You mustn't write to Mum. I don't want any of my real family to know until I'm ready to tell them.'

Her real family? So the Kellys weren't her real family? 'Have it your way,' Rose muttered.

'I intend to.' Joy flashed her a look. 'You haven't been the sister I wished for up to now, so I hope you are going to stand by me, Rose. And Rose, tell everyone in the rows I'm Mrs Donaldson. I consider myself to be Bobby's wife now, and I don't need people gossiping because of the lack of a silly piece of paper, or finding out about me being given away by the Kellys.'

'She can call it a silly piece of paper, but it gives her rights and respect. There'll have to be a divorce and a wedding at some point.' Dad was digging the frozen earth to pull up a boiling of taties for dinner when Rose found him the next day and told him about Joy's evening visit.

'She says the wife won't agree to that. She wants her husband back.'

Dad leaned on his spade. 'We'll have to support her, but we can't be too soft. She's had too much of her own way and needs to learn you can't always keep all the bonnie marbles.'

Rose smiled; she'd heard that from Dad many a time, and maybe now Joy had a father to listen to she would become less selfish. 'If anybody can help her on the right track it'll be you and Grace,' she told him.

Joy was coming on Tuesday afternoon when Dad was at home because of his nightshift and the little'uns were at school, so she would be able to spend time chatting about her future plans with Dad and Grace.

Rose was relieved she wouldn't be there because Joy rubbed her up the wrong way, and she seemed to do the same to Joy. Rose was still grieving for her imaginary sister, the one she had held close in her heart for years who had been kind and had loved her on sight. Ha! that had been a pipe dream.

Dad was watching her closely. 'Rose, we're asking her to stay for a bit of dinner, and when you come in, try to get on and be kind. She hasn't had the easy life you've had.'

Rose swallowed hard. Easy life? Losing her mother, looking after the family, losing Danny? She turned away. Dad expected too much of her at times.

'Rose, hinny. You've been surrounded by love all your life, that's what I mean.'

She turned back. 'Okay, Dad, for you – I'll be the kind big sister and give her a chance.'

It became a pattern that Joy would come twice a week and she would sit back while Grace waited on her hand and foot and Dad sketched her and started on a proper oil portrait of her. She was lovely to Dad and treated Grace kindly like some sort of personal maid, but her comments to Rose always had a bite.

She ignored the little'uns, showing no interest in their tales from school or their games. They'd been told to call her Auntie Joy, and they didn't find that unusual as adults in the rows were often referred to as auntie out of respect.

As they were going home one night, Lily piped up, 'I really don't like Auntie Joy.'

'Why ever not?' Rose asked.

'She moans when Grace makes a fuss of Robbie instead of

running after her, and she ignores most of what *I* say to her until Grandad is listening, then she is sweet. She's sort of false. Is two-faced a swear word, Mam?'

'No, but it's not a nice thing to call someone, Lily.' *Out of the mouths of babes*, thought Rose.

CHAPTER 49

$\mathcal{R}$ose lurched out of a doze when the phone rang out. She glanced at the clock; half past ten. She'd dropped off to sleep for a moment while reading in bed, but the shrill tone had her wide awake in a moment. The bairns are in bed safe, don't panic, she told herself. Nobody rang after ten unless it was an emergency. The pit? An accident? Work? An animal? She rushed into the living room and grabbed the receiver in case it stopped ringing out.

'Rose, it's Frank. Can you get into Ashington soon? We have an injured dog, and it looks like we'll be operating.'

'Yes, I'll be there as soon as I can.' Rose put the phone down and ripped off her nightdress as she headed back to the bedroom. The phone had been provided for just such an emergency and it didn't happen often, but emergency procedures were in place for when it did. She left within minutes, knocked on number one, and when Grace came to the door with her nightdress on and hot water bottle in her hand, Rose handed her the key for her flat. 'Is Dad home tonight?' she asked.

Grace nodded. 'He's just gone up.'

'If he's with Johnnie you can just slip into my bed, and tell the kids I had to go to work when they wake up.'

'Don't you go speeding on those roads, lassie,' Grace called as she rushed towards her car.

She didn't know what to expect when she parked at Woodhorn Road, but when she spotted the Turnbulls' Land Rover her heart sank. Not Peg?

She passed a red-eyed young lad, Farmer Turnbull's middle son, and opened the door to the treatment room. The farmer and Frank stood over a silent dog in a pool of blood. Was she too late?

'We have no time to lose, Rose. Get scrubbed up and prepare the theatre – I'll scrub up once you're ready. I've sedated her so she's not in pain, but we need to move fast to stem this blood properly.'

She heard him telling the farmer to go home and they would call him when they knew more.

When Frank wheeled the dog in she saw it wasn't Peg, but a young bitch from her last litter. Rose could remember their delivery a couple of years ago. She had a badly mangled back leg. 'What happened?' she asked.

'Alf's lad rode into the yard on his motorbike – far too fast, Alf reckons – and he caught her with his back wheel. Sent her flying, so we'll have to check that it's not just her hind leg.'

Frank scrubbed up as Rose prepared the instruments. When he was ready, she placed herself near enough to pass over what he needed and to be an extra pair of hands, but was careful not to overcrowd him. She admired how focussed he was.

The minutes ticked by and it was clear the hind leg would be lost. 'Bessie could be back to herding on three legs within months. She could have a long life ahead of her,' Frank muttered, as if convincing himself.

'You're right. She deserves this chance.'

Frank looked up for a moment and his eyes locked with hers. The slight crinkle at the outer corners told Rose he was smiling.

'This is what we're here for. Turnbull has spent a lot of time training her up to work with Peg, and that young lad will never hear the end of this if we lose her.'

'He should have been more careful – poor Bessie.' Rose hoped the youngster would pull through.

All was going well until near the end, when the young dog's heartbeat became erratic, then stopped. Her own heart pounded in her ears as they worked to resuscitate her. 'Come on, Bessie girl, we can't lose you now!'

'We've got her back.' Frank sounded jubilant. 'She's lost a lot of blood and we'll have to watch her carefully, but we've done it. We've got her back.'

Frank wheeled Bessie back into the treatment room while Rose cleaned up. The theatre had to be ready for whatever came their way. She hoped there wouldn't be another emergency after this one, but they had to be prepared.

She took over observation while Frank got out of his scrubs, then they both sat by the dog.

'I didn't want to amputate, but that fracture and wound would never have healed. Alf Turnbull will be devastated – she was turning into a wonderful sheepdog to take over from Peg in a year or so. I'll drive over to deliver the news, and I'll tell him we'll keep her here for a day or two.'

Rose, close to tears, knew Frank had done his best. 'She almost died back there, Frank.'

'The Turnbulls don't need all the details, just that she's on the mend. That lad will be in enough trouble.'

'I hate motorbikes!' Rose said.

'Everything is safe in the right hands, Rose.'

'You're right – I'm just tired. Shall I make us a brew?'

Frank walked over and enveloped Rose in a hug. 'Thanks for getting here so quickly. When we know she's out of the woods, you go home and have a good sleep. I'll open up and ask Pam to send extra help from Morpeth for the morning surgery.'

'You'll do no such thing. Pam's busy enough, so I'll open up and sort things here before I go home, and you'll go to break the news to the Turnbulls.'

'Just give me a moment, Rose. This one got to me tonight.' He was still holding her tightly, and Rose's arms were wrapped around him.

'We wouldn't be human if a young life didn't affect us, Frank.'

They stood silently, both of them deep in thought, finding strength in holding one another. 'We make a good team, Rose.' Frank broke the silence.

Rose looked up into his eyes. What was there? Love and sadness? Regret? She pulled away. 'Time I put that kettle on.' Her voice came out a bit too brightly.

As Rose drove home, once re-arranging morning surgery was completed, she couldn't help thinking about the hug. They were the oldest of friends, they had a strong bond; but that hug... it had been as though Frank was hanging onto her for dear life. She was worried about him. He had stress at home, she knew, and on days like this he needed support; so if she could give it, she would.

Why couldn't Marjorie be more supportive of Frank? Marriage was a compromise; hadn't she and Danny learned that early on? Marjorie Maxwell had no interest in the practice, and Rose guessed he would tell her nothing of his day and bottle it all up.

CHAPTER 50

*J*oy arrived at number one for a visit, but had a backache. She explained she had come by bus because her car was being serviced. 'Money is tight with Bobby getting casual work, so I'll have to wait to get it out of the garage. You don't know how he can get hold of a good reference, do you? His last employers have his wife as their housekeeper, so their reference is spoiling his chances of decent work.' She wiped a tear from her eye.

She exasperated Rose. You can't just conjure up a reference, and most people don't have a car, she thought. Her own car was for work and she was fortunate to have it, but it wasn't a necessity for Joy, not with a baby on the way and a partner without a steady income.

As it was getting late Rose offered to drive her through to Gosforth, and Joy accepted.

Dad pushed an envelope in Joy's pocket as she left. 'You'll need that car in the coming weeks, hinny,' he said as Joy hugged him.

Rose swallowed hard at the love in his eyes. Joy was playing on his emotions, and Dad didn't have money to burn; they had Terence at university and Johnnie at home.

They travelled the first part of the journey in silence. 'You're annoyed I took that money from Dad, aren't you?' Joy said at last.

'Yes. He has more important things to do with his money than finance cars. He has the boys to consider.' Rose kept her eyes on the road, but could feel Joy's glare.

'He wanted to give it to me. He feels guilty that other people brought me up. He wants to do something for me, and you're just jealous, Rose.'

Rose's cheeks burned. Was she right? Was she jealous, or was she less gullible than Dad?

As they drove along the main A1, Joy said, 'We're not right in Gosforth, we're next door in Seaton Burn, so you can just stop by the Moor House. It'll be on your right.'

'I know it, the white pub on the corner,' Rose replied. The mining village was three miles nearer to them and not exactly Gosforth, but Rose said nothing. Maybe three miles seemed like 'next door' to an Australian who was used to vast expanses of land.

Rose pulled in as Joy pointed along the road. 'I'm over on that street just off Dudley Lane. It's quicker to walk than you to drive me from here.' She got out, and without a thanks she was off. Rose pulled further into Dudley Lane to turn around then make her way back along the A1.

She had already pulled away when she caught sight of Joy's gloves on the passenger seat. The road was quiet, so she could turn around using the bus lay-by ahead and try to catch her. As she was driving back towards the Moor House, she spotted Joy's beige mac. She was crossing the main road, so she wasn't going the way she'd pointed to Rose at all.

Driving slowly, she turned in right and tailed Joy to Chapel Place, a much smaller terraced street hidden behind the Methodist Chapel. She turned off her lights and watched as Joy knocked on the third door along. A shaft of light beamed out as the door opened and a man embraced her.

Joy was secretive; she had led them to believe she was living in Gosforth, and it wasn't as accidental as Rose had first imagined because she obviously didn't want them to know exactly where she lived. Rose made a mental note: third along in Chapel Place. She'd found Rose's hiding place, whether she wanted her to know or not.

Rose didn't mention the incident to Dad when she got back. She knew Dad and Grace were won over by Joy's charm, and she got the impression they thought she was impatient with her sister.

'She's a young pregnant lassie,' Grace had said more than once. Grace had been in the same position and obviously had empathy with her. She seemed to think that Rose didn't.

When Rose was a young pregnant lass of twenty, she had faced up to it and faced the change it would make to her future. It seemed to her that Joy wouldn't face up to anything; she hadn't faced up to breaking up a marriage, she hadn't given much thought to Bobby Donaldson's happiness, she hadn't told her mother or grandparents the truth, and now she wasn't telling them the truth about where she lived.

Joy liked to keep a lot of secrets, and she was nothing like the sister of her imagination. There seemed to be a lot of cards up Joy's sleeve; which one would she pull out next?

CHAPTER 51

They'd had a busy day, and Rose was reaching for her coat when Frank said, 'Do you have to get straight off home or could you pop into The Collier's Arms and have pie and peas? My treat.'

Rose knew Grace would be making tea for them all and she liked to get back to Lily and Robbie straight after work, but Frank looked tired around the eyes and a bit low. 'Okay. Pie and peas and a half of shandy would go down well.'

Marjorie had been in Yorkshire since Monday and was returning tomorrow for the weekend. It seemed like she spent most of the week while Frank was working back there, and the house hadn't been put up for sale.

As they walked along the road, Frank admitted, 'I just couldn't face a tin of soup or beans on toast on my own again tonight.'

'I'm lucky because Grace does most of the cooking in our family.' Rose knew she'd be exactly like Frank if preparing dinner was left to her.

'I really should open a recipe book and learn to cook, because the fridge is full but I don't know what to do with it.'

'Frank, you do enough and work such long hours. If Marjorie is going to stay away all week, find some domestic help for yourself. You can't do it all.'

Frank ordered their food at the bar and brought their drinks to the table. 'You're right about needing domestic help, Rose. I'm always running out of shirts and stuff, and Marjorie won't be going near my laundry over the weekend. I just haven't had time to sort something out. I need a weekday help, that's for sure.'

'Is she going to be in Yorkshire five days a week every week?' Rose asked.

'It looks that way – we haven't discussed it, it just happened. We don't discuss anything, Rose, or it ends in a row or tears, and I can't stand either. What about when Deborah reaches school age? Will she go to school in Yorkshire?' Frank rubbed the back of his neck.

'It's Marjorie you need to talk to about that, not me.' Rose knew he was stressed, but she couldn't help him with this. Frank had seen his father give in to his mother and sister, and he was doing the same. Had he learned this from his father? If he didn't stand up for himself, Marjorie would carry on riding roughshod over him. It was sad to see a marriage break down.

As they ate, they talked about Rose's family and how Terry was doing on his engineering course. 'He loves Manchester and he's working hard. Dad will be delighted to see one Kelly with a degree.'

'You should have gone.' Frank pushed his empty plate away and took a drink of his pint.

'And if I had? We would probably still be here exactly where we are now because your dad promised me a job when I qualified,' Rose said.

'You deserve to have the qualification and letters MRCVS after your name. You know you do.'

'I'll admit it, I'd *love* letters after my name – what an achievement for a girl brought up in the colliery rows! Like many fine dreams, it wasn't to be, and I'm really happy to work with you.' She meant it. She was happy with her lot.

'I don't know what I'd do without you, Rose.'

The wistful tone alerted Rose and she read the look in Frank's eyes, a look from the past. This was dangerous territory. If his sister hadn't scuppered their friendship, they may have ended up courting. This look, even if Frank didn't realise it, warned Rose to tread carefully; they could be friends, but a friendship with a married man needed boundaries. Look at the mess her sister was in! She stood up. 'I have to go now, Frank,' she said.

'So soon?' His disappointment tore at her heart strings.

'Yes, I have the children to collect. You needn't rush. Just sit there and finish your pint and I'll see you in the morning.'

She left the pub. It seemed so natural to be with him, but it wasn't her role to ease Frank's loneliness. Why didn't Marjorie realise how blessed she was to have him, and why couldn't she be there for him?

The children were in bed and Rose sat with the television playing, but she wasn't watching. She was thinking back to her youth, to the time when she got two Valentine gifts: one from Frank and one from Danny. Frank, so clever and handsome, had been the firm favourite then, because she'd thought Danny, with his dark looks and a reputation for getting up to mischief, was a bit wild. Eventually, after she'd lost contact with Frank and thought he'd forgotten her in his new life in Cambridge, she had fallen for Danny.

He hadn't forgotten her, of course, his sister had a lot to answer for, but it was years before they realised what she had done. By then Danny had won Rose's heart, but Frank... she realised now that he still had a place in it. She had part of his heart too; hadn't she seen that tonight? They couldn't rekindle those feelings; that was a road she didn't want to tread. She was free now, but he wasn't. Rose was going to be on her guard.

There was one thing she could do for Frank though. She intended to sort out his domestic muddle.

Rose asked Lottie to call around on Friday evening once they had their children in bed. Lottie often came and brought her home-made cake or biscuits so they could keep one another company. They watched TV and chatted and Rose caught up with the goings on in Linwood. Tonight, she had something to put to Lottie.

'Lottie, are you still after a part-time job?' Lottie had mentioned it a couple of times but Rose wasn't sure whether she was serious or not.

'Yes. I'm bored while Paul is at school, and there are no signs of me having another – so unless I fall pregnant, I'd love to work a few hours a week. They say if you don't think so hard about it you can fall pregnant. I certainly didn't think with Paul, did I? Do you think it's true? When you got a job at Maxwell's, you got pregnant.'

Rose laughed. 'I was already pregnant, but I didn't know. I can't say if a job would help your pregnancy plans, but I think I have one for you.'

'What? I'm all ears.' Lottie put her knitting down and her listening face on.

'This is just a thought. I have to run it past him, but Frank Maxwell is in dire need of somebody with your skills. He needs his house cleaned, his laundry done, and a cooked meal left for him Monday to Friday. You'd need to spend a couple of hours a day there. What do you think?'

Lottie's eyes glinted and she sat up straight. 'That would be perfect! It's on the bus route and it's far enough away so the folk in the rows needn't know my business or where I'm going.'

Rose smiled. Lottie was a gossip in the rows, but she liked keeping her own business to herself. 'There's nothing to be ashamed of being housekeeper to a vet, Lottie.'

'His housekeeper? That sounds better than his charlady, I suppose,' Lottie said. 'I just don't want certain folk around here thinking I can't manage on Dennis's pay. You know how they talk.'

Rose understood that the pride of 'managing' and the opinion of others was of paramount importance in this close-knit community. Opinions didn't bother her because she didn't conform to being a colliery housewife; but Lottie, like her mother and Grace, was highly sensitive to the judgement of others within the five rows. 'Maybe you should think about it and talk it over with Dennis and your mam,' she suggested.

'We could save for a foreign holiday maybe. Dennis would agree to that!' Rose knew Dennis and Lottie loved their yearly trip to Blackpool, so a holiday abroad would excite them both.

'You could save for whatever you like,' Rose laughed as Lottie imagined the luxuries her work could provide.

In the end she said, 'Shall I ask Frank, or do you want some time? I'll have to find him someone soon. If you're up for it, I'll testify to your cleaning and cooking skills.'

'I do want this job, it's exciting,' Lottie said. 'I'll make sure it's okay with Dennis. Just put me forward.'

As she left, Lottie's parting words were, 'I hope I don't get pregnant right away. I want that foreign holiday!'

On Monday morning it was settled. Frank readily agreed to having Lottie Simpson as a part-time housekeeper and she arrived at one the next day to straighten up his life. From then onwards Lottie smoothed away the practical problems, and he looked a lot happier.

If only his personal troubles were so easy to solve, thought Rose. She hated to see her friend looking dejected, as he did every Monday when his wife and daughter left him and drove to Yorkshire.

CHAPTER 52

*J*oy hadn't turned up at First Row for over two weeks. 'Do you think she's gone into labour early?' Grace asked Rose. 'I'm sure she's further along than she says.'

'She could be,' Rose agreed. You were never sure of the truth with Joy. 'Maybe her car isn't fixed? Maybe she felt poorly?'

'I wish we had her address to write to her, or you could have called with a few scones. She likes a fresh girdle scone,' Grace fretted.

Rose didn't mention she knew the address. She'd wait a while to see what Joy was up to.

A few days later, a letter came to say Joy had sold her car, she was due any day, and she would send a telegram when their grandchild was born.

'You can't say fairer than that,' Dad said, and Grace agreed.

In the letter she mentioned having the baby at the Princess Mary maternity hospital. That was where Rose had stayed after having Robbie, but Joy played around with the truth so much who knew where she'd have the baby?

. . .

A telegram came to tell them Joy and Bobby had a daughter. They waited for more news. A letter informing them she wasn't well and wouldn't be up to visitors came a few days later.

'I'm disappointed. I thought she'd want to see us and want us to see the bairn,' Grace admitted to Rose. 'Your dad has gone quiet about it – never a good sign.'

Rose wondered about what to do for the best. She wouldn't be welcome if she knocked on the door of Chapel Place. In the end she took Dad to one side and told him about the night she dropped Joy off.

'You're telling me she lied about her address?'

'Yes, Dad, she obviously didn't want us to know where she lived.'

'I'm going to go. I want to see my granddaughter and to see they're in a fit place to live.'

'Don't make trouble, Dad.'

'Would I ever do that, pet?'

'I recall you gave Danny a fat lip after he married me.'

Dad laughed. 'I was a more foolish father in those days, Rose. I was ten years younger too. I won't go blacking the fella's eyes.'

Rose sat in the car around the corner from Chapel Place on tenterhooks the following Sunday afternoon. She'd dropped Dad off to call on Joy and the minutes dragged as she waited for him to reappear. She had a book but couldn't concentrate. Another glance at her watch told her he'd only been twenty minutes.

The seconds ticked slowly by, until at last she saw him come around the corner. His walk told her he wasn't happy.

He slipped into the passenger seat. 'I wasn't exactly welcome, but I got to know enough,' he said.

'Shall we go for a drink, Dad, and talk?'

'Aye, lassie. Why not?'

The Moor House was nearby so she pulled into Dudley Lane

and found a corner table in the pub, while Dad ordered her a port and lemonade and himself a pint.

'Tell me everything,' she said after taking a sip of the port.

Dad nodded and took a deep drink of his pint. 'The man, Bobby, answered the door. Pleasant he was, but when I introduced myself, he clearly didn't know me from Adam. Joy hadn't told him owt about her background or about meeting us. Can you believe that?'

Rose could imagine that easily. Joy told people selected bits about herself, but you never got the full picture.

Dad carried on in a low voice. 'I passed myself off as a friend of her father's, just like I did with the Goodchilds. I said she'd visited us twice a week until lately. He didn't know about us but knew she had been visiting, Rose, a childhood friend in Linwood.

'I asked how he was managing for work and he said he worked long hours to scrape by. He works at a local bowls club keeping the greens and does extra gardening or farm labouring for as long as he has the daylight to work by, but the nights are cutting in.'

'Where was Joy?'

'She was asleep in the bedroom with the bairn. He made a brew, and I couldn't help myself – I asked him what his intentions were. He looked flustered at that.'

'Dad, you didn't!'

He nodded. 'I had to. "You know our situation then?" he asked. "I do. I know a lot about you from Joy's grandparents, the Goodchilds," I told him.

'He explained he and his wife had a loveless marriage, but she was very religious and would never agree to a divorce. He wants a new life with Joy and his daughter – Margaret they're calling her. To all around them in Chapel Place they are man and wife. He seems a decent enough chap, a steady head on his shoulders except where Joy is concerned. He's in his late thirties so a good few years older, but you know she's flighty and probably needs that.'

Rose squeezed his hand but said nothing. He was deep in thought.

'He took me up the stairs and I tiptoed in and saw them sleeping. The bairn is small and wrinkled like you all were – and Joy, she looked like an angel with her blonde curls all over the pillow. I didn't disturb them.

'He's not daft, that Bobby. As I left, he said, "Mr Kelly, is there more to all this that I should know? Is there more than you just being her father's colleague?"

'"Ask Joy, ask her who the Kellys are to her," I said. I wasn't going to be the one to tell her secrets.'

'Oh, Dad, she's a strange girl.' Rose finished her port.

'That's true, but she's one of us and we have to watch out for her.' Dad stood up and left his drink. 'Come on, hinny, take me home to Grace. Take me home to normal folks.'

*R*ose knew Lottie had some gossip the moment she opened the door to her. She stood there with flushed cheeks and her eyes alive with excitement. 'Are the bairns asleep?' she asked.

'Yes, come in and I'll put the kettle on. I can see something's happened. Are you expecting?'

'No, I haven't come around to tell you that – I've only been working a month, so I don't want to be either. I'm not even dwelling on babies at the moment, and Dennis is delighted.'

'What is it then? There's something.' Rose studied Lottie's face.

'You have to swear to keep a secret, and you have to promise you won't tell me off, and then I'll tell you a terrible discovery about Frank.'

Rose's stomach lurched. 'Frank? Lottie, what's going on?' She switched off the kettle and went to the sideboard. 'Shall we have a sherry? You're worrying me.'

Lottie nodded. 'Good idea. I have kept something totally to myself and it is killing me, so I'm just going to tell you and you can tell me what to do for the best.'

Rose handed Lottie a sherry and took a gulp of her own. She didn't want to know anything terrible about Frank, but she had to know what Lottie had discovered.

'What has Frank done?' she asked.

'It's not him, it's his missus. Oh, Rose, she's a right one, she is.'

The muscles in Rose's jaw relaxed; Frank wasn't the one in trouble. 'Okay, Lottie, tell all.'

'You have to understand that I was cleaning, and you know I'm thorough. Their bedroom hadn't had a proper clean since I don't know when. All top show, she is, with lovely bedding all white and pin-tucked and a candlewick bedspread so thick it'll take a week to dry, and two beautiful side cabinets with drawers and little lamps. It's like a bedroom from a film, but pull those cabinets out and there's dust and fluff that's been there for months.' Lottie paused for breath.

'So you were cleaning the bedroom *and...*?' Rose pressed her to carry on.

'I was pulling her side cabinet out and using her fancy vacuum nozzle – I'd already done his side – when I found something trapped underneath. I thought it had slipped out of the back of the drawers, like it can, you know. Anyway, I pulled the bundle out and it was a few letters.' Lottie stopped and took a sip of her sherry.

Rose's mind was whirling. What was Lottie getting at? 'Lottie? You put them straight back where you found them, didn't you?'

Eyes wide, Lottie nodded vehemently. 'I did... sort of.'

'Sort of?' Rose's suspicions were right. 'Lottie, you didn't?!'

Lottie bit her lip. 'I told you not to tell me off. You know what I'm like. If you employ a housekeeper, they're bound to know lots about you because they see your things.'

Rose tilted her head and studied Lottie's face. 'If you read any of those letters that was snooping, you know it was.'

'Oh alright, Rose, I snooped! I admit it. But *she* deserves being snooped on, I'm telling you, and if you don't want to know I won't say another thing.' Lottie sat back with her arms folded and her lips pursed to give her a self-righteous expression.

'Lottie, you've started so you'd better finish.'

Lottie sat forward again. 'They were love letters. I just glanced through one and the name at the bottom was *Jeremy*. That meant I had to check the postmark and date. It was last year! She received the love letter when she was with Frank. It was to her Yorkshire address, but she's hidden the whole lot here.'

'Things aren't always as they seem. Maybe he was an old flame who got in touch.' Rose didn't want to fly to conclusions.

Lottie nodded in agreement. 'That's what I thought. So I had to read a few more to make sure.' She raised her hand before Rose could say a word. 'I won't tell you the things he said, but he's a mucky pup this Jeremy! Who writes such stuff down on paper? Rose, they're hiding an affair, and I think Frank should know.'

Rose paced up and down. 'Are you absolutely sure? It might all be over by now.'

'It wasn't over last month. I kept that one letter for proof.' Lottie took the letter out of her handbag. 'Do you want to see?'

'No.' Rose shook her head. 'Lottie, you can't just take someone's letter.'

'That Jeremy shouldn't just take someone's wife then. I put the rest back, but I thought if I put this latest one where Frank can find it then he'd make the discovery and sort Jeremy out.'

'Oh, Lottie. You can't do that.' The thought of Frank finding a letter horrified Rose.

'Why not?'

Rose didn't want Frank hurt, and she wished she hadn't heard any of this.

'Maybe Marjorie is going to tell him herself.'

'The letters go back over a year, Rose. Maybe she is just going to string Frank along. He's a lovely man – no edge, appreciates my corned beef pie and my rice pudding more than Dennis, and I really care about him being made a fool of by her. I thought you would too…' Her voice trailed off.

Rose sensed Lottie was disappointed in her reaction. She poured them both a second sherry to gain some thinking time. 'I don't know what to think,' she admitted.

'Rose, I haven't met Marjorie yet because she's always away when I'm there, but *she* leaves me notes to clean this or sort out that. *I'll* leave her a note saying I've cleaned under your cabinet and filed your love letters back under, that's what I should do!' Lottie was outraged.

'That would get you fired.'

Lottie took a deep breath. 'I want to keep my job, Rose – I love it. That's why you have to tell me what we should do for the best.'

All was quiet at the practice for the rest of the week. Lottie kept out of her way and Rose wondered whether she had followed her advice. She'd urged Lottie to return the letter and do absolutely nothing; it wasn't their business. Lottie hadn't been pleased with her suggestion, but what else could she advise?

Rose hadn't slept well with the worry. She knew marriages went through shaky times, and some couples were better apart, but the Maxwells' marriage wasn't their business. She felt annoyed with Lottie for putting her in this position. When she'd kept her mother's secret from her father, it had weighed heavily on her heart and caused a rift between her and her father. This secret was similar in the way it churned up her emotions and created a barrier between her and Frank, because she knew something he didn't.

'What's wrong, Rose? You seem to be avoiding me,' Frank asked on Thursday afternoon.

'Do I?' She felt an uncomfortable warmth creeping up her neck.

'Let's go out together to the Turnbulls'. I'm castrating this afternoon and we can see how Bessie's getting along.'

Rose took a deep breath and nodded. She'd better tuck this all to the back of her mind, or she'd be adding to Frank's worries by behaving strangely.

They pulled into the farmyard and Peg and Bessie came running up to check out the visitors, Bessie nimble on three legs. Rose and Frank looked at one another as she bounded up to them. 'Makes it all worthwhile, doesn't it?' Frank smiled, and her heart felt raw with pain. Frank was kind and good fun, and she loved him. Someone was treating him badly, but she couldn't tell him.

On Friday when Rose arrived at work, Frank was putting a holdall into the boot of his car. 'I'm off to Yorkshire, Rose. Hold the fort.' His face was set, and he wasn't going to say more.

'Has something cropped up? Is Deborah okay?' she asked.

'Deborah? She's fine, but there's something I need to sort out. I'll see you Monday.' Rose watched as he drove off.

CHAPTER 54

*R*ose mulled over what Frank *had* said, or what he had *not* said, right until lunchtime. Lottie was due to start work one until three, so she watched the door for her arrival.

She was busy explaining the best way to squeeze anal glands to a trainee assistant when Lottie slipped in and up the stairs. After finishing the explanation and asking the assistant to try out her technique on the terrier who was with the vet in the treatment room, Rose followed Lottie upstairs.

Lottie was washing up as Rose entered the kitchen. She kept her back to Rose. 'He's found out, has he?'

'I don't know what you're talking about,' Rose said.

'Why have you come up then?' Lottie dried her hands on a towel and stood with her back to the sink.

'To tell you Frank has gone to Yorkshire, so he won't need a meal prepared for tonight.'

'That's because he found the letter. Oh my, I think Hell will break loose in Yorkshire today, Rose.'

'Lottie, what have you done? I told you to leave things alone.'

. . .

Rose went back to her desk with her insides churning. It seemed that earlier in the week Lottie had put back the letter but left part of it sticking out from under the cabinet; she had left it to chance whether Marjorie saw it first or Frank. It had lain with a corner sticking out for three days; Lottie kept checking. She had resigned herself to Marjorie being the one to see it at the weekend, but today it had gone.

When Lottie looked underneath, they had all gone. Frank had found the cache.

Rose didn't know how to still her reeling thoughts. She prayed Frank would deal with Marjorie calmly, yet hoped he would punch Jeremy right into tomorrow. Most of all, she wanted Frank to be alright.

The weekend seemed interminable, and she was unlocking the surgery by eight on Monday. Frank's car wasn't there, and after calling upstairs, she realised he was still in Yorkshire.

The phone rang. 'Maxwell's veterinary practice,' Rose said.

'Rose, it's Frank. I won't be in until one. You'll need to use one of the Morpeth vets to help run morning surgery. Ask the Ashington staff to be ready for a staff meeting at one – include Lottie. Everyone there unless it's an emergency call. I'll see you then.'

'Okay. Is everything—?' He'd put the phone down.

Rose felt nervous all morning. What was going on? She collared Lottie as she arrived at five to one. 'You need to come into the waiting room. Staff meeting.' Lottie's eyes widened and reflected her own. Concern mingled with fear.

At one o'clock Frank strode in.

'You'll be wondering why I've called a meeting. It's to let you all know that Mrs Maxwell and I have separated and will divorce. I may need to take time off to organise my affairs, but I'll try not to let this affect the practice too much. Other than that, I don't want you to ask how I am or how things are – I just want a normal working life. Is that clear to you all? There were murmurs of 'yes' and heads nodding.

'We aren't compatible and we have agreed to part, so no rumours, no gossip, and I know you'll all pull your weight to keep things running because you're a great team.' He managed a smile. 'That's it, back to work.'

Everyone moved off and Rose went towards Frank. 'Back to work, Rose. We have a busy afternoon,' he said and walked into his own office.

Rose was stunned at the clear knock back, but she went back to reception. Lottie came up and whispered, 'Shall I go and make him his favourite pie, or the hotpot I usually do on a Monday?'

Rose sighed. 'Do both. He'll be fending for himself all week.'

CHAPTER 55

Out of the blue, Rose had a phone call from her sister.

'Hello, it's Joy. Can you meet me at the café on Gosforth High Street on Saturday morning? I've sold my car so I can't come to you.'

'Yes, of course,' Rose agreed. She had promised to take Robbie and Lily to the woods, but she could take them later. This was more important.

'Don't tell anyone,' Joy added.

Rose smiled; as usual Joy had to be secretive. What had made her like that? Was it a lifetime of living with a secret keeper? Had it somehow rubbed off on her?

When they met in the café, Joy was on her own.

'Where's the baby? Where's Margaret? I wanted to meet her. She must be five weeks old by now.'

'She's with Bobby – I have enough of her day after day and he dotes on her. He's taken her for a walk before he does a gardening job this afternoon. I'll have her for hours after that.'

'I see.' Rose couldn't help feeling disappointed, but she remembered Lily was hard work when she was weeks old.

'I want to ask you for some help,' Joy said. 'You can say yes or no. I'm not begging but I want some money – I've used up all of my savings, and unless I get help I'm stuck.'

'I'll help if I can,' Rose said. 'What do you mean by stuck?'

'I want to go home to my mother, to Dorothy. She's not well and I want to see her. She'll take the news of the baby better if I see her in person. I still haven't written about her. I want the fare home, Rose. If I get a ticket for the Oriana's next journey, I'll be back with Mum within weeks. It's a lot, I know, but I can't work and Bobby has no savings left, so I can only ask you. You have a good job – have you some money set aside?'

Rose sat back in shock. 'You're leaving Bobby?'

'Yes,' snapped Joy. 'Goodness, don't be so surprised – we're not even married. He can go back to his proper wife who doesn't want to let him go. He's older than me and wants to be settled, but I'm not ready for that. I'm homesick and need Mum.' She started to cry.

Rose studied her. She cried prettily; she cried for her own way. She wanted to say no, but was Dorothy really sick? She'd be desperate to see Joy.

'I'll have to think about it and see how much I can raise. What's the fare?'

Rose left the café with her mind racing. She had to watch her pennies, but she still had the house deposit money set aside in an account for Lily and Robbie going to college, and Jim had repaid her the loan from Danny's winnings so she could use some of that to help Joy. The thing was, did she want a hand in assisting Joy to leave Bobby?

Bobby was married and old enough to look after himself. Maybe a return to Dorothy would be better for Joy and her baby; Dorothy would adore being a grandmother. How could she refuse? Whatever her behaviour was like, Joy was still her younger sister, and she'd have to help her.

When Joy rang the next day, Rose told her, 'I'll do it. I'll get the money and bring it to you next Saturday at the same place.'

'Rose, you're a darling sister. Thank you!'

The words were like honey, but Rose guessed they weren't sincere. Those honeyed words were a lure and could turn to vinegar in a trice.

Joy paid a final visit to Linwood on the Sunday before she left for Australia. She brought Margaret and Grace cooed over her; almost two months, she was a beautiful little doll of a baby and seemed very content.

Joy explained how she was taking two trains to get to Southampton and boarding the Oriana. She had already told Bobby and he'd left the house to set up home and start afresh with his wife. 'The house in Chapel Place is packed up and I'm leaving on Tuesday,' she said. 'I get the train to London and change for Southampton. I'll write when I get there.'

'I hope that baby doesn't suffer with seasickness,' Grace fretted.

Dad gave Joy a long hug. 'Look after yourself, bonnie lassie,' he said, and then strode off to his allotment.

Rose gave them a lift home. Joy didn't hide where she lived this time, but seemed not in the least embarrassed to have changed her dropping off point. 'Bye, Rose,' she called out casually without a backward glance.

Rose felt unsettled. Parting like this didn't sit right with her. Could she have tried more?

The next day Rose checked the London train times and booked Tuesday morning off work.

'Something important?' Frank asked.

'You wouldn't believe it, but I'll tell you one day,' Rose promised.

Frank knew nothing of her secret sister and her shenanigans. He thought his own sister was a trial; one day she would tell him about the trials of Joy.

She had decided to surprise Joy at the platform, give the baby a locket to remember the Kellys by, and to say a proper goodbye. Yesterday she'd bought a gift from Briggs the Jeweller's next to the Ashington surgery. The jeweller had inscribed the tiny silver hinged locket with a message. It opened to reveal: 'To Margaret with love from the Kellys'. She hoped, one day, Joy would explain to her daughter who the Kellys were.

At ten Rose scanned the platform looking for Joy with her pram and case. No sign so far. At last a glimpse of blonde hair tied in a scarlet scarf and a beige mac. That was her!

She rushed towards her and touched her arm. Joy whirled around and her eyes widened. She looked pale. 'What the hell are *you* doing here, Rose?'

'I came to say goodbye, to say it properly, and to give you this for Margaret.' Rose looked for the pram. 'Where is she? Where's Margaret?'

Joy gave her a long stare. 'She's not with me, obviously.'

'What do you mean? Who has her?' Icy fingers seemed to be clutching at Rose's chest.

Joy sighed. 'You have to mess things up, don't you? You have to interfere. Look here, Rose, I'm going back to my mother, but I'm not going back with a child. I want my freedom. Bobby has her. He wanted her and he has her, so he's happy and I'm happy.'

'Bobby? You've left her?' Rose's mouth felt dry, and she could hardly get the words out.

'He's her father and his wife can't have any. He went back to her and took Margaret with him yesterday. His nagging wife is glad to have him back with a daughter she can call her own, and I'm glad to be free of you Kellys. You didn't need to know this. I visited to leave you with nice memories, but you had to come today.'

Rose was left reeling by the news. Was she in the wrong to have come here? 'I wanted to say goodbye.'

'I have to go, here's my train pulling in.' Joy left her and stood by the platform as a train for Liverpool approached.

Rose was speechless. Her unwanted gift in her hand, she watched Joy disappear onto the train without her daughter. She'd been given away as a baby, and now she was doing the same. How could she? Or was it being given away that made it easier for her to do the same? Once again Rose thought about her mother's actions. 'See what you started, Mam?' The ripples of Mam's actions spread wider.

CHAPTER 56

*R*ose made her way to the car park. Had Joy planned this all along? Would she ever write as she had promised, or did she intend to disappear again? She had jumped onto a Liverpool train when she'd said she was heading for Southampton. More lies? Rose wasn't even sure whether Joy was returning to Australia. The Oriana was due to set sail, but would her sister be on it? You couldn't rely on a word she said.

Instead of heading for work, she found herself driving towards Seaton Burn and then turning into the street where Joy had lived. Her house door was open and there was a small van outside it. Rose pulled in and watched.

Eventually a man emerged carrying a large cardboard box. She couldn't see him clearly, but she guessed he might be Bobby. Without thinking, she left the car and walked up to the van.

'Mr Donaldson?' she called.

He turned around. 'Oh, hullo? Do we know each other?'

He was of medium height and a wiry build, with a shock of dark brown hair and clear blue eyes that held her own gaze. A nice-looking chap, a bit older than herself... late thirties? 'We haven't met, but I know about you, Mr Donaldson. I'm John Kelly's daughter, and you met him after Margaret was born.'

'Ah yes. A nice chap, your dad. He was a colleague of Joy's father, wasn't he?

'Amongst other things, yes,' Rose admitted.

'Joy's gone, I'm afraid.' The clench of his jaw and the way his eyes moved from hers to the house showed Rose he felt ill at ease.

'I know that, Mr Donaldson. I went to say goodbye at the station. I've just watched her get on the train.'

'You did? She told me she was leaving tomorrow, but when I got here I saw she'd already flown the coop – no proper goodbye.'

'That's Joy, she tells so many tall tales I don't know how she sleeps!' Rose blurted out.

A smile played around Mr Donaldson's lips. 'You know her well, then. I've just come to discover that side of her. She has me dizzy with her changes of mood and her different tales.'

'Is it true you have Margaret? Is that part true?' Rose dreaded hearing she'd placed Margaret in an orphanage. He gave her a long look followed by a nod of his head, and Rose let out a sigh of relief.

'You seem to know a lot.' The man placed the box in the van and turned back to her. 'Did Joy confide in you?'

'I don't know what you know, Mr Donaldson, but maybe we should have a chat and compare stories.'

He closed the back door of the van. 'Call me Bobby,' he said. 'Let's sit on that bench by the chapel and have a chat.'

Rose followed him to a wooden bench that was damp. 'I've got clean sacking, hold on.' Bobby returned from the van and placed the sacking on the bench. 'Do you mind if I smoke?' he asked, and when she shook her head he brought out an old clay pipe to puff on.

Rose smiled. 'You don't look old enough to puff on a pipe.'

'It's a gardener's thing. We have a rest and puff on a pipe.'

'Do you like working outdoors?' Rose asked.

'I love it. I like wandering the countryside when I'm not gardening.'

He seemed to be a nice-natured man and loved the outdoors, so perhaps he'd be a good father to Margaret.

'What are you staring at?' He interrupted her thoughts.

'Oh, sorry, I was just thinking about Margaret and you bringing her up.'

'And why are you so interested, Miss Kelly?'

'I'm Mrs Dodd, but please call me Rose. I have a surprising tale to tell you, but if you're going to bring Margaret up you need to know it so you can tell her if she ever asks.'

Rose told him about Joy's background and how they were related. She told the story as clearly as she could, and Bobby puffed on his pipe and listened. There was silence when she came to the end.

'Well I never. The tales she told to go and see you, the tales she told about why she had to leave Australia, but I heard none of this. I love that lass with all my heart, but she doesn't know truth from fiction.'

'You mean she tells whopping lies,' Rose said.

He nodded. 'I do mean that. She played with me, I see that now. She got a shock to find she was expecting, because... well, we didn't think that could happen.'

Rose shuffled in her seat. 'So that bit was true, about you and your wife being unable to have children?'

'Yes, that's true, Rose. Lizzie is a cold fish so it was never very likely, but she longed for a child and did try to make it happen in our first years of marriage. Nothing happened, so she gave up and blamed me. I was unhappy, and I'm making no excuses, but my head was turned when I met Joy.'

'What about the age difference though, Bobby? You must've known she was too young for all this.'

'Joy is in her mid-twenties and she'd already been engaged but called it off. I wasn't her first man, Rose. My only regret is that I was still married in name, even if it was a broken, loveless marriage.'

'Bobby! Didn't she tell you she's only nineteen?'

Bobby's face turned ashen. He didn't know. 'Nineteen? But she said she was twenty-five when we celebrated her birthday in March. She seemed older – she was a woman who knew her mind. That's what I thought. More lies.'

Rose's heart went out to the man. He hadn't really known Joy at all. Who did know her?

'Can I give you this?' She handed him the gift box for Margaret. 'I want to give Margaret a keepsake. We didn't give up on Joy and we won't forget Margaret.'

'I'll take it for when she's older. For now she belongs to me and Lizzie, and that will give her a good foundation. She'll learn to tell the truth, and she'll be loved but not spoiled.'

'Is your wife happy to take on another woman's child?'

'She sees her as her own. She prayed and her prayers were answered in a strange way. That's her take on it all. She's very religious, and wouldn't give up on the marriage even though there is no love between us. I will go back to her because I will do anything to keep this bairn. Going back to Lizzie means I can work and provide for my family, and we both get what we want. The bairn will be loved and cared for.'

'What if Joy changes her mind?' Rose asked.

'I can't see her coming back. The getaway was planned before I knew about it. When I think back to the birth, she insisted on being registered at the hospital as Mrs Donaldson, and she insisted on using Lizzie's name on the birth certificate. I worried it wasn't rightly legal, but Joy said she wanted her daughter to be registered to a properly married couple, and as I was the father I should add my wife's name.

'I did it to keep the peace. Margaret is registered to me and to Lizzie. We're her official parents on paper.

'We're moving to Elswick and starting afresh. Lizzie has persuaded our boss to give me a reference, for her sake really. With a proper reference I should find decent work, and nobody will know any different.

'Lizzie is a good housekeeper, she's well-spoken with standards but she's happy to live in an Elswick terraced house to have her own little lassie. Margaret is there now, and I'd better be going. Lizzie doesn't trust me out of her sight, of course, and who can blame her.'

'This is the parting of the ways then,' Rose said.

'It is.' Bobby thrust out his hand. 'I hope the lassie turns out like her aunt. You have a kind heart, Rose.'

'Thank you.' Rose's eyes blurred with tears. 'I've put down one or two addresses and tucked them under the velvet of the locket box. Just in case… you never know.'

'I think bygones like this are best left as bygones, but I'll keep the addresses there, Rose.'

'Thank you.' Rose walked back to her car.

Joy was gone, and Margaret was with her father. Her dream of having a sister had not gone to plan, but at least her niece was in loving hands.

How would she explain this to her dad?

John Kelly did what he always did; he went to his allotment and lit a bonfire. After a few hours, Rose walked along to check he was alright. He was sitting on a cracket, watching the fire and feeding bits of canvas into the flames. Rose pulled up a seat and watched as the flames licked over Joy's face. He was burning the portrait it had taken him months to complete. 'I think we've been here before, Rose. She hurt me as much as her mother, and this is all I can do to cleanse myself of the pain.'

Tears rolled down Rose's cheeks; tears for Dad, for Joy, for baby Margaret, for Mam, for Bobby and his loveless marriage. She didn't cry for herself; she was lucky she'd known a real love and had two precious children. She didn't have to hide behind lies.

rank had changed. It was all business and no lunchtime chats. He used the other assistants in a rota to run his surgeries with him, and kept suggesting she work extra days in the Morpeth surgery to help out Pam and the team. Rose was hurt, of course she was, but she didn't show it. People dealt with their troubles in different ways, and Rose had felt very anti-social after losing Danny. Not with her close friends though.

Rose racked her brains to think of ways in which she could have offended him. He surely couldn't think she had encouraged Lottie's plan?

Lottie, stricken with guilt, had made a confession in church about finding the letters and leaving their discovery to chance. Part of her penance was to own up to her employer.

She had told Frank, expecting to be fired, and over a cup of tea she poured out her relief to Rose. 'He just laughed at how long he'd walked by them, and told me their discovery was the best bit of luck he'd had in a long time.'

'He's not cut up about it then?' Rose was perplexed.

'Not a bit. Him and me, we have the house running like clockwork, and he says the only thing he misses is time with Deborah. She'll visit every other weekend and a week each holiday.'

It couldn't be the discovery of the letters because he was friendly with Lottie, so what was it that had him treating her so distantly?

Rose threw herself into promoting the Pit Pony Champions charity. She kept herself busy to stop brooding about Frank, and to stop thinking about her sister's return to Australia. She had imagined having a close relationship with Joy for so long. As for Frank, she had taken his friendship for granted and had never imagined they'd ever grow apart, but there was no doubting he avoided her like a dose of the strangling angel nowadays.

The Jems performed at Newcastle City Hall and Jemsmania hit the area. A queue formed overnight for the tickets when they went on sale, and extra police had to be called in to manage the crowds of fans without tickets who stood outside on the night.

Rose and Lily and Helen and her three were sent tickets. They got there early to say hello to the lads, and they were taken to seats on the balcony with a great view; but as soon as the group appeared, they couldn't see a thing. Everybody stood and jostled their way to the front, and they couldn't hear a note because of fans screaming out the name of their favourite.

Helen and Rose took their children out before the encore and agreed it had been quite scary. They were glad Daphne had declined a ticket.

'She'd have gone onstage and marched her lad off until there was order,' Helen said.

'The staff had a hard job to do. I think Lily's next concert will be when she's older. There are as many people outside as there were inside.' Rose held Lily's hand tightly until they got to the car park.

The group had put out charity donation tins and they sent the tins along with their fee to Vera for the charity.

When Rose visited Vera to discuss the accounts, Vera thrust the entry at her.

'Look at the noughts on that entry!' Vera exclaimed. 'All of that for an hour or two of music. I phoned the number on the letter that came with the cheque to say there must be a mistake and a manager's assistant talked to me. She said the donation would save them tax or such-like.'

Rose was glad The Jems were doing well. By helping Jim and the ponies, she had done some good. After all, she'd prayed for a challenge in her life, and now she had it.

CHAPTER 58

1966

They hadn't seen Jim for a while, but they received phone calls at strange hours in the day. News of The Jems playing all over the world filled the scrapbook kept by Lily and Daphne. Late one night, towards the end of March, Rose got a call from Jim telling her he was flying by helicopter to Blackthorn Farm for a few days. He was landing after dark and being picked up the same way, so press and followers wouldn't know about the visit. He wanted her to attend a meeting.

Daphne phoned the next day to say, 'Jim's coming with his manager and a solicitor and they're staying in Newcastle but visiting the farm for an important meeting, Rose. He wants to see you and the bairns at the weekend, but I daren't make arrangements until I see the whites of that lad's eyes and know he's here in his own room for a day or two.'

'He called me too. He asked if I could come along on Friday afternoon after work, Daphne. He said it was about something important.'

'His meeting with the bigwigs is at four. Maybe he wants you as a witness to sign something. We're family so we couldn't.'

'A contract or something? You're probably right,' Rose agreed.

'I won't get to you until five thirty though, Daphne, so tell him that.'

Rose kept her curtains open on Thursday night in case she caught sight of a helicopter crossing over the sea and heading for Seabottle, but she saw nothing. She'd thought no more about the meeting since chatting to Daphne, but that night she lay out her best trouser suit and a business-like blouse. She didn't want to let Jim's team down. She might have to be a witness and add her signature on a big record deal.

At five on Friday Rose checked her appearance before locking up and driving to Blackthorn Farm; hair in a French plait, make-up applied carefully, and nails freshly done at lunchtime courtesy of Pam and her pink polish. She added a spritz of perfume to finish off the look. She was quite the respectable witness.

The roads were clear, and she was pulling into the farmyard by twenty past. It had rained and the yard was extra clarty, so she had to place her feet carefully as she walked to the door. She was about to put her hand on the knocker when the door opened and Helen, face flushed and eyes glistening, pulled her inside. 'Thank goodness you're here. What an afternoon! I'll tell Daphne you're here. She's making a brew in the kitchen, but you get straight into the dining room. You'll never believe what's going on.'

Rose felt her heart flutter just looking at Helen. 'Is everything okay, though?'

Helen nodded. 'You look all done up. Did you know this was happening?'

'What do you mean?' asked Rose.

'Oh, never mind, just go in. They're all waiting for you.'

Rose made her way to the dining room. She had only been into the room a couple of times to get extra chairs. She opened the door and was taken aback by the smoke in the room and the number of people around the large table.

Jim, in jeans and a T-shirt, lounged on a chair next to his dad. Ted was in his work shirt and braces, no jacket, and the man drawing on a cigarette at Jim's other side was in a denim jacket. Matt Wilson, still in his work clothes, sat opposite Jim, and she would have felt overdressed except for the portly shiny-faced chap at one end of the table in a dark suit and a bow tie who was smoking a pipe, and the sober-suited man beside him.

The conversation stopped when she entered. 'Ah, Rose, you're here at last. Come and sit here beside me.' Jim beckoned her over. 'Charlie, you go and sit by Matt.'

Charlie stood up and offered her his hand. 'Pleased to meet you. I'm The Jems' manager and I'm glad you could make the meeting, Rose.'

Daphne came in with a tray of tea and a pile of steaming hot girdle scones. 'Rose has just finished a day's work and will need a cup of tea. You can open that window behind you, Jim, so we can all breathe.' She frowned at Charlie's cigarette.

Rose took a cup. 'What's going on?' She turned to ask Jim, but he was at the window. 'I'll put you in the picture, hinny,' Ted said.

'Jim is taking over Blackthorn Farm after all, thank the lord. He's after me retiring and living in a purpose-built house down the far end near the Ayrshires. We'd be overlooking the sea, and now there's the new housing down that way we'll have no bother with a road and electricity and suchlike.

'*That's* not all. He's going to build himself a house down by ours, and he's going to build a recording studio and practice rooms for The Jems and their music.

'And *that's* not half of it, Rose. He wants Matt to move here into the farmhouse and go into partnership with him. Matt here...' He pointed to Matt as if Rose didn't know who he was. 'Matt here will make the farm arable and we'll just keep enough Ayrshires for milk for ourselves and to show, so we'll sell off most of the dairy equipment and the Holstein cattle. Are you following so far?'

Rose nodded. 'I am. It all sounds well thought out, but why am I here? Am I to witness the contracts?'

Jim laughed. 'Don't be daft. You're here for the next part of the discussion, isn't she, Dad?'

Ted nodded and Rose wondered what could be coming next.

Jim came back to his seat beside her. 'Tell Rose what we would like to do with one of the spare fields and the small barn, Dad.'

Rose waited patiently as Ted ruffled some papers and pushed them over to her. 'The field, the small barn, and the area outlined in blue, Jim wants to turn it over to a charity to convert it into a pony rescue centre for retired gallowas and the stock from any pit closures that come up.'

Rose's head whirled. The blood pounded in her ears. The field and the barn were perfect. It would be an expense to run a large centre, but the NCB would help and the charity was doing well.

'What do you think, Rose? Jim put his arm around her. 'Will it do? Will it work?'

'Will it do? Oh, Jim, I never imagined!' She burst into tears.

'I never imagined I'd have a number one or tour the States and have money to support a charity, but you gave me a leg up when I needed it. You believed in me when it counted, and I believe in the work you're going to do for these ponies.'

'Well, that was quite a speech, Jim. Can we get back to who runs what now?' Denim Jacket said.

Jim punched his arm. 'We can, Charlie, we can.'

The meeting restarted and Rose was introduced properly to Charlie Chapman and the solicitors. She listened as plans for transferring deeds and applying for planning permission carried on.

When it was the turn for the pony rescue to be discussed, Rose realised the magnitude of Jim's plan. The charity and Jim would share costs and Jim would employ a manager who would live at Corner Cottage once Helen and Matt had moved into the farmhouse.

'It's a specialist job,' Rose commented. 'You'll need someone with a sound knowledge of ponies and their care, the willingness to allow visitors and use volunteer help, and the perseverance to raise money to keep going.'

'I'm looking at the only person I'd trust with the role,' Jim said. His eyes held hers. 'This is your dream, Rose, and you have to grab it with both hands.'

CHAPTER 59

*R*ose left the farm at ten o'clock. Driving home, she thought about Jim's plan. His parents would live by the farm and Ted could look out on his Ayrshires; Jim would have a house next to them, so Daphne would see him when he was recording. The studio was handy for all the lads; Eric, Mick and Stuart were all in favour of spending a few weeks near to their own families when they were recording new material. Matt couldn't ever have bought Ted out, but he could earn a share in the farm, and Helen had the farmhouse she longed for.

Her heart flipped when she thought of moving into the Corner Cottage. That homely yet spacious cottage with three bedrooms and two rooms, as well as a kitchen downstairs. She'd enrol Robbie into Seabottle School and Lily would have an easier travel to Morpeth Grammar. Her old school had been relocated to a modern building up Cottingwood Lane, and if Lily passed her eleven-plus she would go there in September.

Rose would work with the retired ponies, rehoming some locally when she could and keeping the rest here. They'd have visitor's days and fundraising days, and her head filled with plans for the future.

There was one hurdle: she'd have to hand in her notice at Maxwell's. She could sacrifice seeing their clients and the animals, but how would she get on without seeing Frank every day? There had been a cool distance ever since he started divorce proceedings; pleasant, but not the old close friendship she'd come to treasure.

She wondered if he'd lost his trust in women; he was quite cool with all of the female staff. Rose didn't like to examine her feelings about Frank too closely, but without work they wouldn't see each other at all, and that saddened her. She'd keep a tight lid on her emotions, but she knew she'd miss Frank Maxwell more than anyone would ever know.

Rose had already booked herself in to check on the Blackthorn ponies' teeth on the morning of Jim's departure. She did this every few months to keep their mouths healthy and make sure the old horses could feed properly.

An older pony's teeth kept on growing but the teeth could be irregular, so the pony would have the teeth 'floated'. This meant the sharp bits were filed smooth. She didn't sedate without the vet, so anything more serious than a file she'd set aside for Bruce at the Morpeth practice and then she'd come back to help him.

Jim came to meet her in the yard. 'Hi, Rose. I told Dad I'd give you a hand. I've enjoyed being back and doing the roof, so I thought I'd go and say hello to old Spike and Jonty and the lads.'

Rose laughed. They were the two grumpiest and most likely to give him a kick. 'If you're sure.'

'I'm sure. While we're on, I want to check you're okay with everything we discussed about the farm's future.'

They set off for the ponies' field. 'I am so stunned, it's like a dream. There's a lot of paperwork, but the fact you're going to give us the space and some funding is a huge commitment, Jim.'

'When it's up and running, I see it as a way for kids around here who don't have their own pets to be around animals and learn to care for them – learn about the amount of work it takes,' he said.

'Showing volunteers the ropes takes time, but it builds up a workforce that takes pleasure in doing the job. The retired horse-keepers will do their bit, and show the young people the right way to go about it.'

'When we've got that going, we might get a couple of riding ponies. I know the pit ponies can't be ridden, so a couple who would enjoy giving the kids a ride would be a great addition. I want to give back to the community, Rose.'

'Whoa, Jim, let's not trot before we canter.' Rose could see his vision, but it would all take time.

He laughed. 'The recording studio, I have plans for that too. I'm going to meet my old music teacher to see if he's willing to get the plans off the ground. When we're not recording, we'll open the building to young musicians – give them a facility to create music.'

Rose was concerned. 'Jim, you have wonderful ideas, but it all costs money – houses, studios, stables, staffing them. None of it comes cheap.'

It was Jim's turn to laugh. 'Rose, I'm embarrassed by the fortune our LP has made, and what we're going to get from the USA and world tour. I have the money, even if I don't have another hit. All the Jems are in on the studio idea. We've seen too many friends get high on fame and high on drugs and have nothing to show but a catalogue of songs – we are going to give kids like we were something to do. We'll all come back here to live, one day. There's nowhere like Northumberland.'

It began to rain, and Jonty came up and nudged at his pocket.

'Nowhere like Northumberland? You'll not mind getting wet and helping me to gag Jonty and check his teeth then. We have a full morning ahead.'

CHAPTER 60

*R*ose handed in her notice to leave Maxwell's at the end
of April. It was going to take a lot of work to get
Blackthorn Farm Centre up and running, and one or two local
mines had been ear-marked for closure later in the year. There
was no time to lose.

Frank said nothing all day, but called her into his office when
she was about to leave that night. 'Setting up the centre is a
wonderful opportunity, Rose. I was expecting this, because Dad
and Vera said the charity needed you full-time. I'm glad your
rescue idea is going from strength to strength.' Frank's eyes met
hers briefly. Did she see a flicker of regret, or was it just her vivid
imagination?

'It's Jim Fairbairn of The Jems we need to thank for giving the
charity a boost. He's been a tower of support, and to give us land
and facilities on Blackthorn Farm for as long as the charity runs,
it is just so generous of him.'

Frank looked away. 'I wonder why he's being so generous in
giving away land that belonged to his family for years?'

Rose felt defensive on Jim's behalf. 'He's taken over the land
from his father, but he's putting lots of money into the farm. He

wants to do something for the community and he's building his parents a new home, so his father is delighted. Why should you mind, Frank?'

'He seems to be buying your gratitude, that's all.'

'You couldn't be more wrong!' Rose stood toe to toe with Frank 'Jim doesn't need my gratitude. We are close and he wants what's best for me, as well as what's good for the ponies. What is wrong with that? I think, that for some reason, you're jealous of Jim Fairbairn.'

Frank took her by the shoulders. 'Maybe I am,' he admitted, and his lips were on hers. He was kissing her, then with his arms wrapped around her, he whispered into her hair, 'I spoke out of turn. I like what Jim is doing for the area, but I am jealous of him spending time with you when I can't be with you.'

Rose pulled back, her cheeks crimson, her heart pounding, and her lips wanting to find his for more. 'You haven't wanted to spend time with me for months, Frank Maxwell. Don't think I haven't noticed how cool you've been. This is just because *you* think I care for someone else.'

'Do you?' Frank stepped forward and gently took her face in his hands. 'Is there something special between you and Jim?'

Should she give in and kiss him? She wanted to. No. She pulled away. 'Do I care for someone else? That's my business and it's certainly none of yours.'

She strode out of the office with jelly legs and a galloping heart, but she had her pride. Frank had only shown an interest in her when she sang Jim's praises.

CHAPTER 61

oving into the cottage on Blackthorn Farm with Lily and Robbie was an upheaval, with all hands on deck; all hands except Frank's. Lottie and Paul helped, and Lottie explained that her boss was away for the whole weekend. Rose tried to put his absence out of her thoughts, but she was disappointed he hadn't asked to help.

Though they all missed being across the way from number one, Lily and Robbie loved the space, and Rose never tired of the view of wide skies and countryside.

Helen left the cottage in an immaculate condition, so there was none of the scrubbing that was needed when she took on the flat above Mrs Lawson's salon. Nevertheless, Grace came laden with cleaning products and a pinny. Her cleaning took no time at all, because even Grace had to admit the place was ship-shape.

It was to be a summer of new beginnings. Rose would run the Blackthorn branch of PPC, Robbie was due to start school at Seabottle in September, and Lily, who had passed her eleven-plus, would be starting at Rose's old school in Morpeth.

Over the summer Dad had taken over part of the shed in the garden and came often to sketch or paint. 'When I retire at sixty-five, I'll be here so often you'll be fed up with me,' he said. He sketched and painted watercolours of the scenery and the pit ponies; they were to be sold in the little charity shop that they were erecting in a corner of the refurbished milking shed. 'If my paintings sell and bring happier days for those gallowas, then I've done my bit.'

Only part of the milking shed was used for the Ayrshire's that Ted was keeping on, so this was partitioned off and the rest of the shed was given over to the centre.

Building began and the plans became a reality. Littlehorn colliery was due for closure in October, and there were eight more gallowas joining them, so they had to be ready for then.

Part of the milking shed was converted to house a large kitchen, where Helen and Daphne put on bread-making demonstrations, churned butter and held jam and chutney-making classes. They sold chutneys and jams and all the excess produce at the shop alongside John Kelly's paintings and made a steady profit for the charity.

Just as Rose would manage the pit pony rescue strand, Jim's semi-retired music teacher was to manage a music area. It was to be set up so young musicians had space to practice playing their instruments and to make use of the recording studio.

Jim was toying with the idea of an arts block the next year for local potters and artists like John Kelly. 'The potential is there, Rose. I want Blackthorn Centre to be synonymous with opportunity.'

He had big ideas and Rose loved to see how Jim's confidence had grown. Matt, who now managed the farm, agreed with Rose. 'The crops are doing well and we're trying out new farming ideas. He's a good partner is Jim, because if you're the expert, he leaves you to it.'

Ted Fairbairn spent many hours with his Ayrshires who provided top quality milk for the farm and those they knew. 'I'd never want my milk from anywhere else now,' Grace said after baking a rice pudding with the rich milk they produced. At long last, one of his Ayrshires won first prize at the county show that spring, and Ted proudly hung the rosette in their new kitchen overlooking the field.

He was proud of his son too. 'He flies in by helicopter like others drive a car,' he marvelled to Rose.

He told Jim on one of his flying visits, 'Son, it was a dream come true, winning that red rosette. I'll die a happy man, now.'

'Get away with you, Dad. You've years of winning yet. You can't rest on your laurels. I didn't stick at just one chart-topping record, did I?'

'Maybe you're right, lad.'

It was a push to get ready in time for October, but they made it. Their six retired ponies would be joined by eight more sprightly companions from Littlehorn colliery, and there was an atmosphere of anticipation on the farm in the week leading up to their arrival. Extra supplies were ready, rotas were drawn up, and a group of men from Littlehorn would be on hand to see that their equine marras were settled into their new home.

The animals were due to arrive at eleven, and after Lily and Robbie left for school, Rose set off to pin bunting to the gate of the farm. It had rained all week, so this was her first chance to make their arrival welcoming. There would be balloons flying from the gate too. Her heart sang at the way things had worked out.

'Take it down, Rose.' Ted came panting up the track and

rested on the gate, trying to get his breath back. His face was grey and he had tears streaming down the deep wrinkles of his cheeks.

Her gut twisted. Ted didn't cry. 'Robbie? Lily? What is it? Tell me?'

'The pit!' he gasped. 'Bairns... come back to the farmhouse.'

The pit? Bairns? What did he mean? Rose dropped her hammer and ran. She raced to the farm and burst in on Helen and Daphne, who were in tears. 'Tell me! Ted can't speak.'

'Aberfan... a tragedy, all the bairns,' cried Daphne. 'It's on the radio.'

The nightmare of Aberfan, where a generation was wiped out by a slag heap sliding down the mountain onto the village school, unfurled as the day went on.

The pit ponies of Littlehorn were settled into their new home by grim-faced miners and Rose's heart felt leaden with the size of the tragedy. She didn't need pictures to see how the event would have occurred; she had lived beside Linwood's pit heap most of her life. How could such a vast waste tip move like that?

Every mother in Seabottle was at the school gates to hug her bairns when the school closed that day. The children ran out excited about it being blackberry week, the half term when they picked wild blackberries from the hedgerows, and their parents hugged them. Parents the nation over would be relieved it wasn't their child or their school that had suffered today, and distraught that it had to happen anywhere.

In the village of Aberfan, a hundred and sixteen bairns didn't come running home from school.

Rose's dad brought Johnnie to see the new ponies on Saturday. 'We're used to pit disasters, Rose, but this one... it's the unthinkable. Not miners, but their bairns. They were sent to school and should have been safe. How did it happen?'

'There'll be an enquiry, Dad.'

'I'm glad neither of my older lads have to go down the mine, and this one won't either,' Dad vowed to Rose, as they watched Johnnie feeding carrots to the ponies.

Sorrow gave way to anger, and a grieving industry discovered that the tragedy had been waiting to happen. A spring ran underneath the heap and The National Coal Board tipped waste onto a powerful source of water. When heavy rain made matters worse, the slurry slid down onto the village of Aberfan and buried the school.

CHAPTER 62

1967

*R*ose couldn't have wished for a better job; her two children were thriving on the farm and doing well at school, and she had good friends in Daphne and Helen. It had taken almost a year to get everything running smoothly and she was busier than ever.

She had called on Meg Mason to help with the cottage and she arrived by bus every day to restore order to their lives and have a hot meal ready when they got home. Rose's job wasn't nine 'til five, and she loved it. Robbie mucked in with the farm tasks after school, while Lily took more interest in Meg's cooking while she tackled her homework at the large kitchen table.

'Thank goodness somebody in the family will be able to cook a decent rice pudding when I retire,' Meg said.

It was when Lily and Robbie were in bed, and she was bone weary but still not sleepy, that Rose felt a bit empty. The pain of losing Danny had changed. She was sorry he was missing seeing their wonderful children growing up, but when she looked at their wedding photo now, it seemed so long ago and he was so very young. He would never age. 'What would you have made of this life, Danny?'

On one restless night she walked out into the dark garden, looked up at the full moon and wondered, *Is this it? Is this my life?* 'You should be content. What else can you possibly want?' she asked herself.

Rose still helped out at Linwood on Sunday morning. Unless there had been a problem in the week, it only took an hour or so to check the ponies and see that the rota was running smoothly. Frank came on the first Sunday of the month, and although things were cool, she lived for those mornings when she could work alongside him and know he was alright.

On the first Sunday in April, Bruce arrived instead of Frank.

'Hello there, Rose, I'm here to help out. You'll have to show me the ropes.'

Her insides lurched with disappointment. 'What's wrong with Frank?' She tried to sound cheerful.

'He has his hands full with Deborah every other weekend and I offered to take the ponies on. What's better than looking over a few ageing feet on a grizzly grey day?' he joked.

Rose swallowed her disappointment and it sat heavily in her belly like a cold tapioca pudding. She'd lost her only contact with Frank. He wasn't just keeping a distance; he'd pulled up the drawbridge and shut her out of his life.

She was quiet all day.

'Is there something wrong, lassie?' her dad asked.

'I'm just a bit tired this week, Dad.'

'You work too many hours because you live on the job,' Grace told her.

'I'm glad to fill in the hours,' Rose said wearily. She reached for her coat on the back of the door. 'I'm going for a walk before I drive us all home.'

'It's getting dark, you watch your step,' Grace called.

The steps she took were familiar. She hadn't known where

she was going when she set off, but Rose found herself at the door of Linwood Chapel. It was still open, even though the evening service had ended half an hour earlier; the doors were seldom locked.

While she tended the horses, Robbie went to Sunday School, but she didn't go to the Sunday service anymore. The passing years had lessened the raw pain of being without Danny, but when she thought of those bairns of Aberfan, she still felt that singing God's praises would be too much to ask of her.

She sat on the back pew and soaked in the silence as she had many times in the past. *All you have to do is ask.* The clear message she was receiving was just ask. It was hard for Rose to ask for anything for herself. She sat a while longer. What was the use of prayer? She *was* a believer. She found comfort just sitting here, but she didn't think God always got things right.

Rose stood to go. The moonlight shone through the stained glass above the chapel door. The cool colours glowed over the back of the church and she looked up at the familiar figure of Jesus as a shepherd, tending his flock as he had always done since she was a little girl. Tonight he seemed to be looking at her as though she was one of his lost sheep who had come home for help.

She stood in the dim glow. 'Okay, I have a full life, but I'm still lost. I'd like to have someone to share my life with. I'd like a happily ever after. It can't be the happily ever after that was snatched from me, but I don't want to journey alone forever. Is that asking for too much?'

CHAPTER 63

*B*udding daffodils signalled that warmer days were finally approaching. This spring had arrived late in Northumberland. Alf Turnbull called to the farm to see Ted and bumped into Rose. 'Bessie is working well on three legs, thanks to you and Frank, and she's taken over from Peg as our main sheepdog. She's just had a litter and I'm keeping one, but it's hard to choose. She's had beauties. You should bring your little'un to see her pups.'

Rose took Robbie over to the Turnbulls' after school one night while Lily was doing her homework. Bessie proudly showed off the wriggling pups who were almost ready to leave her.

'Could we have one like this one day when you're not so busy, Mam?' Robbie asked. He was holding a wriggling red and white pup with bright eyes that was eager to climb round to his shoulder.

The litter pulled at Rose's heart strings, but Robbie's request pulled at it more. When she wasn't too busy? She was always on the go, but that didn't mean her boy shouldn't have a dog. She looked at Alf, who gave her a wink.

'Which would you choose, Robbie?' she said.

'This one, little Red, because he's chosen me.' The pup licked Robbie's ears.

'Okay, he's yours.'

'Really? Honest? Thanks, Mam! Thanks, Farmer Turnbull!'

'You'd better thank Bess there,' the old man smiled.

'Thank you, Bess.' He crouched down and patted Bess. 'Oh, Mam, look. Bess just has three legs.' His surprised expression made Farmer Turnbull laugh.

'A four-legged pup from a three-legged bitch. That's an unusual pet you're getting, young Robbie. Let me tell you that Bess can do more on three legs than most dogs can on four. Never lets her disability hold her back.'

Red came to live with them two weeks later and brought disruption to the family routine, along with lots of love and laughter. Meg Mason complained about having him under her feet but fed him titbits, and Robbie took his training, with Ted Fairbairn's help, very seriously.

The centre planned to organise their first big event at Blackthorn. They would celebrate the second successful year of the Pit Pony Champions charity and the first Summer Fayre of Blackthorn Centre early in July.

Posters advertising the date were ordered to go up all around the neighbouring towns. The entrance fee was going to the charity and a percentage would be given to their Linwood offshoot to pay rent to the Bateys for their field.

The fayre was to be held on the Saturday before the schools broke up because they were keeping it to locals for this trial run. 'In future years it'll be bigger and better!' promised Jim. He was arriving under cover of darkness the day before the fayre, and The Jems were ending the day with a short concert outside the milking shed.

Frank had never visited the farm, and Rose wondered whether to invite him or not. It wasn't as if they weren't speaking; they just didn't speak any more, and she missed him.

On the day of the fayre Rose would be supervising the ponies and would invite lots of local children to assist in grooming them the week before because there was going to be a best groomed pony competition. The ponies' manes and tails were always cropped short when they were working underground and some of them turned into beauties when they grew back, but it required work to keep them that way.

She would be busy on the day, but she wanted to cook something to sell at the charity shop. She thought about digging out her mother's recipe book and making a batch of cinder toffee. Yes, the kids would like that, and she could make it in advance so it wouldn't go wrong and spoil her day.

Rose decided to give her toffee a trial run. As she got to a crucial point in the proceedings, the post landed on the mat. She couldn't leave it there or Red would destroy it. She wrestled a slim white letter from his sharp teeth and put the chewed post on the windowsill. The post could wait while she finished the cinder toffee.

The tricky part was adding bicarb to the bubbling mixture of syrup and sugar. My, how it erupted into a molten golden volcano, filling the kitchen with its sweet toffee aroma. She poured it onto the greased tray and watched it spread in ripples to cover the surface. It looked perfect.

When it was cool, she would try it out on Dad seeing as he was here today to do some sketching. As she looked out onto the back garden, he was chasing after Red who was running round with what looked like one of Dad's painting rags in his mouth.

She glanced at Danny's picture smiling down from a shelf of the dresser and remembered how he had brought her first dog, an abandoned injured pup, to her to fix. She'd taken it to Maxwell's vets, and wasn't it strange how one event led to another? 'It's a different life without you, Danny. We're all sorry for the times you've missed out on.'

After cleaning the kitchen of the toffee making mess, she tested a piece of cinder toffee; perfect, just like Mam's. She was about to call her dad over to try some when she spotted the envelope. What was it that Red had almost ruined?

It wasn't a bill. It was a good quality envelope and addressed to her. She opened it and almost choked on her toffee. She had to sit down and read the words again.

She was being asked if she would accept a place on the Queen's birthday honours list in June. Who had put her name forward for such a thing? If she accepted, she had to reply and answer a few questions, then keep it secret until the list was revealed on the Queen's birthday.

Apparently members of the community had asked the Queen to recognise her contribution to veterinary nursing and her charity work, both nationally and in their local community. For this work, she was to be awarded an OBE.

Would she accept? Of course! Dad would be so proud, and she would be truly honoured to be Rose Dodd OBE. Letters after her name at last, thanks to the people she knew and worked with. She was filled with a sense of pride and thankfulness for her unnamed supporters.

She had to keep it secret. How could she keep this just to herself? But there was one person she would never keep a secret from again. 'Dad!' she called. 'Come inside and read this.'

CHAPTER 64

*L*ater in the week Rose decided to drive into Morpeth, then Ashington to drop off posters and some leaflets at both of Maxwell's practices. She might see Frank and have a word about the event.

The Morpeth branch was quiet. 'Can you distribute these leaflets to clients and put the poster on the waiting room wall?' she asked Pam.

Pam took the bundle, saying, 'I certainly can. Just leave the Ashington bundle and I'll take it tomorrow. I'm looking forward to visiting Blackthorn after all your hard work.'

'There'll be cows and horses and it's uneven underfoot – so no heels, mind you, Pam,' warned Rose. Pam was always well-dressed and had quite a collection of shoes.

'I'm coming along for the jams and chutneys, and I see you have a bread-making demonstration so I'll stay for that. Keep me way from the fields and flies,' she said, pinning the big poster to the noticeboard. 'I'm due a break now if you fancy coming upstairs for a cuppa.'

Rose glanced at her watch. 'Okay, I have time for that.'

She followed Pam up the familiar staircase into the staff kitchen she knew so well.

It held memories of late nights when she nursed sick animals, of Danny making her hot chocolate and of having long discussions and putting the world to rights with Frank.

Seeing Rose glancing around, Pam said, 'It's in need of redecorating but it's homely, isn't it?'

'Yes, it is. I lived over the practice for a while, and it holds lots of memories for me.'

While Pam made a pot of tea, they caught up with the comings and goings of the staff. She handed a mug to Rose and asked, 'Are you and Frank back on the same page yet?'

'What do you mean? We're not on any page – I've hardly seen him since I left. We used to catch up with one another when he checked the Linwood ponies on a Sunday morning, but he handed that over to Bruce a few weeks ago.'

'You don't know his divorce has come through at last then? It was just last week, but I thought he might get in touch or make some sort of move to get things back on track.'

'No, Pam, I didn't know about the divorce. It's a good thing for them all, I suppose. What do you mean by getting things back on track? There's nothing to get on track.' Rose was puzzled as to why Pam should think that.

'He hasn't called? He's hopeless.' Pam rolled her eyes. 'We all knew he had to keep well out of your way while Marjorie was gunning for him, but the staff here have had bets on about how long it would take him to go along to Blackthorn Farm afterwards. The man is head over heels in love with you. You must know that.'

'Head over heels? I don't think so.'

'We all know so! He never stops mentioning you, casually asks who has seen you, uses you as an example of everything good, tells the assistants to read your handbook thoroughly, got everybody together to apply— Oh, I could go on.'

'It's a shame I never saw that side of him.' Rose gave Pam a wry smile. 'What did you mean about getting people together?'

Pam put her mug down. She looked serious. 'Oh, that? It's something and nothing – forget I said it. I'm not joking, Rose, he loves you. It's been the divorce that's kept him away. When they started divorce proceedings, Marjorie hired a detective. She didn't want the divorce to be because of her – oh no, she wanted Frank to be blamed, and she had this detective chap who was out to dig up any dirt.

'A real snooping Sid, he was. He asked all sorts of questions to the staff. We closed ranks, but we knew he was always prying into things – he even rummaged in our bins. He was after any evidence to show Frank was friendly with you or one of the assistants – or even me, and I'm twice his age.' Pam laughed and Rose could only shake her head in amazement. She had known nothing about this.

'He wanted anything he could find to pin the blame on Frank, so Frank had to be distant with any female he worked with, and especially you because Marjorie had her sights on you. The only female who the detective didn't bother chasing was Lottie. She's a bonny lass, but maybe Marjorie thought that Lottie, having access to her things in the house all that time, might have information that would backfire on her.'

'I wouldn't know about that,' Rose said. Pam was astute. She'd even guessed correctly about Lottie. Was she right about Frank? 'I wasn't aware of any detective, Pam. Why didn't Frank say?'

'He wanted to keep staff out of it all, but I cottoned onto the detective straight away. It's a sordid business when the likes of him become involved. Would you have stayed away if he'd asked you to? Anyway, now this horrible time is over, he's free.'

'He hasn't been in touch, but I have been cool whenever I've seen him. I was hurt. I didn't realise what was going on.'

'I'm glad I've had a chance to put you straight then, because you two are perfect for one another, you must know that.'

Rose blushed. Pam laughed and said, 'I'll leave it at that,' and they drank their tea.

Rose left with a light step. It all made sense; Frank was protecting her from the mess of the divorce. Why hadn't she seen that? Pam was right, and Frank had known her too well; if he'd asked her to stay away, she would have ignored him.

What was it Pam had said? She'd mentioned him getting people together, an application, and then she'd dismissed it. Rose had a feeling this was to do with her award. Maybe her past colleagues and friends wouldn't be so surprised when the honours list came out in June. Was it Frank who had tried to make sure her work was recognised and she had letters after her name at last?

Rose thought about Frank all night. Pam's offer of delivering the Ashington bundle meant she had no excuse to call around. Should she ring him up? They hadn't spoken in months. She couldn't just ring out of the blue and ask him to come to the fayre in July, could she?

She was inspired with an idea. Why didn't she offer him a judging role on the day? It was an excuse to get in touch, anyway. She picked up the phone, her heart thumping. She put the receiver down; she couldn't.

She paced the floor and picked the receiver up again. She dialled before she could change her mind.

'Hello, Frank?'

'Rose, what's wrong?'

'Nothing's wrong, Frank. I'm just ringing to ask if you'd like to come to our fayre at Blackthorn Farm in July, and judge our best-groomed pit pony contest.'

'I'd love to.' No thinking, he'd answered in an instant.

'That's good.'

'Rose?'

'Yes?'

'Could I come over and look around the centre sooner? I'd like to visit on a normal working day.'

'Yes, of course you can. I mean... when? When would you like to come?'

'Tomorrow? I'm free first thing.'

Rose couldn't stop a grin from stretching across her face. He wanted to come tomorrow! 'Tomorrow morning is fine, Frank.'

'I've missed you, Rose.' She detected a catch in his voice.

'I've missed you too, Frank. See you tomorrow.' She rested the phone on its cradle. It wasn't *what* they'd said, it was the tone he'd used.

We're on the same page thanks to you, Pam, she thought.

Rose opened the back door and walked into the cool garden; it was dusk and the fragrance of night-blooming jasmine filled the air. Sadness left her, and the light happy feeling filling its place made her want to dance. Frank Maxwell missed her, and he was coming to see her in the morning. How would she sleep?

She was up at break of day and cooked pancakes for Robbie and Lily. 'These are good, Mam.' Lily's eyes widened in surprise as she bit into the wafer-thin pancakes drenched in sugar and lemon juice. Rose held out a battered old cookbook. 'I used Grandma Ginnie's recipe. I wrote all her recipes down when I was a girl, and I don't know why I don't use the book more often.'

Lily looked through the pages. 'I recognise Grandad's sketches in the margins and your handwriting,' she said.

'I'll try more of the recipes, then you'll recognise Grandma Ginnie's cooking too,' Rose promised.

After breakfast Lily took Robbie for a walk to see Jennifer, and Rose tidied up as she waited for Frank. She'd made a batch of singing hinnies from the recipe book too, and the plate was sitting on the table ready for them to be dropped onto a sizzling hot griddle.

She heated the griddle and smeared it with lard, then peeped out of the front door for it must've been the tenth time. She returned to a smoking hot griddle and dropped the scones onto it before going back to the front door. She had just poked her head around when his car pulled up. Out he jumped with a huge bouquet and an even huger smile.

'Frank!' She opened her arms, and he was there embracing her and kissing her cheek. She moved back and looked into his eyes, and somehow her mouth met his. They kissed on the path and Rose didn't want the feeling to end. She belonged in his arms.

'Come into the kitchen, I'm making singin' hinnies,' Rose said as she took the beautiful hand-tied bunch of flowers from him.

'Oh no,' Frank groaned. 'I wasn't expecting your cooking today, Rose.'

She gave him a look. 'I'll have you know it's Mam's recipe, and foolproof.'

He followed her into a kitchen already filling with smoke and some shrunken, blackened offerings. She pulled the griddle off the stove, saying, 'Open the back door quickly. This isn't my fault, it's you and your kisses.'

He opened the door and she took the griddle outside and it smouldered on the ground. She turned to look at him, feeling hot and flustered and annoyed that another recipe hadn't gone to plan. 'They were supposed to sing, not scream.'

He took her in his arms. 'Come here, Rose. Did I tell you you're beautiful and you're a marvel with animals?' He kissed her. 'Did I tell you you're perfect as you are?' He kissed her again. 'I love you, Rose.'

CHAPTER 65

*W*hen the birthday honours list was published on the second Saturday in June, she took a copy of the paper to Linwood.

Dad read aloud, 'The Queen has been graciously pleased on the occasion of the Celebration of Her Majesty's Birthday to signify her intention of conferring the Honour of OBE on the undermentioned.' He ran his finger down the list. 'Here you are! Rose Virginia Dodd. Founder of the Pit Pony Champions charity for services to veterinary medicine and animal welfare.'

'You kept that under your hat, our Rose,' Grace said, and Dad gave her a wink.

News spread and she was besieged with congratulations. Vera phoned her saying, 'About time too, I'm delighted.'

'You've worked hard to make the charity a success too, Vera.'

'Nonsense, you deserve it. You've not only written a veterinary assistant's handbook that's been a set textbook in training and widely used in veterinary practices, you've donated all the royalties to animal welfare. You've founded The PPC charity and your continued efforts to raise awareness of the need to rehome retired and redundant pit ponies in all the mining areas of the UK has resulted in better facilities.'

'How do you know the reason so well, Vera?' Rose asked.

'Ah, you've caught me out. Between you and me, the two Franks worked on the application ages ago. Everyone they asked contributed and recommended you. It's a well-earned accolade from those who know you.'

She would be presented with her medal at the palace by the Queen, but that invitation hadn't arrived yet. What a day that would be! She wanted to take Dad with her. Two guests were allowed, so she'd ask Frank Senior who had helped her with her handbook and so much else over the years. She knew her own Frank would want to come to London, but he'd take a step back so his father could attend the actual ceremony.

Her own Frank. She realised that gaining his heart was better than any award. She was in love, and she hadn't thought it was possible to feel this way again.

Maybe Grace and Vera would travel to London with them too so they could make a real celebration of it afterwards? There were so many people she could include!

To involve everybody, Rose decided to celebrate receiving the award with a party after the fayre, and everyone at Blackthorn Farm was on board with her idea.

Helen, Daphne and Meg got together to plan for the huge buffet they'd serve in the kitchen of the shed that they used for demonstrations. They'd put up trestle tables to accommodate all of their families and a few friends, and whoever The Jems brought along.

Jim called to congratulate her and to say The Jems would play. He mentioned to Rose he might be bringing a girlfriend he was keen on if he could persuade her to come. 'She was born around here but can't remember much about it because the family moved away when she was young. I think you'll really like her, Rose.'

'If she makes you happy, I'll like her,' Rose assured him.

Lottie offered her services for washing up. 'I'm offering to help so I can stay for the party and see the band,' she confessed to Rose.

Rose gave her a hug. 'You are invited anyway, you doylem. You're one of my oldest friends, and look how well you've looked after Frank.'

'I'll let you in on a secret. I won't be doing that much longer, Rose. I'm pregnant – I'm having another at last. It was Frank who suggested I see a specialist. I had that little op, and now...' she patted her flat tummy, 'we're having another.'

The day they chose couldn't have been better. After a week of rain, the clouds cleared and the ground dried and visitors arrived in droves. The shop sold out of cinder toffee and that pleased Rose. *See, Mam, your recipes are still going strong*, she thought.

Frank judged best pit pony, but they all got a rainbow of rosettes. Deborah told Rose she'd had a lovely day and would love to come again to see Red and Robbie. Teaching Red tricks had made her and Robbie firm friends.

'Come whenever your dad will bring you, sweetheart,' Rose said as he led her off to find her grandad and Vera. She was staying over at her grandad's so Frank could stay late at the party.

Lottie arrived with Dennis. She explained she'd arrived late in the day so she wouldn't be too tired for the evening celebrations. 'I'm over the sickness, thank the Lord, but I can't bear the smell of Dennis's aftershave. He's had to wash it off. Do you think that means it's a girl?' she whispered to Rose.

'I'm sure that's not a sign. Does Paul know yet?'

'We're telling him soon, now I'm safely over the three-month mark. Won't he get a surprise?'

They looked over at Paul who was sitting on a bale of hay in the corner of the shed. He was chatting and laughing with Lily, Jennifer Wilson and her brother, Mattie.

'It doesn't seem ten minutes since we were that age. You, me, Danny and Dennis,' Rose said.

'I'm feeling weepy. Stop it,' Lottie sniffed.

'I've been told to put cloths on the tables in the shed then mingle, so I'll do that and we'll chat later.' Rose went in search of tablecloths.

Daphne caught her and had a quick word. 'You've done enough for the event, The Jems are playing their surprise set in a moment, and when they finish the last of the day visitors will leave. They'll do another set later in the evening after the food. Once you've put cloths on the tables, slip away to get changed and come back here in an hour or so to enjoy yourself.'

The Jems started playing outside and the shed quickly emptied. 'Their music will be heard in Alnwick! I hope they're not *this* loud tonight or I'll never sleep,' Ted complained to Daphne, who led him away.

Rose watched them walk off arm-in-arm and smiled. Ted was proud of his son, but loved to complain.

Daphne walked Ted towards the stage. 'Don't you say a word, Ted Fairbairn. Wear some earplugs tonight if you must. I don't want you nagging Jim – he's already upset because that girl he's keen on has suddenly pulled out of the trip, and he wanted us all to meet her. She had some sort of a family crisis in Australia to sort out, so he bought her a ticket for a flight home. He's asked me not to mention it to anybody.'

'Don't look at me, I won't. He's too young and hasn't the life-style to be settling down with a girl, anyway.'

· · ·

310

Rose popped home to shower away the smell of ponies and change into a green dress for the party.

After her shower, she held the dress to her. Frank liked it, thought the colour matched her eyes. It was a minidress with long sleeves for when the night got cooler. She loved the puffed sleeves that ended in a very wide cuff with six tiny covered buttons, but they were hard to fasten. She'd pair the dress with low-heeled black Mary Jane shoes that were good for dancing.

Rose brushed her hair loose, put on some make-up, and was fiddling with the buttons on the cuff of the dress when there was a knock at the front door. 'Who is it?' she called through the open bedroom window.

'Frank.'

'The door's open, come on up.'

Frank opened the door and bounded up the stairs in three or four leaps. He stood in the doorway. 'You look beautiful,' he said.

'Thank you. I can't fasten these bothersome buttons.'

'Here, let me.' He took her wrist, but before he fastened the buttons, he kissed the inside of her arm.

A spark of fireflies swarmed through Rose. He was so close, and she wanted him. She longed for his kisses.

Frank traced up her arm with tiny kisses right to her neck and she let out a moan.

'Do you want me as much as I want you, Rose?'

She took his face in her hands and kissed him. If he asked her too, she'd take off the dress, forget the party and lock out the world.

He clasped her to him. 'Marry me, Rose. I want you to be my wife.'

Her heart raced. She wasn't expecting those words today, but she knew there would only ever be one answer. 'Yes. Yes, I'll marry you.'

They kissed. She melted into his hard body and wanted the kiss to last forever. Slowly he drew away. The look in his eyes showed his desire for her. 'Do we have to rush to the party? Will anyone notice if we turn up late?' he asked.

'We won't be missed for a while.' She moved closer, longing for his touch, hungry for his kisses and knowing that this love was all she needed. This man was her happily ever after.

GLOSSARY

Bevin boy – a conscripted miner named after Ernest Bevin
  Champion - excellent, wonderful
  Clarty – muddy or dirty. Clarts means mud
  Connie – conscientious objector shortened from conscientious
  Cracket – a low stool with a hole in the middle for carrying it.
  Doylem – a foolish person
  Fret - a mist coming in from the sea
  Fettle - a mood, eg: a fine fettle or a bad fettle
  Gallowa - any pit pony not just a Galloway pony.
  Haar - a cold sea fog
  Hinny – a term of endearment like 'honey'
  Hintend – hind end, backside
  Linties – fast running birds so used to describe anyone rushing about.
  Lowse – finishing time, the end of a miner's shift or drinking up time at a bar. A sharp lowse is an early finishing time.
  Marra – a workmate or friend
  Masting – the brewing of tea in a pot
  Netty – lavatory. Some say it is a shortening of 'necessity'

Nowt – nothing

Owt – anything

Pig's ear – a mess – you've made a pig's ear of that.

Proggy mat – a homemade mat made from pushing strips of cloth into a hessian backing with a progger

Scullery – a room off the kitchen or main living room with a sink and bench and some shelving and sometimes a larder

Stottie - a round of bread baked on the bottom shelf of the oven

Taties - potatoes

'Tute – the working men's institute, a social meeting place

Yammer – to moan and groan

Who were the Pitmen Painters?

The pitmen painters were a group of artists who formed in the 1930s. In The Colliery Rows series, John Kelly is a fictional character from the group.

Lee Hall of 'Billy Elliot' fame has written a successful play, 'The Pitmen Painters'. It has toured nationally and internationally.

A large collection of the group's work is on display at Woodhorn Museum in Northumberland. As well as holding a fascinating exhibition of the pitmens' paintings, this old colliery site is packed full of the social history of mining and well worth a visit.

RECIPES FROM THE BOOK

Border Tart - baked by Helen and Daphne

Enjoyed by families both sides of the border between Scotland and England.

Preheat the oven to 180c fan gas Mark 6 and have a 20cm greased tart tin at the ready.

Step 1 Make the pastry case

(nowadays there is a shortcut because you can buy a sheet of ready rolled pastry)

Ingredients

175g plain flour

90g butter, cubed

25g caster sugar

30ml cold

• sift the flour into a bowl

• add the diced butter and rub into the flour with your fingertips until the mixture resembles fine breadcrumbs Add the sugar and punch of salt and gently mix through

• add 2tbsp water and mix to a firm dough. Add another tbsp water if needed but not too much

• Knead the dough briefly and gently into a ball on a floured surface

• Roll out the pastry to the thickness of a copper coin, fit the sheet into the greased tart tin and trim excess from the edges using a knife

• Prick the bottom of the tart with a fork

Helen hint -It is a good idea to line the pastry with grease proof paper and weigh the base down with a few clean coppers or dried peas. This stops any air bubbles forming while you

bake the pastry case in the oven for 15 mins

Step 2 While the pastry is baking, make the filling:

Ingredients

1 large egg

75g soft brown sugar

50g butter

120g currants

50g glacé cherries, chopped

2 tspns lemon juice (optional)

30g chopped walnuts (optional)

• Beat the egg and sugar together in a mixing bowl

• Melt the butter in a pan over a gentle heat and then pour this into a mixing bowl with the soft brown sugar and the egg.

• Mix together well then add all the other dry ingredients and stir together to combine them.

Step 3

When the pastry case has baked, spread the mixture into the case and bake in the oven for 25 minutes.

Remove from the oven and allow to cool completely.

Step 4

Once the Border Tart has cooled, prepare the icing to decorate. Be patient because the icing sugar will just disappear into a warm tart.

Ingredients

150g sifted icing sugar

2-4 teaspoons cold water

(Helen adds a squeeze of lemon juice but it's optional)

• Sift the icing sugar into a bowl, slowly add water and mix until the icing is smooth and glossy.

• Spread the icing evenly on top of the Border Tart and leave it to set.

Serve.

This Border Tart slices into eight pieces. It will keep for a few days in an airtight container

* * *

Ginnie's Cinder toffee -made by Rose

You might know it as honeycomb, is a traditional British treat loved by the bairns in the colliery rows.

Prepare a greased baking tray for the hot toffee and have a whisk ready

Ingredients

caster sugar 10 level tbspns (200g)

golden syrup 5 level tbspns (100g)

1 level tsp bicarbonate of soda

Step 1

• Put the sugar and golden syrup into a saucepan and set it on a very low heat.

• Warm gently for 10 minutes until all the sugar has melted, stirring occasionally with a wooden spoon.

Step 2

• When it has melted, turn up the head and allow it boil. Leave to bubble without stirring until it turns golden-brown. 2 or 3 minutes.

Ginnie tip- Test by dropping a small amount of syrup into cold water it is ready if forms hard, brittle threads,

Step 3

• Turn off the heat under the pan. Add the bicarbonate of soda and quickly whisk it into the toffee. This only takes a second or two. The mixture will froth up and, as it's extremely hot, it is recommended to wear an oven glove

Step 4

• Pour the hot mixture into the middle of the oiled baking tray.

• Do not spread it out or touch it in the tray. Let it spread out itself. Leave it to cool and harden

• Break into bit size pieces.

It's eaten quickly but any spare pieces can be saved for another day in an airtight container.

ABOUT THE AUTHOR

Hi from Chrissie!

Thank you for choosing one of my books. If you enjoyed it, please consider writing a review because it helps me to find other readers just like you who will like reading my northern stories.

You are very welcome to join my reader's club where you'll receive the occasional newsletter whenever I have special news or book offers. On signing up, you'll be given a free and exclusive prequel about Rose Kelly's early years. Just use this link and scroll to the green button on the Chrissie Bradshaw home page. www. chrissiebradshaw.com

Chrissie Bradshaw, 2016 winner of the Romantic Novelist's Elizabeth Goudge writing trophy, has always loved match-making a book to a reader. Writing the kind of book she loves to read takes this a step further. When Chrissie is not writing or reading, you will find her walking Oscar on the beach, trying to avoid the gym and spending time with her family and friends. She loves to keep in touch with readers.

ALSO BY CHRISSIE BRADSHAW

If you enjoyed 'Rose's Ever After', you might want to try one of these:

Rose's Choice

A heart-wrenching wartime saga of love, family and secrets (The Colliery Rows Book 1)

Rose makes a discovery that could destroy her family. Does she keep her mother's secret? It's Rose's Choice.

The Unwelcome Angel

An emotionally gripping wartime novella. (Linwood Colliery Novella) A diphtheria epidemic sweeps through Linwood. Which children will get home for Christmas?

The Dunleith series

A Jarful of Moondreams

This compelling, modern family saga, set in Northumberland, links to the Linwood Colliery books. A must-read if you want to know what happened to Joy and Bobby's daughter. What shocking secrets are about to spill out of the moondream jar this summer?

The Barn of Buried Dreams

A riveting contemporary novel set in Northumberland. Erin and Heather Douglas are struggling after their mother's death. Losing her has left a void in their family, and everyday life has side-lined the sisters' dreams. When will their dreams see daylight?

ACKNOWLEDGEMENTS

I couldn't possibly list all of the people who have helped and encouraged me on the way to following my dream career because I'd worry about missing someone out.

Let me just say that, over the last few years, I have appreciated the professional expertise, practical help and emotional support I've been given by so many people. I have learned so much and had fun along the way.

For their work on this book, a special thank you to Laura Gerrard, a gifted editor, and JD Smith who has created such an eye-catching cover.

I am grateful each day for the writer friends and family who cheer me on and for my dog, Oscar, who persuades me to leave my desk at regular intervals.